Also by Michael Talbot
The Bog
The Delicate Dependency

MICHAEL TALBOT

William Morrow and Company, Inc. New York

This one's for Mitzi and Pam, with love

8-88 BA 1500

Copyright © 1988 by Michael Talbot

All of the characters in this book are fictitious, and any resemblance to persons
living or dead is purely coincidental.

Library of Congress Cataloging-in-Publication Data

Talbot, Michael, 1953–
    Night things / Michael Talbot.
      p.   cm.
    ISBN 0-688-07163-5
    I. Title.
    PR6070.A36N5   1988
    823'.914—dc19   88-9680
                                                                CIP

Printed in the United States of America

First Edition

1 2 3 4 5 6 7 8 9 10

BOOK DESIGN BY BARBARA MARKS

Contents

*For we wrestle not against flesh and blood,
but against principalities, against powers,
against the rulers of the darkness. . . .*
—The Epistle of Paul to the Ephesians

PROLOGUE

New York City, 1870

When the woman awoke she knew immediately that something was wrong. She did not know what had alerted her to the fact. She had not heard anything. She knew only that one moment she was sleeping soundly and the next moment she was completely awake and alert. Clutching instinctively at the top button of her nightgown, she sat up in bed and stared into the darkness.

In the moonlight streaming in through the windows the room was ghostly and still. Anxiously she surveyed the shadows, half expecting to see some intruder lurking there. Beside her her husband slept, and in the distance she could hear the ticking of the hallway clock. Nothing seemed amiss, yet she knew that something was terribly wrong. There was an ominous edge to the darkness, a palpable air of danger.

Quickly she put her slippers on and padded over to the window. The lawns surrounding the great house appeared dreamlike in the bluish glow of the moonlight. In the distance, in the light of the gaslights on Fifth Avenue, she could see the huge wrought-iron fence that surrounded the estate. Her heart pounded.

She fumbled at her dressing table until she had managed to light a candle and then went into the hall. She knew somehow that if she did not hurry a life would be lost. But whose life? Who was in danger? And then she realized. It was her daughter.

As she raced toward the nursery she wondered how she could have been so stupid. Who was the most vulnerable member of the family? Whom had she struggled for the past eight years to nurture, to protect, even from her husband? She reached the nursery and flung the door open, hoping against hope it was not true. But she found what she had feared and already known. The sheets had been clumsily cast aside and the bed was empty. Frantically she searched the room, under the bed, in the closet, but the little girl was nowhere to be found. Gasping and already crying, she raced back to the hall and called for help.

Slowly the household awoke. On the floor above, the light of a gas jet coming on shone like a beacon down the servants' stairs, and at the far end of the hall her husband stumbled grouchily into the hall wrestling with his robe. His immense mustache, usually so carefully waxed and shaped, jutted out at strange angles, giving him a comical look which belied the anger in his expression.

"What is it?" he demanded. "What's wrong?"

"It's Sarah again," the woman gasped. "She's gone." She gestured toward the empty bedroom and then looked back desperately at her husband.

"This cannot go on," he said, shaking his head. "I told you something had to be done."

"I will not have my daughter put in one of those places."

"But she's sick. She needs to be under the care of doctors."

"She is not sick!"

"Then what is wrong?" he challenged, and her gaze
drifted to the floor. She did not know what was wrong
with her daughter. At times the little girl appeared completely normal, running and playing as any eight-year-old
might. But then there were the other times when she went
into strange trances that would last for hours, or had sei-
zures followed by animated descriptions of where she claimed
she had been and what she alleged she had seen. And there
were other such alarming incidents.

Something stirred within her, giving her the courage to
look back at her husband. He could be selfish. Cold. Concerned only with the intricacies of his business and the
power he wielded. She would not let him force her to stop
caring, force her to give up her daughter. She met his fiery
glare head-on, and something in the erectness of her bearing told him he had better back down.

He looked at the circle of servants gathered around them.
"She's disappeared again," he said wearily. "Search the
house."

The servants dutifully dispersed.

Taking the hem of her nightgown in hand, the woman
rushed toward the staircase to join in the search. When she
reached the banister she paused and looked back at her
husband. Reluctantly he grunted and followed.

They searched everywhere, in the cellar, in the attic,
even in the laundry and the coalbin of the huge and stately
house. Periodically they called out to each other to see if
anyone had found any clues, but it was to no avail. It was
as if the little girl had vanished. Finally, after exhausting
all other possibilities, they returned to the nursery. It was
there that the woman discovered what at first only piqued
her curiosity, but then quickly filled her with horror as
she realized its implications. The latch on the window of
the room was unlocked.

Letting out a cry, she rushed to the window and flung it
open. Her heart pounded as she madly surveyed the moonlit

grass several stories below and imagined the twisted and inanimate form of her daughter lying on the carefully manicured lawn. But she was not there. Unable to bear it any longer, the woman buried her face in her hands and started to sob.

She felt the pressure of her husband's hand upon her shoulder. She sensed the insistence of his grip, even the terror.

"There," he said in a hush.

She looked at him wonderingly and was taken by the stillness of his gaze as he looked out the window.

"*There*," he repeated with even more emphasis and nodding his head.

Slowly she followed the line of his vision until she too saw what he was looking at, and when she did, her heart stopped. For there, some twenty feet off and standing at the very edge of the roof, was their daughter. She stood as motionless as a statue, gazing raptly off into space.

"No—!" the woman cried, lunging forward, but her husband pulled her back.

She looked at him imploringly. "What are we going to do?"

He looked back at their daughter, and his faced filled with dread over the task before him. Beads of sweat formed on his brow. He pushed his hysterical wife into the arms of one of the maids, and he took off his slippers. Looking one last time at the ground far below, he rolled up his sleeves and crawled out the window.

The little girl became aware of the commotion taking place around her. She even heard the sound of her parents' voices and realized that they were upset about something, but she paid them no mind. She was too entranced by the swirling shapes before her. It was the first time they had come so clearly. Faces that drifted in and out like the glistening veils of the aurora borealis. She had been visited by the faces before, but never so many as this. Even their voices were clearer, the voices which had first come to her in her dreams, and which had once been little more than a chorus of mumbling. Now they spoke plainly, and although they occasionally sibilated in unison, they told her many amazing things.

What was strange was that although she knew the voices were saying something important, she was not really sure what they were telling her. It was as if her consciousness were not really present, only some deeper portion of herself, like the person she was in a half-remembered dream. Suddenly the murmuring of the voices intensified as if informed by some unknown urgency. The luminous cloud of being became turbulent as the voices crescendoed, and a flood of images suddenly swirled and tumbled before her. All at once, in a scintillant burst of energy, the vision vanished as the viselike grip of a hand closed around her arm.

She turned, and to her astonishment she saw it was her father. Confused, she took a step forward. He cried out, yanking her brusquely toward him. For a moment she thought her arm had been wrenched from her body, and it was only after he had gathered her up in his arms that she understood where she was.

She began to cry, but instead of comforting her her father only cursed under his breath as he slowly made his way back across the eaves of the house. How had she gotten here? she wondered. What had she been doing on the roof? And then she remembered . . . the voices . . . and the swirling light.

But as her daze evaporated and she drifted slowly back into the stifling logic of reality, she realized two things. First, and quite unexpectedly, she realized she was special, chosen. She had perceived an order of things invisible to most human beings, and to her great surprise she had been allowed to glimpse her role in that order. Second, and most astounding of all, she had been shown a shape.

Here her vague understanding of what had happened to her ended. For although the vision still shimmered in her mind, she knew only that she had seen something both possible and impossible: a form never before fathomed by mortal minds.

I

THE HOUSE

And oftentimes, to win us to our harm,
The instruments of darkness tell us
truths. . . .
—Shakespeare, *Macbeth*

"Are we almost there?" Lauren asked excitedly as the Porsche shifted gears to negotiate the increasing steepness of the mountain road. The highway they were on was one of the old two-laners, and together with dazzling mountain scenery and the verdant walls of tamaracks and pines that surrounded them, it seemed like a scene right out of a picture postcard.

"Almost," Stephen said, grinning from ear to ear and still refusing to tell her anything about the house he had rented for them in the Adirondacks for the summer. He reached out and squeezed her hand lovingly.

A warm tingle enveloped her as she returned the squeeze and smiled. She still could not believe that she, Lauren Montgomery, had married Stephen Ransom, famous recording star, king of the pop charts for the past three years. Only four short months before he had been merely a celebrity to her, the pop superstar of such megahit albums as *Ransom of the Heart* and *Ransomed for Love*. But one

afternoon Annie had called her in to say she was giving
her the writing assignment of a lifetime: the opportunity
to spend an entire week with Ransom, to follow him around
and do what Annie called a real meat-and-potatoes piece
on the guy.

What a week that had been, she remembered. When she
had first entered Stephen Ransom's suite of rooms at the
Plaza she had been nervous as a schoolgirl. But there was
such an instant rapport between them, such a feeling of
closeness and uncanny familiarity, that within a half hour's
conversation it was as though they'd known each other
for years. To her enormous surprise—for such behavior
violated all of her personal and professional standards—
they made love their very first evening together. Indeed,
from that day on they spent every available moment together, and scarcely two months later, on the morning
that her article about him came out in *People Beat*, he called
her up and told her he wanted to marry her. When she
giddily asked him why, he said it was because he liked the
way she described him in the article as having "impish,
boy-next-door good looks with just a hint of something
dangerous in his eyes." They went down to city hall that
same day.

She looked at herself in the car mirror, at her blond hair
and delicate features. She had been told that she looked
like Julie Christie, but she had never believed it. Until she
had met Stephen it had been difficult for Lauren to believe
that anything truly good might happen to her.

It was not that she was a pessimist, really, at least not
when it came to the world in general. Whenever the cyn-
ical old fogies at *People Beat* began spewing apocalyptic
claptrap about nuclear holocaust or the inevitability of the
decline of good journalism it was always she who challenged them, she who argued that there was something
inherently good in the human spirit, something that, no

matter how dark the world became, would never let it sink into the mire of total moral turpitude.

And she believed it. She did not know why. Perhaps it was some past-life thing—for she had certainly not been raised in a religious environment in this life. But whatever the cause, there was a deep and abiding conviction in her that there was something akin to grace in the universe, that the cards of fate were stacked ever so slightly on the side of innocence and that good things were just a little more likely to happen than bad.

Except when it came to her.

Her reasons for excluding herself from this mantle of grace were deep, lost in the painful fragments of her childhood, but she knew that one of the fragments was her father. Her earliest memories of her father were of a proud man, handsome, outgoing, and always in command of the situation. Born to parents who had emigrated from the south side of London to New York's Hell's Kitchen, he had risen from poverty to ownership of his own tool-and-die business and by the time Lauren was born had purchased quite a nice home for her and her mother in the Forest Hills section of Queens.

Lauren's memories of those early years were rapturously happy, and although she did not see her father much, she remembered the brief stretches of time she was able to spend with him as almost luminous, they were so qualitatively different from the rest of her life. She could still remember the brands of candy he would bring her when he came home from work, and how she would endlessly trace and retrace the design in the kitchen linoleum as she waited for him to finish showering in the basement—her mother never let him come into the house proper until he had showered and changed out of his work clothes—and come upstairs at the end of the day.

It had nearly killed her when one day he didn't come

home and for weeks her mother refused to tell her anything. When she was seven and after nearly six months
had passed, her mother finally explained to her the meaning
of the word "divorce" and told her that her father would
never be coming home again. As for why, Lauren was
given only sketchy fragments about there being another
woman involved and about how her father had decided to
live with her instead of them. But because these fragments
were beyond the comprehension of a seven-year-old, Lauren could only imagine that somehow the divorce had to
do with her, with something she had done. And perhaps
also with some secondary and less consequential crime
committed by her mother.

In time Lauren became convinced that if only she could
see her father she might be able to make amends for whatever it was she had done, but her mother told her that after
the divorce her father had moved out West and had left
no forwarding address. Her relationship with her mother
had never been good, and after the divorce it too got worse.
Although Lauren recognized now that her mother's increasing inability to cope with Lauren or with even the
most trifling of everyday events was due to her own dev-
astation over the divorce, it only intensified Lauren's feeling that somehow she was the victim of some terrible
mistake, that if only she could locate her father she might
be able lift the horrible curse that had befallen her.

Her feeling that she was the victim of some dark spell
increased when she was eight and her mother was confined
to a wheelchair with severe rheumatoid arthritis. From that
point on until Lauren went away to college at the age of
seventeen, she was her mother's chattel and slave—a nurse
when her mother became too ill to take care of herself,
and a punching bag when her mother recovered enough
to recall the pain and bitterness that had placed her in the
wheelchair in the first place.

It wasn't until Lauren was in her early twenties and had

landed her first job—as an assistant to a staff writer at the *Village Voice*—that her mother accidentally let drop that her father had not moved out West but was living in Westchester. At first she was furious at her mother for withholding the information from her for so long, and they had a terrible argument. But then afterward Lauren was ecstatic and her dream of reclaiming some of the lost happiness of her youth was rekindled.

Another year passed before she finally reestablished contact with her father. Perhaps because it was a moment she had looked forward to for so long, she just didn't want to rush into it. Or perhaps she wanted to wait until she had a more impressive job (and she did, for by that time she had become a staff writer at *People Beat*). Whatever the case, it was with both joy and profound nervousness that she visited her father's spacious home in Westchester.

The meeting was anticlimactic to say the least. Far from being the luminous and larger-than-life figure she remembered, her father was short and paunchy. In fact, he was exactly the sort of man she usually detested—perfectly coiffed hair (stiff with hair spray and carefully combed in a large wavy sheet to conceal a burgeoning bald spot), shiny and manicured nails, oppressive cologne. And of course there was the cigar, a Dunhill Montecristo No. 1.

Nor was he even the warm and affectionate man she remembered, let alone the knight to wipe clean all the ruinous memories of her childhood. He was stiff and ill at ease. Rather than being impressed at her successes, he seemed resentful of them. They spent an uncomfortable afternoon together, and when it was over Lauren was appalled to realize that she had felt more relaxed with his wife, a darkly tanned and vaguely blowsy redhead named Tiffany, than she had with him.

Her father was not the only man with whom she had had an ill-fated relationship. About six months after the Westchester fiasco a girlfriend invited her to go to a gallery opening, and there, while looking at sculptures created by placing bundles of multicolored wire beneath the wheels of subways and while drinking white wine out of a clear plastic wine goblet, she met the the man who was to become the second significant male figure in her life, a Hungarian painter named Miklos.

As with Stephen, her attraction to Miklos had been immediate. Miklos was not as handsome as Stephen was, but he possessed a certain panache. Tall, thin, and given to wearing only the newest Italian fashions, he cut a most striking figure. He was also one of the best-read human beings she had ever met, and what with his intoxicating accent and her discovery that he was a staggeringly talented painter, her heart was quickly lost to him.

For the better part of a year their relationship proceeded without a hitch. Although she had had several boyfriends in college, he was the first man to bring her regularly to orgasm. He was also the first man she had ever met who was sensitive to every one of her foibles, and they quickly developed such a rapport they both started remarking that it seemed almost as if they could read each other's minds.

That Christmas they were married, and two months later she found out she was pregnant. It was, however, the beginning of the end. Despite Miklos's initial excitement at the prospect of having a child, as her pregnancy advanced he became increasingly irritable. Although they had both agreed on having a baby, he fought bitterly when she tried to convert a portion of their loft to a nursery, and by the time the baby was born he had become totally convinced that being a successful father and a successful painter were two mutually incompatible things.

They toughed it out for another few months before Lauren took their son, Garrett, and moved into an apartment of her own. Although it wasn't until another year had passed that she filed for divorce, she never really saw Miklos again.

Throughout Garrett's childhood, her bad luck with men continued. After Miklos she met Peter. Peter worked for a rival magazine, and her relationship with him ran smoothly until he stole a story idea from her that she thought she had discussed with him in confidence. After Peter she met Julian, who turned out to be one of the worst hypochondriacs she had ever met. And after Julian, Stan, a stockbroker who seemed perfect in every way, until he was indicted on an insider-trading charge.

And after that things continued pretty much the same. Sometimes she would go for months without dating at all. And whenever she did meet someone she was interested in she knew that at some point, before the relationship became too serious, she would discover some fatal flaw. Sometimes she would find out the man was married. Sometimes she was forced to end the relationship out of sheer boredom. But whatever the reason, she seemed destined to meet nothing but jerks and losers.

Until she met Stephen.

Her first several weeks with him she was as nervous as a cat, fearful that at any moment she might discover some terrible crack in his seemingly perfect personality. But there was none. She even speckled her conversations with him with subtle and carefully worded questions designed to draw him out, but always he gave the right answers. More than that, every day with him, every hour and second, was an experience too wonderful to be true. During the day he would take her shopping at Bendel's or to the designer boutiques at Saks and allow her to buy anything she wanted. At night they would go to parties at the Palladium, or at the home of some famous writer or movie star, and the next day they would have front-row seats for a private performance of a Broadway play. Indeed, just when she thought she had had the most nearly ultimate experience possible, Stephen would top himself again. He would fly them both to Paris on the Concord for lunch.

Or fill her apartment with ten dozen red roses. Or leave a pair of diamond earrings from Cartier's on her pillow. Or tell her he loved her at precisely the moment she needed to hear it the most.

In the brilliant afternoon sunlight that filtered in through the window she looked at him, at his sculpted profile and curly black hair. It was an added plus that he was as good-looking as he was. He was tall and muscular and had the intensity of a young Marlon Brando, with a Roman nose, square chiseled chin, and limpid and arresting green-gray eyes. He was also one of the most alive people she had ever met. Constantly on the move and never tiring at the prospect of exploring something new, he always had a sparkle about him. He could be soft and tender when the moment demanded. He could be intellectual and discuss everything from Proust to a Gilbert and Sullivan operetta. But he could also just as easily drop the polite and boyish facade and exude a brute masculinity, a raw, take-charge sensuality that, although it embarrassed her to admit it, nearly took her breath away.

She gave his hand another squeeze. Had someone told her a few months back that she would be quitting her job at *People Beat* and getting married again, she would have laughed in his face. She would miss working at the magazine, and she recognized what a profound change marrying Stephen had made in her life, but she was glad she had made the decision. She loved him more than any man she had ever met, and the fact that he loved her made her feel like the luckiest woman alive.

From the backseat came the sound of a page turning, and she turned around to glance at her son, Garrett, his nose as usual buried in a book. Her only concern was how the eleven-year-old was going to adjust to all the changes that had taken place in their life. It had taken her days of talking just to get him used to the idea that she had married Stephen. When she told him they would also be leaving

New York and spending the summer in the mountains, he had just about died. It was an understandable reaction. After all, she was all the family he had, and now he was going to have to get used to having a stranger for a father and to adjust to an entirely new environment as well. In the end he had begrudgingly consented to the move, but she knew that he was still far from happy about it.

"What are you reading?" she asked, caring less about the subject matter of his book than about how he was feeling.

"It's about UFOs," he returned.

"UFOs?" Stephen said, puzzled.

"It's space," she explained. "Ever since he saw *E.T.* he's been obsessed with anything that has to do with outer space."

Stephen looked back at Garrett. "So what do you think about the Adirondacks so far?"

Garrett leaned forward with a scowl. "There haven't been any houses for hours."

"But that's just the point," Stephen countered. "I rented a place for us up here for the summer so we could get away from everyone else, be someplace where there's lots of peace and quiet."

"But will we even be able to get television up here?"

"Sure we'll be able to get television. We'll have all the comforts of home. Marty's seen to everything. You're going to love it up here. Just wait and see."

"Yeah, I know," Garrett huffed as he slumped back into his seat.

Lauren looked quickly at Stephen. She hoped that he had not taken Garrett's peevishness too personally, that he realized Garrett was reacting not to him but to the upheaval in his life in general. It worried her slightly that Stephen had never had any children of his own—had never even been married before—and she hoped he understood that contending with such displays of mood was all part of being a father. In addition, Stephen's schedule was so hectic and demanding and he was on the road so much that he and Garrett had not really spent much time together yet. That was one of the reasons she had been so excited about their moving to the mountains for the summer. She hoped it would give them all the opportunity to spend some time together and become a true family.

She was just about to try to initiate some further conversation among the three of them when suddenly the Porsche hit a bump and they turned off the road. She looked ahead and saw that they had pulled into a narrow driveway pitted and gullied by endless rains and so enclosed by trees that it seemed as if they had entered a dusky green tunnel. Difficult as it was for her to believe, the drive was even steeper than the mountain highway they had just turned off, and even the powerful Porsche strained to make the climb.

They continued on for several minutes until at last the leafy tunnel opened onto a vast and breathtakingly beautiful mountain lake. On the far shore, standing majestically on a prominence of rock, was a house. Even at a distance it was clear that it was immense, a stone fortress encrusted with turrets and gables and studded with countless dark and gleaming windows. Surrounded by towering balsams and pines it seemed more like an alpine hotel than a house for a single family.

"It's called Lake House," Stephen said. "What do you think? I flew up here on the sly to check it out after Marty told me about it."

"It's incredible!" she gasped. "When you said you had rented a lodge in the Adirondacks I thought you meant a cabin or something."

"No, no," he laughed. "Lodges in the Adirondacks are like cottages in Newport. They're also known as 'great camps.' You see, in the latter half of the nineteenth century the Adirondacks became a Mecca of sorts for wealthy East

Coast families. It became an issue of status to see who could build the largest and most palatial summer retreat. The Rockefellers, the Vanderbilts—they all built homes up here. Lake House was built in the 1890s by Sarah Balfram, the daughter of the railroad magnate Josiah Balfram. I think Marty said the agent told him her fiancé jilted her and she decided to isolate herself up here in magnificent splendor. Wait until you see the inside. You're going to love it."

She looked at the house worriedly. "But how will I ever be able to keep it clean?"

He laughed again. "Well, first of all, Marty had a cleaning crew give the place a once-over last week so everything would be shipshape when we moved in. Then in a week or so, after we've had some time to ourselves, we'll hire some permanent help. You keep forgetting you're a lady of leisure now." A devilish sparkle came into his dark eyes. "Besides, I didn't marry you for your cleaning skills."

"Oh, *Stephen*," she chided playfully. But she realized he was right. It was going to take some time getting used to having people like Stephen's manager Marty to take care of most of the busywork of everyday life.

"What's the lake called?" Garrett asked.

"Lake Ketcimanitowa. It's an Indian name and it's all ours."

Lauren looked at him with astonishment. "You mean this entire lake is also part of the rental?"

"The lake and two hundred acres of land surrounding it. I told you I had gotten us a place with lots of privacy."

She looked back at the expanse of wilderness before them and marveled that anyone might have the financial resources to rent such an immense tract of land. Yes, she thought, it was going to take her some time to get used to Stephen's life-style, but what a marvelous challenge!

As they continued on the narrow drive she watched eagerly as still more details of the house became visible,

and with every passing moment she became impressed
anew with its colossal size and beauty. It would have been
inaccurate to say that the house was sprawling, for like the
mountains behind it it was citadel-like, with most of its
mass concentrated around a central core. But out of this
central core sprouted so many interconnecting peaks and
gables, so many battlements and towers and tangled un-
dergirdings of Gothic tracery, that it was impossible for
her to even imagine how many rooms the house might
contain.

She also noticed several other things. Although it had
not been clear from a distance, surrounding the house was
a great pillared veranda, and in addition to the main structure there appeared to a complex of service buildings set
off to one side and artfully concealed behind a grove of
trees. As they approached she saw also that the huge shelf
of land on which the house sat was not just barren rock
but was lushly carpeted with grass and dotted here and
there with hedges.

Finally they reached the house, and Stephen pulled the
Porsche to a stop beneath a colonnade of majestic black
spruce. "End of the line. Everybody out."

They all piled out, and as soon as Lauren stepped out
of the air-conditioned enclosure of the Porsche the deep
resinous smell of the pines flooded her nostrils. Combined
with the peaceful grandeur of the mountains it nearly took
her breath away.

"You still haven't told me what you think of the place,"
Stephen prodded.

She looked at the house towering above them. Under
other circumstances she might have found its imposing
size a bit intimidating. But this was what her new life
would be like, and she'd just have to get used to it.

"Oh, Stephen, it's fantastic! In my wildest dreams I never
thought I would ever live in a house like this. I love it."

He grinned. "I knew you would."

She looked down at Garrett. "Isn't it great, Garrett!"

From his expression it was clear that he was also impressed, but as soon as she looked at him he quickly resumed an air of indifference. "Yeah, it's okay."

She smiled, realizing that at least they were making some headway.

Stephen went around to the back of the car and opened the trunk. "Come on," he said, handing them a suitcase each. "I want to show you the inside." As he had explained to her earlier, Marty had already arranged for the heavier baggage to be waiting for them in the house.

He took out a suitcase for himself and a case containing his guitar, and as they started up the drive a mischievousness came over him. "There is something else that you should know about the house." There was a touch of Dracula in his voice.

"What?"

"Well, Lake House isn't just a normal house. You see, Sarah Balfram was something of an eccentric. Apparently she had all sorts of strange things built into the house— stairways that go nowhere, hallways that end at blank walls. The house is actually quite famous. The rental agent said that it's even been written about in books."

"Wow, that sounds neat!" Garrett suddenly perked up again.

The revelation took Lauren by surprise, however. "What do you mean, stairways that go nowhere? How can we live in a place like that?"

"Oh, you don't have to worry," Stephen comforted. "The house is huge, and most of it is quite normal. It's only around the edges that some of the rooms are a little wild." Stephen's eyes positively sparkled as he said the last words.

"I should have known." Lauren rolled her eyes and

laughed as they reached the house and started up the steps of the pillared veranda.

"The place is gonna be great. Just wait," he said, setting his suitcase down and fumbling for his keys. He stuck one into the lock, but it refused to turn.

Lauren admired the oak entrance door surrounded on all sides by narrow stained-glass windows, which depicted grape arbors and lush foliage.

"What does that say?" Garrett asked, looking up.

For a moment Lauren was so mesmerized by the delicate tangle of leaves and vines in the windows that she did not see what he was talking about.

"What does what say?"

"That," Garrett repeated.

She followed his pointing finger until she saw what he was looking at. Chiseled into the granite keystone above the uppermost window was an inscription written in Latin, and although dark and discolored with age she could still make out the words: *In girum imus nocte et consumimur igni.*

"I don't know," she returned. "Do you know what that says, Stephen?"

He shrugged. "No. Probably just some sort of greeting or something."

The lock clicked, and Stephen smiled as he pushed the door open and gestured for them to follow.

They were greeted by an entrance hall of impossibly grand proportions. The walls were richly paneled in walnut, and at the back an elaborately carved staircase extended to a balustraded floor above. High overhead an amber pendant chandelier tinkled in the breeze that rustled past them, and on all sides elaborate spindlework archways led to cavernous and equally resplendent rooms beyond. To the left of the door was a coachmen's waiting room, a relic from a time when carriages had been the main mode of transportation for inhabitants of the house. The entire hall was pervaded by a magical emerald light. It was several seconds before Lauren realized that the green glow was caused by the late-afternoon sun streaming through the stained-glass windows behind them.

Stephen was now so excited he seemed like a little kid on Christmas morning. "Let's put our bags down here for the time being. I want to show you some more of the house before we take them up to our rooms."

He motioned for them to follow him through the spindlework archway to the right, and after passing through a small sitting room they entered an enormous drawing room some twenty feet wide and sixty feet long. The ceiling of the vast chamber was of vaulted oak, and on the floor was one of the largest oriental carpets that Lauren had ever seen. At the far end of the room two eighteenth-century griffins stood guard on either side of a massive granite fireplace, and on the walls an octet of reindeer heads gazed dumbly at the various arrangements of sofas and wing chairs that filled the expanse. But the most striking feature of the room was the solid bank of leaded windows that lined its southern side, affording a spectacular view of the lake and mountains.

She turned around dizzily. "Oh, Stephen, it's beautiful. It's one of the most extraordinary houses I've ever seen." She ran over and hugged him tightly as Garrett contrived to examine a stuffed pheasant.

"Check this out." Stephen pulled her over to what looked like a door leading off the drawing room and swung it back to reveal that it opened onto a solid brick wall. "This is the real door," he said, closing the first and opening another several feet away.

Lauren shook her head and closed her eyes as if the craziness and wondrousness of it all was simply too much for her.

"The kitchen's this way," Stephen said, walking through the real door.

He continued to lead them on a tour of the outer rooms

of the first floor, through the kitchen, pantry, and larder, through a ruby-red dining room with velvet walls, through a library with walls of green Spanish leather, a Moorish-styled billiard room, and numerous other sitting rooms and parlors and two long completely enclosed sun porches running parallel to each other on opposite sides of the house and appointed with identical but oppositely arranged wicker furnishings.

Through all of it Lauren became increasingly enchanted by the house as well as the many magnificent possessions it contained, windows bedecked in diaphanous curtains with cobweb edging, tables draped with seventeenth-century French lace with minute, perfect men and animals embroidered among their gossamer threads, globes of Favrile glass, lamps in the form of brass mermaids holding nautilus shells, Tiffany inkstands, and bright-green Russian malachite boxes.

Throughout their tour they encountered still further examples of Sarah Balfram's architectural eccentricities. In the kitchen Stephen gleefully pointed out a set of servants' stairs that went nowhere (the real set was concealed in what looked like a utility closet). In a parlor near one of the sun porches two doors led onto hallways that were really dead ends; and strangest of all, the floor and walls of a sitting room near the library were actually built at slight angles, creating a subtle feeling of vertigo in anyone who traversed the room too quickly.

"This room is like being high without dope," Stephen said, prancing around and pretending to be so dizzy that he fell to the floor.

As they continued, Lauren noticed two other things. First, in spite of the great number of rooms they passed through, it appeared that they had covered only a small part of even the first floor. Always there seemed to be more rooms beyond, corridors opening onto other corridors and stairways, real or illusory, extending deeper into the seemingly endless recesses of the house. Second, despite Lake House's great age, everything was in a remarkable state of preservation. Here and there the carpets were slightly worn and the floors creaked a bit, but all in all everything was in surprisingly good condition. Nowhere did she see even so much as a loose piece of molding or a peeling patch of paint. Even the great diamond dust mirrors were free of the unsightly blemishes that usually afflicted old looking glass as if they, along with everything else in the house, had somehow been frozen in time.

"For as old as this house is it certainly is in good shape," she commented. "Who takes care of its upkeep?"

"Sarah Balfram's estate," Stephen returned. "Apparently Sarah Balfram was so pleased with Lake House when it was finished that she decided she wanted to try to preserve it forever. So she transferred ownership of both the house and the land to a perpetual trust and arranged that there would always be enough funds to take care of it."

"You mean the house doesn't really have any living owners?"

"Nope. It was Sarah Balfram's wish that the house never be sold, only rented."

"Why only renters?"

"Because that way she could make sure that no one ever altered the house or tore it down. In essence, by assigning ownership of the house to a perpetual trust she was able to oversee its destiny forever."

Lauren once again surveyed the entrance hall and marveled at the love Sarah Balfram must have felt for her house to have gone to such lengths to preserve it. Seeing her admiration, Stephen stepped forward and embraced her.

"Are you happy?"

She smiled. "Deliriously."

They kissed and for a moment just rocked in each other's
arms. Then she noticed Garrett standing off to the side and
staring down at the floor.

Lauren gently loosened herself from Stephen's embrace.
"I think it's time we showed Garrett his room. Is everything ready?"

Stephen seemed not to detect the special emphasis in her
voice. "Yes, of course it is."

Lauren looked at him meaningfully as she struggled to
contain a smile. "I mean *everything*."

For several seconds he continued to look at her perplexedly until at last the meaning of her inquiry dawned
upon him. "Oh, right. Yes. Everything's ready."

She winked before retrieving her suitcase. "So which
way to the bedrooms?"

"Ours is the first one on the right up the stairs. Garrett's
is two doors down from that."

She walked over to the walnut staircase and noticed an
electric light switch set into one of the scrolls of the walnut
paneling. Given the age of the house she deduced that it
must have been added at a later date. She clicked it on,
but nothing happened.

Stephen explained, "I'm afraid we won't have electricity
until tomorrow."

"Why?"

"Well, Marty's had a portable generator set up to keep
all of the food in the refrigerators fresh, but most of the
power for the house comes from a battery of generators
in one of the service buildings out back. The only problem
is that the generators are so old someone pretty much has
to watch them all the time, and the applicants for the job
don't show up until tomorrow. Until then I'm afraid we're
just going to have to rough it."

She looked up a little uneasily into the shadowy recesses
of the house.

He smiled impishly. "It'll be more romantic spending our first night by candlelight."

Lauren poked him and started upstairs. Garrett had grabbed his bag and started to follow her when Stephen stopped him. "Hey, sport! Maybe later you can bring down your football and you and I can go outside and throw a few."

"I don't own a football," Garrett returned grumpily.

"Well, why not?"

"Because I don't like football."

The words took Stephen by surprise. "You don't like football? What all-American kid doesn't like football?"

"I don't," Garrett repeated, his ire increasing.

Stephen backed off. "Well, that's all right." He shifted nervously. "What do you like?"

"I like to read."

"He likes chess," Lauren stepped in, offering assistance.

"Hey, I love chess. Maybe we can play some chess later?"

"Yeah, maybe," Garrett said halfheartedly and then raced past his mother up the stairs.

When Garrett reached the top of the stairs he walked a few steps farther until he was out of sight and then stopped. A sinking feeling moved sluggishly through his stomach. He was well aware that his mother had been trying all afternoon to draw him out and cheer him up, and he knew that he had cruelly sidestepped her every attempt.

It was not that he wanted to hurt his mother. It was true that he was unhappy about their move to the mountains for the summer, but this was not the major reason for his discontent. What troubled him now, indeed, what made him feel almost as if he were falling off a cliff, was something he had only recently figured out. Although he now recognized that some part of him had known it for months, it had only been in the last several days that he had realized with certainty that Stephen did not like him.

He did not know how he knew this. Stephen had not said or done anything which overtly indicated this was true. And yet Garrett sensed it in the way Stephen looked at him, sensed it even in the way Stephen had handed him his suitcase when he had unpacked the trunk. And this strange intractable coldness he felt coming from Stephen frightened him.

It frightened him because of the uneasiness he felt in Stephen's presence in general. Stephen's fame and wealth lent him an aura of mystery and power. Thus to Garrett he represented an unknown, and the possibility of his disfavor frightened Garrett all the more, for he did not know what such disapproval augured.

But what frightened Garrett most of all was that his mother seemed so oblivious to it all. She was clearly so taken with Stephen and so willing to go along with whatever decisions he made that Garrett suddenly felt very alone. He knew his mother loved him, but her blindness to Stephen's true feelings toward him made her love seem fragile and insignificant. For the first time in his life he felt truly threatened.

Panting, Lauren reached the top of the stairs and looked at him. "Youth," she said enviously.

Garrett turned around, not wanting her to see the unhappiness in his face. Unaware of the interior struggle he was going through, Lauren continued down the hall. As he followed her, he started to observe the features of the second floor. The wallpaper was a rose color and gave everything a pinkish hue. Everywhere he looked were winding staircases and spindlework archways that bespoke still further rooms and corridors in the labyrinthine house.

When they came to the first door on the right of the hall, Lauren stopped. "This must be my bedroom," she said, turning the knob and walking in. The room beyond was awe-inspiring. Like everything in the house the master bedroom was built on a baronial scale. The walls were hung with a restful blue-gray damask silk, and on the floor was a French Aubusson carpet. At one end of the chamber

a mammoth canopied bed of the same blue-gray damask
was flanked on one side by a marble fireplace and on the
other by a Louis XV dressing table, and on the far left of
the room two elaborately carved amboyna-wood ward-
robes dominated the wall. The door to one of the ward-
robes was ajar, and Garrett noticed that his mother's clothing
had already been deposited neatly inside.

Lauren set her suitcase down as she looked at the bedroom with amazement. "Goodness, it really makes you
wonder what your bedroom's going to be like, doesn't it?"

Her reference to one of the rooms in the house as being
his reminded him again of his plight, and he looked down
at the floor.

She seemed mystified by his reaction. "Oh, come on,
Garrett, I know you think this place is as neat as we do.
Aren't you just a little bit curious about your new bed-
room?"

The words made him feel all funny inside. He was interested. In fact, perhaps the single most distinguishing
feature of his personality was his voracious curiosity about
virtually everything he came into contact with, and Lake
House was certainly no exception. Ever since they had first
pulled up the drive he had burned to know more about
the house. What unknown vastnesses and further architectural oddities did it conceal? And mingled with his curiosity and making it more delicious was a mote of fear.
Lake House was so enormous and its architecture so evo-
cative of old horror movies that he fancied just about anything might be hidden in its innumerable closets and
passageways. But all these feelings were overshadowed by
the thought that still loomed foremost in his mind—that
it was Stephen's house, part of Stephen's world, and this
dampened his enthusiasm.

Out of the corner of his eye he could see that his mother
was eyeing him with annoyance, but he refused to meet
her gaze head-on.

"Well, *I'm* curious," she said as she strode into the hall. He followed, and when they came to the first door past the damask bedroom they peeked in and saw that it was another master bedroom. As his mother shut the door, Garrett wondered why Stephen had not given him this room as his bedroom, but before he could say anything they had moved on. When they came to the next room, Lauren stopped and went inside.

He hesitated for a moment, reluctant to make the commitment of actually viewing his room, but after a sufficient display of dilatoriness he followed her in. As soon as he did so he saw why Stephen had given him this room instead of the second master bedroom. It was smaller and less grand than the first two rooms, but it was clearly much better suited to be the bedroom of a boy. The wallpaper was brown and gilt, and a large bay window filled most of the room's southern exposure, providing the same majestic view of Lake Ketcimanitowa as the drawing room on the first floor. An immense oak bed dominated one side wall. His possessions were already in residence; most visible among these were his *National Geographic* Map of the Heavens framed neatly on one of the walls, his Commodore computer sitting on a desk across from the bed, his models of the Starship *Enterprise*, the space probe *Mariner*, and the space shuttle *Discovery*, and his sizable collection of books and paperbacks.

But one sight startled him and filled him with both rapture and mystification: a telescope standing in the middle of the bay window. He looked at his mother with amazement, for it was not just any telescope but the Lieder 4000. He could not even begin to estimate how many times he had stood at the window of F.A.O Schwarz on Fifth Avenue and desperately tried to imagine what it would be like to own it.

He ran forward with disbelief to examine all of the features that had made the telescope seem so desirable and so unattainable—the 1,200-millimeter lens, the precision electric motor which enabled it to continuously adjust for the rotation of the earth and keep it aimed at an object in the heavens. Suddenly he felt very contrite over the way he had been behaving. "Oh, Mom, I didn't even think you knew that I wanted it."

"Oh, sure. You only kept steering me over to F.A.O. Schwarz every chance you got."

"Only twice," he defended sheepishly. He looked back at the telescope, almost afraid to touch it.

"So why don't you try it out?" she prodded.

He blinked at her, still unable to believe that the Lieder 4000 was his. Cautiously he removed the lens cap and inserted the eyepiece. He opened one of the bay windows and aimed the telescope at the mountains in the distance. It took him a few minutes to get the hang of focusing it, but when he finally succeeded, he discovered to his delight that its magnifying powers surpassed even his loftiest expectations. Not only could he see the trees on the distant mountains as clearly as if they were in his own backyard, but he could even see the red crest of a cardinal as it fluttered around in the branches of a silvery birch.

"This is excellent!" he exclaimed. And then he remembered the hefty price tag the telescope had displayed as it sat in the window of F.A.O. Schwarz. "But where did you get the money to buy it?"

"Honey, Stephen and I bought it for you."

His stomach tightened as he looked at the telescope less fondly. This time he wasn't able to conceal his distress.

"Garrett, what is it?" she asked.

"Nothing," he said, his heart pounding as he tried vainly to keep from showing his feelings.

She sighed. "Come on, you've been beetle-browed all afternoon. I know something's bothering you. So instead of making me coax, why don't you just tell me about it now?"

He looked at her despairingly, fearful she would not

believe what he had to say, but before he knew it the words came tumbling out.

"I don't think Stephen likes me."

She looked at him with astonishment. "What on earth makes you say that?"

His mind raced. What could he say to her? That he did not like the way Stephen looked at him? "I don't know. It's just a feeling I get," he stammered. As soon as the words left his mouth his heart sank, for he knew that he had not communicated the full extent of what he felt.

"What sort of feeling?"

"A feeling like he's being nice to me only because you're there. But if you weren't there . . ." His voice trailed off.

She smiled. "Oh, Garrett, I'm sure all your feeling is just the newness of your relationship. The two of you haven't even spent enough time together for him not to like you."

"But how do you know it's not going to be like before?" he snapped.

"What do you mean?"

"You said the same thing about some of your other boyfriends, and looked what happened."

His remark angered her. "If you mean Tim, we've already been through all that. I know it was a mistake to let him move in with us, and I'm sorry. But you can't continue to hold that against me forever."

He looked down stubbornly, but before he could say anything else she put her arm around him and sat him down beside her on the bed. "Listen, Garrett, you and I have always had a sort of understanding. We've always respected each other's wishes. I know it hasn't been easy on you with me being away so much on writing assignments, but you've been really good about it. And strange though some of your interests are, I've always supported them and tried to see that you've had everything you've needed for your hobbies. Now I know it's not going to be easy, but you said you were going to give Stephen a chance. So for my sake, won't you put this idea out of your head and at least try to meet him halfway?"

Her request merely caused the sinking in his stomach to intensify, but as he looked into her eyes and saw how much it meant to her, he realized he had no choice. He knew that if he continued on his tack of moody obstinacy he would only alienate her further.

"Okay," he said quietly, hoping she did not detect the pessimism in his voice.

She hugged him. "I knew I could count on you."

Almost on cue, there came the sound of Stephen clunking his suitcase down in the bedroom down the hall, and Lauren stood up. "Well, I'm going to go do some unpacking. Do you want to come with me or do you want to stay and tinker with your new telescope?"

"I'll stay," he said.

"Okay." She kissed him on the forehead and then went out.

Left alone, Garrett looked back at the telescope. Knowing now it had been purchased with Stephen's money, he considered never touching it again. But then he looked at all of its special features and recalled how remarkable its powers of magnification were. He approached it slowly and allowed his finger to trace down its sleek black exterior. What could he do about his failure to convince his mother about Stephen? Since simply telling her had proved so unsuccessful, he had to find another way to accomplish the task. And although he did not know what that was, something told him it was going to require every last ounce of resourcefulness he possessed.

When Lauren reached the master bedroom, she found Stephen unpacking his suitcase.

"That was Marty," he said when she entered. "He called to tell me that the new single jumped ten places on the charts last week."

"Oh, you knew it would," she said happily as she sat down on the bed and bounced a couple of times to test its firmness. To her delight, despite the obvious age of the bed its mattress seemed new.

"Did you get Garrett settled in his room?"

"Yes."

"Did he like the telescope?"

"He loved it," she murmured distantly as she thought again of Garrett's assertion that Stephen did not like him.

"But . . . ?" he countered, sensing her pensiveness.

"Oh, it's nothing. It's just something Garrett said."

"What was that?"

She pursed her brow, not wanting to hurt his feelings. "Well, you know how difficult all this has been for him. Somehow he's gotten into his head this crazy idea that you don't like him."

As she had expected, Stephen seemed surprised. "He thinks that?"

"Yes, but you know how eleven-year-olds are. He was probably just seeing how I would react. Gauging my feelings. I'm sure it had nothing to do with you."

"No, maybe it does," Stephen said unexpectedly, and this time it was her turn to be surprised. She looked at him silently, waiting for him to continue.

"The truth is, I'm not really used to kids. That's probably why I forgot all about the telescope downstairs when you were dropping all those hints about it." He turned to her beseechingly. "I told you when we got married I didn't have the foggiest idea how to be a father. I'm sure that's what Garrett is sensing. I can get up and perform in front of twenty thousand people, but when it comes to carrying on a conversation with an eleven-year-old I just don't know what to say. Maybe just being up here and spending some time together will help."

"That's what I told him," she comforted. And then, seeing the brooding look in his eyes, she crossed the room and put her arms around him. "You know, I do have a certain amount of experience in these areas."

"What do you mean?"

"I mean that I haven't spent eleven years as a mother for nothing. If you like I can give you a few pointers."

"Like what?"

"First, don't worry about how to carry on a conversation with him. The key is just to get him started. That's the first thing you have to know about talking to eleven-year-olds. Once you get them started, they'll do all the rest."

"And how do I get him started?"

"That's easy," she said. "Just ask him something about spaceships or extraterrestrials."

"Extraterrestrials?" he said, raising an eyebrow and grinning.

She laughed and poked him in the ribs. "Yeah, just show him that you have even the slightest interest in anything weird or creepy and you'll have him eating out of the palm of your hand."

"Well, I think I'll practice on you," he said as he returned the poke and then chased her back to the bed. She squealed, trying to get away, but he caught her and tried to pin her against the mattress. They wrestled around on the bed for several minutes, laughing and kissing, and then she lay in his arms, his astonishing clear green-gray eyes fixed on hers, and she was mesmerized by their uncanny depths. She shuddered with the thrill of being mastered by something or someone you couldn't quite control, and wondered what she had done to deserve this magnificent man, about whom she still had so much to discover.

After she finished unpacking, Lauren spent the rest of the afternoon opening windows and allowing the cool smell of the pines to disperse the mustiness of the house, and poking around in the refrigerators and the cupboards, taking inventory of the ample provisions Marty had laid in for them. However, she confined her wandering only to those rooms Stephen had already shown them, for despite her desire to know everything there was to know about this wonderful house, darkness came quickly to the forest and she reasoned it would be wiser for her to wait until they had electricity before embarking on further exploration.

Finding that Marty had also seen to it that the gas stove was operable, she took some boneless chicken breasts out of the kitchen's huge walk-in refrigerator and sautéed them in butter and wine. She also found a fresh loaf of French bread, the makings for a salad, and even a case of champagne, and by dinnertime she had not only prepared them all a meal fit for a king, but also filled the ruby-red dining room with enough candles to illuminate a cathedral.

After she set the food on the table, she looked out the expanse of dining-room windows and again became transfixed by the awesome beauty of the place. In the last rays of the setting sun the formerly dark-blue waters of the lake had become a pointillist explosion of golds and vermilions, and a pair of loons swam near the shore. Their mournful cries echoed in the stillness of the twilight. With the coming of the cooler evening air a veil of mist started to rise off the water.

Realizing that the food was going to get cold if she did not force herself out of her reverie, she called Stephen and Garrett down to dinner.

"It certainly is beautiful out here at night," she said, gazing out the window at the smattering of stars that had begun to flicker in the sky. She looked at Garrett, his face aglow in the lambent light of the candles. "What was it you were telling me the other day about why stars twinkle?"

He kept his eyes trained on his plate as he pushed his fork into a piece of chicken. "They twinkle because of fluctuations in the earth's atmosphere. If you looked at the same stars from outer space they wouldn't twinkle at all."

"Where did you learn that?"

"At a lecture at the planetarium."

She blinked, impressed. Although the precocious range of his knowledge was a natural result of his curiosity and his love of books, some of the information he possessed still amazed her. She looked at Stephen and saw that he had also paid attention to what Garrett had said. "Garrett's teachers say that he has quite an aptitude for science," she informed him.

Stephen looked at Garrett in an obviously interested way. "Your mother tells me you'll make good use of that telescope."

"Yes, thanks. I really like it," he said stiltedly.

Stephen glanced at Lauren and took a deep breath. "So what was that book about you were reading earlier? UFOs?"

Lauren smiled. With a motherly glance too subtle for anyone but a son to notice she prodded him on.

"Yes, UFOs," he returned.

"So what's the verdict?" Stephen continued. "Are spaceships from other planets really visiting the earth?"

For the first time Garrett showed a hint of enthusiasm. "Of course they are. Thousands of people see them every year."

Stephen smiled. "You mean thousands of people see something every year. But can't most of the things people see be explained away as weather balloons and things like that?"

Garrett frowned, annoyed. Although he was aware of the notion that UFOs could be explained away as weather balloons and other prosaic objects, most of the books he had read tended to eschew such mundane explanations. To his mind such interpretations were irritatingly irrelevant. "They're not weather balloons," he groused. "I've got a book upstairs by a NASA scientist who goes around interviewing people who say they've seen UFOs, and he says that under hypnosis some of them can even remember having gone aboard flying saucers."

The impassioned conviction of his answer seemed to disconcert Stephen. It also somewhat embarrassed Lauren, although she still felt a flush of maternal pride at her son's wide-ranging interests.

Stephen pressed on, determined to maintain the conversation. "Well, if so many people are being taken aboard these things, why don't we ever hear about them until after the fact? I mean, why doesn't anyone ever witness the people being taken aboard the UFOs *before* the person starts to ramble on about it under hypnosis?"

"Because the UFOs always choose such isolated places to come down," Garrett returned confidently as he took another bite of chicken. "You know, uninhabited stretches of highway and mountaintops and stuff. Places where they won't be seen."

Again Stephen looked as if either the self-assurance of

Garrett's delivery or the information itself caused him some discomfort. "If spaceships from other planets were visiting the earth, and if they were coming down in isolated places, I don't know why anyone would be crazy enough to get aboard one." He delivered the line with a certain amount of stiffness and to no one in particular as he took another gulp of champagne.

Garrett looked at Stephen perplexedly. "Why would it be crazy to go aboard a UFO?"

"Because if you were walking through the mountains and you came upon a spacecraft from another world just sitting there, how on earth would you have any idea what was waiting for you on the inside? You don't know whether the creatures occupying it are going to be friendly or not. You don't even know if the way they think is going to resemble the way we think. They might be so alien that concepts such as good and evil mean nothing to them. You may be no more than an insect to them, or worse, a microbe to be looked at under a microscope and then preserved in formaldehyde in some intergalactic natural history museum."

Garrett was genuinely surprised. His beliefs about beings from other planets had been forged primarily by recent movies, and it had simply never occurred to him that the inhabitants of UFOs might be anything untoward. In his mind they were all like E.T., shy, ancient, and benevolent. At the moment they seemed infinitely more congenial than the humanity across the table.

Here was just the kind of thing that made him dislike his new stepfather. Stephen's attempts to engage him in conversation were so transparent and patronizing. He obviously had no real interest in UFOs and was skeptical about their very existence. Garrett perceived in Stephen's retorts a hint of the same subtle hostility he had sensed previously, and it suddenly occurred to him that this might be precisely the opportunity he had been looking for. He realized that if he could draw Stephen out, lure him into launching an even more overt attack, then his mother might see for herself once and for all what Stephen's real feelings toward him were. He was racking his brain to determine what he might say to initiate this plan when his mother intervened.

"Stephen, wouldn't you at least be curious?"

"If you came upon some sort of alien spacecraft sitting in the middle of nowhere, would you blunder inside?"

"No, but—"

"I would. I wouldn't care what happened to me," Garrett blurted out. The words came tumbling out of his mouth so quickly they surprised him almost as much as they seemed to surprise the adults. Although it had never really occurred to him before, his unhappiness over his mother's marriage made him realize how much he longed to meet his own E.T., to have a magical, all-powerful friend who would both understand and protect him and perhaps even take him off to some better and more hospitable world. As soon as he uttered the words he felt hopeful he had stumbled upon the provocation he had been looking for, because the expression on Stephen's face instantly became one of perturbed disbelief.

For several seconds Garrett waited, but then, to his great disappointment, instead of attacking him Stephen simply shrugged his shoulders and settled back in his chair. At first Garrett felt thwarted, but then he looked at his mother and saw his reply had earned from her a look of unabashed horror.

"What do you mean, you wouldn't care what happened to you?" she challenged, and the distress in her voice confirmed for Garrett what he already knew, that his plan had backfired and he had managed to alarm her far more than annoy Stephen. Her continued stare told him that she really expected some sort of response, and this left him in a quandary. On the one hand he did not want to upset her

further, but on the other, being forced to retract his statement in front of Stephen seemed equally disagreeable. Finally, forced into a corner, he opted for honesty.

"I don't," he repeated softly as an uneasy silence fell
over the room, and as if in response to the moment one
of the candles suddenly sputtered, casting strange shadows
on the wall.

This confession filled Lauren with horror. It showed her
how upset her son truly was. In addition, his interest in UFOs
disturbed her more than she cared to admit. Perhaps it was
more than just a childish fantasy. She realized that this was
the first time she had encountered an example of her son's
thinking that so radically departed from her own. Whatever
the reason, she had a problem on her hands, but she feared
by pursuing the topic she would topple whatever headway
Stephen and Garrett had made by talking together.

She suppressed her own misgivings and pushed herself
away from the table. "I think it's time for dessert," she
said. She took a large Sacher torte from the sideboard and
served them each a piece. She watched as they ate it, hoping
the rich chocolate confection might dispel the somber mood,
but conversation remained desultory. When they finished
she tried a different approach.

"You know, it's an awfully pretty night out," she said,
looking out the window. "What do you say we all go out
and sit on the veranda for a while?"

The suggestion seemed to appall Garrett, but it was
Stephen who spoke first. "Great idea, honey! But first I
gotta make a call. When I talked to Marty today he told
me that one of the junior execs at the record company
okayed an ad design for a teen magazine without running
it by me first. I promised Marty I'd call him back tonight
so we could figure out what to do about it."

"But that won't take long, will it?"

He grinned sheepishly. "I hope not. But you know how
Marty is."

Once the plan no longer included Stephen, Garrett became more amenable to Lauren's suggestion, and after she finished cleaning up they went out onto the veranda to sit. To Lauren's delight the night was now alive with the stridulations of insects and the cool mountain air was even more redolent with the smell of pines than before, but all of this seemed lost on Garrett. He remained as withdrawn as ever, so much so that by the time she tucked him in that night, leaving him to contend with the darkness of the house armed with no more than a First Alert flashlight, she had grown quite concerned.

When she entered the master bedroom, her own flashlight clenched tightly in her hand, she saw Stephen had left only one large candelabrum burning on a nightstand and was already in bed.

"So how did your phone call go?" she asked.

"Fine."

"Did you get the ad withdrawn?"

"No, I got the junior exec fired."

She looked at him with surprise. "Over one mistake? Isn't that a bit drastic?"

He smiled at her gently. "Honey, that's the way the game is played. Part of the reason I've gotten where I am today is that I've controlled my image very carefully. The only way I can maintain that sort of control is to run a tight ship. I just can't afford to allow slipups like that."

She understood his reasoning, but the severity of his action seemed a little extreme. Finally, realizing she had much more pressing concerns than worrying about the fate of the junior exec, she returned her attention to the matter at hand.

"Stephen, I'm worried about Garrett," she said as she slipped off her shoes.

He rolled over in the sheets, his face half eclipsed in the circle of light cast by the candelabrum. "Why?"

She clicked off the flashlight and started to unbutton her blouse.

"I don't know . . . after the way the evening ended I just felt a little funny leaving him all alone in a strange house without electricity."

"He's not all alone."

"You know what I mean," she said as she slipped out of her dress.

Stephen snorted and then reached out to pull her into the bed. As he did so he pulled free from the sheets. The golden sheen of the candlelight on his naked and well-muscled torso was arousing, but she avoided his grasp.

He seemed to get the point and sat up in the bed. "Okay, so did Garrett say he was afraid?"

"Nooo," she drawled as she took off the last of her clothing and put on a light silk robe.

"Then what's the problem?"

"The problem is that I'm not so sure he would tell me if he was afraid. He can be a very proud little boy. Sometimes its like trying to pry secrets out of the devil to get him to talk."

Stephen exhaled loudly. "So what do you suggest we do?"

She looked at him, a trifle irritated, then suddenly it hit her that perhaps he had been more unnerved by what Garrett had said than she had realized. "Garrett's little talk about getting aboard UFOs really got to you, didn't it?"

"Sort of," he conceded. "Didn't it bother you a bit?"

"A bit, but it's all part of being a little boy."

"I understand," he said too quickly, and something in the tone of his voice seemed unconvincing. "Well, why did *you* get upset by what he said about UFOs?"

The question intrigued her. In fact, she had been puzzling over its various and possible answers all night and had finally started to form an opinion about it. "I think it might be because of the time period I was raised in," she said enigmatically.

Her answer confused him. "What do you mean?"

"Well, you know, when we were growing up all the monsters and alien spacemen in the movies were bad. Now they're all good guys. If you see a movie in which a kid meets something coming out of a spaceship, you know it's going to be his best friend. I guess it's just a different way of looking at things."

"But is it a good way of looking at things?" Stephen countered.

Lauren gazed meditatively off into the distance, the cogs of her writer's mind now turning. "I don't know. At some level of the collective human psyche we seem to have decided it's a good way of looking at things. At least that's the attitude we're allowing to surface in our modern myths, our movies. But is it a good way of looking at things? I mean, if we really were to learn that a flying saucer was approaching the earth, should we ignore the possibility it might be hostile and allow it to land without interference?

Or should we deem that too great a risk to take and shoot
first and ask questions later?"

Stephen snorted. "Sounds safer to shoot first, I think."

"But what if it *was* friendly?" she asked. "What if it
possessed the knowledge and wisdom to propel us light-
years ahead in our evolution and welcoming it with open
arms turned out to be the best decision we ever made?"

"That's a long shot."

"But how can you be so sure?"

"They'll probably be from the extraterrestrial equivalent
of Hollywood, so by nature they'll be aggressive." He
laughed.

"Oh, Stephen!"

"Oh, what?"

She was just about to say something else when he reached
for her again and this time managed to catch hold of her
and pull her onto the massive canopied bed.

"Stephen!" she objected with surprise, but before she
could say anything else he had drawn up over her and was
staring at her with such intensity she fell silent. She wanted
to talk some more, but as she looked at the way the candlelight gleamed on his hair and the musculature of his
shoulders she felt her resolve slipping away. An amused
glint came into his eyes as he seemed to sense the power
he had over her, and with one deft move he pushed her
robe back over her shoulders. With mesmerizing grace he
traced his finger down her neck and along the side of her
breast as he started to kiss her, first gently, but then more
roughly.

Becoming increasingly aroused, she grabbed his chest
and moved her hands down the sides of his rib cage, but
when she reached the well-defined muscles of his legs and
then went to reach between them, he stopped her. "Don't
worry about me," he whispered as he kissed down the
side of her neck. "Tonight I only want you to be happy."
He gently eased her back into the pillows as he continued

to move down her body, kissing first her breasts and then her stomach as his hand moved up the inner surface of her thigh.

He continued to move over her with such skill and sensitivity that by the time they were locked together and were rocking back and forth in the feverish, almost frantic tempo of their lovemaking, she was racked with waves of pleasure.

The candles had long since burned out when they finally finished, and after he had collapsed and drifted beyond exhaustion and into sleep beside her, she lay awake for a little while longer and simply savored the memory of how he made her feel.

Stephen made love better than any man she had ever been with, even Miklos. Every time was different. Sometimes he advanced slowly, engaging in only the gentlest foreplay until she was so excited she could barely stand it. Sometimes he read poetry to her, or seduced her by arranging just the right romantic setting. And sometimes, like tonight, he was forceful, almost brutish. But always he seemed to know exactly how to go about fulfilling his own needs while still being sensitive to hers. He touched her in just the right places. He intuited when and where he needed to be gentle, and when he could be rough.

She looked at him in the moonlight. She loved him so much she almost ached. This pleased her, but it also frightened her. Every time their lovemaking reached some new height, she realized anew how much power he had over her, and sometimes she even found herself wondering how he had learned to be such a consummate lover. How many women had he known before her? She had never asked, but she knew there had to have been many. His prowess as a ladies' man was well known, and she had seen the legions of groupies that waited for him whenever he performed. For a few seconds this thought troubled her, and she snuggled up closer to him. But she was able to reflect on it only a moment longer before she too drifted off to sleep, lulled by the plaintive and distant cries of a whippoorwill.

For Garrett, falling asleep was difficult. For several minutes after his mother tucked him in he brooded about how badly he had botched his attempt to get Stephen to reveal himself. But then slowly, as his attention shifted to the fact that he was all alone in the darkness of the room, he began to get scared. At first he tried to ignore his growing unrest. He assured himself that there was nothing to be afraid of. But as the chatter of his own thoughts quieted, he became increasingly aware of the sounds of the night, the scratchings of the pine needles against the sides of the house, and the *chree chree* of the katydids and other insects.

He considered sleeping with the flashlight on, but it occurred to him that if the batteries ran down before morning he might wake in the middle of the night with no light at all—a possibility too horrible even to contemplate. Next he considered calling out to his mother, but this seemed to offer only a temporary reprieve at best, and it also meant revealing his fear of the darkness to Stephen, which was simply out of the question. Finally, not knowing what else to do, he pulled the sheet, blanket, and bedspread up over his face and fashioned them into a sort of mask, leaving only an open space around his nose so that he could breathe.

Enclosed in his cocoon he resolved to make an earnest effort to fall asleep and for a few moments felt secure. But then the sounds of the night closed in on him once again. Outside he heard something splash in the lake, and the wind rustled mournfully through the pines. The house itself seemed to take on new and eerie life. Here and there it creaked and popped as if it had only been slumbering— the darkness had awakened it and urged it now to flex its sinews and its joints. Somewhere in the distance something snapped. A minute later and farther away a window rattled. And farther still, deep within the very bowels of the house, timbers creaked and moaned as if stressed by forces they were only barely able to contain.

With each new sound his fear increased until he was gripped by such panic that he thought he would have to scream. He was also starting to become unbearably hot under the weight of so many covers and wanted more than anything to kick them off. But he was too frightened to move. It seemed like an eternity before he finally drifted into the comforting oblivion of his own unconsciousness.

He did not know how long he had been asleep when something woke him.

For a moment he was disoriented and stared confusedly around the room, wondering why everything seemed so unfamiliar. But when he finally pieced together where he was, a dark tide of terror swept over him once again.

Had he heard a sound?

He listened and heard nothing save for the whispering of the pines outside.

But then, as he lay awake in bed, his hands sweating and his heart pounding, he became aware of a movement.

It was still some distance away, and the sound it made was not the sound of footsteps, nor even a faint scraping or rustling. In fact, it was not a sound at all. But somehow he knew that something was in the hall to the right of the room. He could discern the slow and measured pace of its approach. And yet the precise nature of his perception remained a mystery to him.

Was it his imagination?

No sooner had the thought crossed his mind than every fiber of his being told him it was not. Desperately he tried to decipher how or why he knew what he knew, and suddenly it occurred to him that he was *feeling* the presence of the thing, its proximity—just as one might feel the

nearness of a heated object, a hot poker. Only it was not
heat that he was sensing, but power. Whatever the thing
was, it was so powerful that its presence could be felt even
through the wall that separated his room from the hall.

And still it drew closer.

His terror growing, he considered yelling for help. But
it occurred to him that perhaps the thing did not know he
was there. Perhaps it was only making some routine transit
of the house and by calling for help he might alert it to
his presence.

Suddenly he remembered the flashlight. It was just a few
feet away on the night table. If he could reach it without
making the bed creak . . . . Perhaps he could blind the
thing with the beam of light long enough to allow him to
escape. His senses told him the thing was now only about
twenty feet from his room and closing in fast.

He started to pull his hand out from under the covers,
but the mattress springs squeaked slightly, and he stopped.
He once again inched his hand upward, but he knew he
had to move quickly. Now the thing was only about ten
feet from his door. Finally, he pulled his hands free of the
blanket and felt a rush of exhilaration, but it was too late.
The door to his bedroom burst open with such force he
expected to hear it bang into the wall. Only it did not.
There was only an eerie silence as the thing swept into the
room.

For a second he thought he had screamed. At least he
felt his mouth had opened wide with terror. But then he
realized his larynx, indeed every muscle in his body, was
paralyzed. Only his eyes were free of the deadly spell, and
in the moonlight he could see quite clearly the open door
and the darkness of the hallway beyond. And for the first
time he saw the intruder.

Standing in the doorway was something like the figure
of a man, only composed solely out of a turbulent and
seething darkness. In height the thing towered well over

six feet, and occasionally in its murky and vaporous form there appeared the suggestion of massive sinews. But whatever was human ended there, for instead of a face it possessed only an impenetrable darkness. Now that it was no longer shielded by the walls it exuded a staggering raw force and power; it almost seemed to Garrett as if he were in the presence of a hurricane. Only he was not, for there was no sound or movement of air coming from the thing, only a pounding, all-consuming silence.

Despite the figure's lack of a face, Garrett sensed that the thing was looking at him. Indeed, no sooner had the thought crossed his mind than suddenly the thing started forward once again. For a moment Garrett thought his heart would stop as it moved right up to the very edge of the bed and then circled slowly as if to study him. But for what purpose? Deciding which limb to rend first? Or whether to kill him now or wait until later? He did not know. He was so weak with terror he was afraid he was going to faint.

In the tumult of his thoughts he summoned up the will-power to mutter a silent prayer, for he was certain he was going to die.

But then to his great surprise the thing withdrew, churning like a storm cloud and pulling its awesome power back with it. As gently as if it were his own mother, it pulled the door softly shut and drifted back into the cavernous house.

He was alone in the darkness once again.

The next morning when Garrett felt a hand close upon his shoulder he screamed and somersaulted out of bed. It was only his mother.

"Good Lord, Garrett, what is it?" she asked, her eyes wide with alarm.

He blinked as he looked confusedly around the room. He half expected to see the thing still standing in the doorway, but instead his eyes were met with the brilliance of the early-morning sun streaming through the window. He was so relieved day had finally come it that it took several seconds for him to realize his mother was still waiting for him to explain.

"Last night something came into my room!" The words fairly flew out of his mouth.

She frowned. "What do you mean, something came into your room?"

"Last night in the middle of the night something opened my door and came into my room."

She looked at him skeptically. "You mean someone came into your room? A person?"

He shook his head as he tried to find the right words to describe his experience. "No, not a person really. I mean, it looked like a person, a man, only instead of being made out of skin and stuff it looked like he was made out of a cloud of black smoke."

Her expression became slightly annoyed as she started to make his bed. "Are you sure it wasn't Stephen? Maybe Stephen looked in on you last night."

This time it was Garrett's turn to be skeptical. Even ignoring the preposterousness of the notion that Stephen might care enough about his welfare to look in on him during the night, the thing had clearly not been Stephen.

"I told you, it was a man who looked like he was made out of black smoke. He didn't even seem to have a face. Besides, he was a lot taller than Stephen. And bigger too."

She stopped making the bed. "Then it must have been a dream."

"No, it wasn't a dream!" he insisted.

His obstinacy finally got to her, and she swung around angrily. "Then what are you telling me? That you saw a ghost or some kind of creature from outer space?"

The question took Garrett off-guard, and he considered it with some seriousness. It had not occurred to him that the figure might have been a ghost, for in his mind ghosts were white and translucent and gave off light. His nocturnal visitor had been unghostlike in these respects. Could the thing have come from a UFO? But just as he was about to consider this possibility, he saw how upset she was becoming. He wanted desperately to convince her of the reality of his experience—the prospect of spending another night in the house without her knowing about its presence seemed unthinkable. But on the other hand, the fear in her eyes reminded him just a little too much of the way she had reacted to his dinner conversation the night before, and this was something he wanted to avoid at all costs. He mulled over his options and then finally, reluctantly, he acquiesced. "No, it wasn't a ghost or anything. I guess it was only a bad dream."

Her relief was visible. "Of course it was," she said as she resumed making the bed. She even began to hum, and when she finished she said brightly, "Now go wash your face and hands and hurry and get dressed."

"Why?"

She smiled even more broadly as she tousled his hair. "Because I'm making your favorite breakfast. I'm making pancakes."

Although Lauren was certain his experience had been a dream, his description of the thing bothered her. An entity made out of a cloud of black smoke just did not seem like something a child would spontaneously come up with, and by the time Stephen came out of his shower and put on a bright-blue velour robe, she felt compelled to tell him about it.

"Garrett just said something a little strange," she said.

"What's that?" Stephen asked as he looked in the mirror and fluffed his curls so they would dry properly.

"He said something came into his room last night."

He knitted his brow. "What came into his room?"

"He said it looked like a man made out of black smoke."

Stephen's curiosity faded. "Oh, you mean he had a bad dream."

"But that's just it," Lauren countered. "Don't you think that's an unusual image for a little boy to come up with in a dream?"

"What image?"

"To describe someone as being made out of black smoke?"

"No, I don't—at least, not for someone as imaginative as Garrett obviously is."

"You're right, I guess," she said. But still something

about Garrett's description of the thing gnawed at her. Finally, after convincing herself she was only being silly, she smiled. "Hey, since it's our first real day in the house, why don't the three of us do something together? You know, something like a picnic?"

"A great idea," he returned.

For Garrett, breakfast started out more pleasantly than he expected. True to her word, his mother made pancakes, and even Stephen seemed in unusually good spirits. Garrett had decided to make a show of tolerating Stephen. This meant being polite, if not exactly warm. After the fiasco of the evening before he did not want to alienate his mother any further. However, he also still did not trust Stephen. He decided the best approach was simply to bide his time and pray that eventually something would happen that would cause his mother to see Stephen's true colors.

When the meal was over, Stephen and his mother launched into such a gushy display of affection that he was forced to flee to the drawing room. He sat in one of the wing chairs next to the fireplace. Upon reflection he realized he was still too unsettled by his encounter with the thing to even think about going back upstairs alone. Such a venture would be tempting fate, at best. But as he continued to dangle his feet over the faded oriental carpet and mull over his experience, several things occurred to him which caused him to reconsider.

It crossed his mind that since the thing in his room had been composed of darkness, there was perhaps a certain logic in assuming it came out only after dark. After all, it had provided no hint of its presence until well after nightfall. Similarly, given that shadows were dispersed by sunlight, and most ghosts and monsters had a long and well-known history of coming out only at night, it seemed likely that venturing about the house during the daylight hours would be safe.

As the experience of the night before retreated further and further into the misty half-reality of memory, his curiosity about the house and its architectural peculiarities returned. Was there some sort of connection between the thing and the other strange features the house possessed? And if not, what purpose did they serve? His longing to know the answers to such questions outweighed his fears, and he decided to go exploring.

He left the drawing room and went upstairs, but when he reached the second-floor hallway a wave of misgiving passed through him once again. He suppressed it, but did make one concession. Remembering that the thing had come from the right, from the part of the hallway beyond his bedroom, he decided not to proceed in that direction and turned left instead.

As he walked down the hall he noticed it looked very much the same as the hall in which their bedrooms were situated. The wallpaper was the same rose color, and everywhere he looked were still more bedrooms. Uninterested in exploring these, he continued on until he came to a small vestibule at the far end of the hall. On one wall was a large circular window, and on the other walls was a profusion of doors. Choosing one at random, he turned the knob and cautiously crept in.

Inside was an upstairs drawing room. Its walls were paneled with elaborately carved oak squares, and on one wall a row of leaded-glass lancet windows looked out on the forest beyond. Like all of the rooms in the house it was richly furnished, and dotting its perimeter were a number of doors and a few staircases.

Seeing nothing untoward, Garrett padded into the room, but by the time he had walked about halfway through he was overcome with such a feeling of dizziness he had to veer sharply to the left and collapse onto one of the sofas. At first he thought he might be coming down with something, but then he remembered the sitting room on the first floor that had made them all feel dizzy, and he examined the room's architecture once again.

As he had suspected, careful scrutiny revealed that the floor, walls, and ceiling were all slightly askew. Indeed, its geometry was even more out of kilter than the sitting room's. But what rendered its pronounced distortion invisible to the human eye was that everything, from the carving in the oak panels to the length of the legs on the furniture, had been carefully designed and reproportioned to conceal this fact.

Giggling with delight at such trickery, he stood and started through the room again. But again the room started to spin around him, and before he realized what was happening he was lurching headlong toward one of the doors. He lunged for the knob and blundered through. Inside he suddenly found himself face to face with a wild boar. Terrified, he screamed and started to run, but in his panic he tripped and fell over his own feet. When he turned around he saw the boar was stuffed.

His heart still pounding, he righted himself and saw the boar graced what appeared to be some sort of trophy room. The walls were covered with panels of birch bark, and everywhere he looked were stuffed animals and mounted animal heads. By a giant stone fireplace at the far end of the room stood a stuffed bear. Over the fireplace was the head of a moose, and gazing dumbly from around the room were deer heads, mountain lions, pheasants, and ducks. Even the rugs on the floor were fashioned out of various animal pelts, all bearing mute testimony to long-ago hunts. The room possessed a stale preservative smell he recognized from the taxidermy displays of museums.

On another occasion this stuffed display might have captivated him, but given his experiences in the house thus far, the smell and the frozen accusing stares of so many dead an-

imals made him uncomfortable. Seeing a door to the left of
the fireplace, he quickly crossed over and turned the knob.
It opened onto a narrow set of stairs leading down.

To his surprise the stairs led him once again to the main
entrance hall of the house. Miffed at ending up where he
had begun, he walked across to the main staircase and went
back upstairs. Now he was doubly determined to find out
more about the house.

This time when he reached the vestibule at the end of
the hall he chose another door. Inside he discovered what
appeared to be a large linen room. He passed through a
maze of smaller rooms branching off it and was once again
forced to go down a flight of stairs that emptied into one
of the sun porches. At least he had avoided returning to
the entrance hall. Still, he had been unceremoniously dis-
charged into one of the outer first-floor rooms.

Again and again he tried to make his way through the
house, but each time he encountered some hindrance or ob-
stacle that foiled his effort. Sometimes the strange and
twisting architecture of the house itself obliged him to take
certain directions. Sometimes a beguiling maze of halls could
not be resisted and led nowhere, into a cul-de-sac of rooms.
Sometimes a corridor seemed too dark to venture into.

Whatever the case, after about half a dozen such attempts
a remarkable realization slowly dawned on him. Far from
being haphazard or merely eccentric, the layout of the
house had a curious rhyme and reason. It was almost too
fantastic to believe, but it appeared the house·had been
carefully designed to prevent anyone from venturing too
deeply into its inner recesses.

As frustrated as he felt, he was very pleased with himself
for having figured this out. But as he sat on the entrance-
hall steps and gazed up into the spiderweb of stairways over
his head he realized his discovery only brought with it more
questions. Why had Sarah Balfram devised such elaborate
strategies to control and influence the route a person took

through her house? And what might he find if he managed to outwit her various stratagems and travel deeper into its interior? This last question sent a chill through him.

After finishing the breakfast dishes and seeing Stephen off to ready the generator building for the job applicants, Lauren decided to do some exploring of her own. However, she was still so fascinated by some of the rooms she had already seen she decided that the first thing she was going to do was take another stroll through the first floor.

Again what drew her attention as she wandered through the rooms were the many treasures the house contained. In the butler's pantry she lingered admiringly over the large collection of Georgian silver and Meissen porcelain, and in the Moorish-styled billiard room she was astounded to find what appeared to be an authentic Sung-dynasty vase. But as she continued on, what started to strike her as odd about the house was how strangely anonymous it was. The rooms were opulently furnished; even the smallest details had been carefully thought out and attended to. But nowhere was there any sign the house had ever really been lived in. There were no portraits of Sarah Balfram or any other members of her family. Even the pages of the books in the library were still uncut—obviously no one had ever actually used the library as a place to read.

Unsettled by the discovery, she went upstairs via the servants' entrance off the kitchen. Wandering through some of the servants' rooms she searched for some sign they had once been inhabited, but again she found nothing. There were no old letters stuffed behind any of the mirrors, no stray coat hangers left in any of the closets, no old magazines, no medicine bottles, not even any lining paper in any of the bureau drawers.

Still, there were other signs the house had been used.

Floorboards had been rubbed smooth by the passage of feet, and carpets had started to go threadbare in what appeared to be the most heavily trafficked areas. But why, she wondered, had none of the house's inhabitants ever really left a personal mark upon the place?

Spurred on by this question, she decided to go deeper into the house, but quickly became lost in a crisscrossing of hallways with no avenue out but a narrow set of stairs. After going down them she found herself in the front entrance hall of the house and saw Garrett sitting solemnly on the main staircase. She smiled at him, but continued to look up at the house perplexedly.

"So the house dumped you out too," he said.

She looked at him confusedly. "What do you mean?"

"You were walking around upstairs and got lost, and the only way out was to come down that set of stairs and into the entrance hall, right?"

"Right, but so?"

"So, the house did it. It doesn't like people walking around too much in it. It always sends them back downstairs."

She looked at him skeptically. "Are you trying to tell me the house is alive?"

He sighed patiently. "No, it's not alive. It's the way it was built."

"Don't be ridiculous, Garrett. Why would Sarah Balfram build her house that way?"

He greeted the question with utmost seriousness. "That's just it," he said staring contemplatively up into the house. "Why *did* she do it?"

Before she could react further, the sound of a car arriving distracted her and she went out onto the pillared veranda to see who it was. A young man in a checkered shirt was stepping down from a dilapidated pickup truck. Although she had heard no other sounds of people arriving, to her surprise she saw that a small crowd had gathered near the generator building. By a tree an older man smoking a pipe had apparently arrived on a bicycle. Two other men, brothers it seemed, stood by an old Ford Mustang, and a man with disheveled black hair and the whitest skin she had ever seen seemed to have come on foot.

She decided to go find Stephen and see how things were going. As she started down the front steps of the house she noticed Garrett was tagging along beside her. However, before she had reached the doors of the generator building she felt a little sting on the back of her neck. Slapping the area instinctively, she looked at her hand and saw a tiny black smudge, all that apparently remained of a mosquito. Within moments the spot at the back of her neck started to itch, but before she could scratch it she felt another bite on the back of her arm, and then another on her leg. She looked around at the gathering of men and was chagrined to see that none of them were similarly afflicted.

"You need some Deep Woods Off," the older man smoking a pipe advised.

"What will that do?"

"Keep 'em from bitin'. It's what I use."

By this time Stephen had come out of the generator building and was watching what was going on. "Where can I get some Deep Woods Off?" she asked.

He took a languid puff on his pipe. "The nearest place to here is Clearwater."

She looked at him perplexedly.

"It's a great camp that's been turned into a lodge," Stephen interjected. "It's about twenty miles down the road. There's a gift shop there. I guess Mr. Foley means you can get some there."

Mr. Foley nodded.

"Well, will you take me there?" she asked, looking at Stephen.

"Honey, I can't. I've got to take care of this. But why don't you go?" He reached into his pocket and tossed her the keys to the Porsche.

"Which way down the road?"

"That way," Mr. Foley said, waving his hand to the right. She looked at Garrett. "Do you want to go?"

He nodded.

"Then come on," she said, scratching herself furiously and heading for the car. When they reached it she opened the door, but before she could get inside Stephen had run up beside her.

"Hey, don't I get a kiss?"

"Well, I guess," she said, putting on a fake pout.

They kissed, but as she started to turn away he stopped her. "So did you enjoy last night as much as I did?" he said with a sly smile.

"Of course I did, silly." She giggled and poked him in the ribs.

Stephen suddenly jerked his arm away from the car and screamed.

"What is it?" she said, jumping in the same direction.

"Bug," he returned, and when she followed the line of his gaze she saw that on the hood of the car was one of the largest spiders she had ever seen.

He looked around for a stick and then approached the spot on the car where the spider was sitting.

"Don't kill it! Don't kill it!" Garrett yelled as he ran around to their side of the car. Picking up a stick of his own, he coaxed the spider onto it and then tossed it gently into the bushes. "Spiders eat other insects, so it's good to have them around," he informed them.

Lauren noticed that Stephen was annoyed and seemed about to say something. But before he could speak, Garrett had started up again. "You know, a spider's blood is green, and since they don't have circulatory systems like we do, it just squishes around inside them."

The remark caused a wave of gooseflesh to rise on Lauren's arms, and from the disconcerted look on Stephen's face she realized it had had a similar effect on him. Stephen just shook his head and walked away. "See ya later," he said.

"Why do you do that?" she asked after they had gotten in the car.

"Do what?"

"Say such creepy things?"

He looked at her confusedly. "What creepy things?"

"Like about that damn spider!" she exclaimed, but she could tell from his expression that he had no idea what she meant.

As they drove away from the house he piped up again. "So why do you think Sarah Balfram did that to her house?"

"Did what?"

"Designed it so that when you try to walk around in the upstairs it always sends you back downstairs?"

"Nothing made me go back downstairs!" she snapped. "I just decided it was the easiest thing to do."

"But that's just it. Each time you go through, something happens that makes you realize it's the easiest thing to do. She did it on purpose, Mom, I can tell."

She exhaled loudly. "Okay, Garrett, suppose she did do that. Why would she do such a thing?" This question caused him to lapse into such silence she became a little uneasy. She knew him well enough to know he didn't take challenges lightly.

For the next several minutes she tried to put everything out of her mind and concentrate on enjoying the scenery. As they traveled, she realized how truly isolated they were at Lake House. Several roads turned off the highway, but none gave any indication of leading to other houses. There weren't even any other cars on the road. She was just about to comment on it when finally they passed a small dirt road with a crudely painted "Keep Out" sign posted beside it.

It was another twenty minutes before they saw any further evidence of civilization in the form of another sign that read: "Clearwater Lodge—Next Right." Pulling into the driveway, Lauren was pleasantly surprised to see that Clearwater Lodge was quite a big place. Like Lake House it sat on the edge of a sparkling lake, but here any similarity ended. Instead of gothic, the lodge was built in the traditional Adirondack lodge style, sprawling in every direction. It was also crawling with people: backpackers heading up mountain trails, boaters, children in life preservers splashing in the shallows of the lake, and picnickers sitting at tables under the spreading canopy of the trees. The sight of so many people made Lauren feel good.

She parked the Porsche in a concrete parking lot outside the main pavilion, and they both got out. Inside, the lodge looked very much like a big-city hotel. The entrance hall had been converted into a huge lobby, and bellboys assisted new arrivals with their bags. Beyond an arch to the right she saw a display of stuffed toy animals, and she knew she had found the right place.

"Come on, Garrett," she said, gently steering him by his shoulder through the crowd.

Walking in, she saw that the store was filled with all the sundry items one expected in such establishments: souvenirs, toiletries, travel books, candy bars, camping supplies.

Seeing a display of comic books, Garrett raced off to the opposite side of the store as Lauren went up to a plump, rather cow-eyed girl standing behind a nearby counter. On her blouse she wore a button that said, "Hi, my name is Amy and I'm here to help you."

"Excuse me, do you sell Deep Woods Off?" Lauren asked.

With almost mechanical efficiency the girl reached up to a shelf behind her and withdrew a green aerosol can. "Sure do," she said, sliding the can across the counter to Lauren.

"How much is that?" Lauren asked.

"Two ninety-five."

Lauren reached into her purse for her wallet.

"Oh, you don't have to do that," the girl said. "You can just give me your room number and I'll put it on your bill."

"No, you don't understand," Lauren said. "I'm not a guest here."

"Are you campers?"

"No, we've rented a house here for the summer, a lodge really. It's called Lake House."

The girl's already sizable eyes opened even wider as she snapped out of her professional demeanor. "Lake House! You're kidding. What is that old place like on the inside, anyway?"

"Oh, it's quite nice really."

Taking Lauren's matter-of-fact response as an invitation to become even more familiar, the girl leaned forward amiably on the counter. "Is it really as strange inside as they say?"

Both her question and her chatty air made Lauren a little uncomfortable. "It's a little strange around the edges," she said, repeating the same line Stephen had used. "But most of it is quite livable."

"Gosh," the girl said.

For some reason her incredulity annoyed Lauren. "Why, does that surprise you?"

The girl fluttered her large eyes and became a little flustered. "Oh, no. It's just that I've always associated Lake House so closely with what happened to Sarah Balfram that . . ." She stopped as if it had finally occurred to her she might have strayed across the fine line between customer relations and impertinence. ". . . well, that I never really thought of 'livable' as a word someone might use to describe Lake House."

She said the last line quietly and with a trace of trepidation, but whatever indignation Lauren felt previously was suddenly replaced by curiosity. "What do you mean, what happened to Sarah Balfram? You mean about her fiancé jilting her?"

"Jilting her?" The girl snorted. "Who told you that? Her fiancé was murdered."

The words struck Lauren like lightning. "You mean he was murdered in the house?"

"So they say."

Lauren scanned the store nervously and was relieved to see Garrett was still glued to the comic-book display. She was glad he was not hearing what the girl was telling her.

"You mean you didn't know about Sarah Balfram's fiancé being murdered before you moved in?" the girl asked with disbelief.

"No," she said feeling a bit foolish. She wondered if Stephen knew. "Do you know which room in the house he was murdered in?" she asked.

The girl shook her head. "That I don't."

Lauren fingered the collar of her blouse nervously. "Do they know who killed him? I mean, it wasn't Sarah Balfram, was it?"

"Well, there's a mystery to that," the girl said, her eyes sparkling. "You see, they say Sarah Balfram built the house when she was young with money her mother left her. Of course, at that time I guess she was already considered a spinster, and added to the fact that she was nutty, everyone assumed she would live out her days as an old maid."

"You mean she built the house before she got engaged? People considered her crazy even before she got jilted?"

The girl nodded. "Yeah, but they say she was a strange kind of crazy. Clever crazy. I mean, I guess she was smart enough to give lectures and stuff and people would come and listen, but I don't know what she talked about. Weird stuff. Anyway, apparently it drove her dad nuts that she spent so much money on building such a crazy house, but I guess the two of them never got along anyway, and so he just stayed in New York and lived his life and she stayed up here and lived hers. Only that all changed when she met this guy Oelrich.

"Oelrich had a reputation in New York for being a sort of creep. You know, he just wanted to marry some woman for her money. So when Sarah Balfram accepted Oelrich's proposal her father evidently came up here to try to stop her. According to the story, he shot Oelrich."

"What do you mean, the story? Wasn't Josiah Balfram ever brought to trial?"

"No, that's the strange part. After he killed Oelrich he vanished without a trace. Some people say he drowned himself in the lake. Some say he ran away to Mexico. The only person who ever knew what happened was Sarah Balfram, but she refused to say. She just went on living all alone in the house, and a couple years later she got some sort of illness and died. Some people say she died of heartbreak."

A shiver ran up Lauren's spine, and her dismay was so obvious the girl looked at her anxiously. "Gee, I'm sorry. I didn't mean to upset you."

"No, it's okay. I wanted to know." In order to get her mind off what she had just been told she glanced around for some sort of distraction. She saw a book entitled *Great Camps of the Adirondacks* and placed it on the counter beside the Deep Woods Off. She also placed a handful of candy bars on the counter, a copy of the latest issue of *Cosmopolitan*, and a book of hiking trails through the Adirondacks. Then she saw a revolving rack of postcards and remembered she wanted to write to some of her friends back in the city.

To her delight as she turned the rack he saw some of the postcards were photographs of famous people from the past who had visited the Adirondacks. There was one of Teddy Roosevelt hunting on Pharaoh Mountain and even one of Jack London standing in front of Clearwater Lodge. But what really caught her eye was a fabulous picture of the 1920s film star Mae Norman riding in an open sleigh through the snow. She turned the card over and saw that the caption read: "Miss Norman is never seen

in anything but an open sleigh no matter how cold the
weather; with her brilliant coloring and dark furs she always makes a most charming portrait."

Lauren smiled at the bygone wording of the caption, but
when she turned the card back around and looked at the gay
and reckless Miss Norman she saw something she hadn't
noticed before. Behind the sleigh was a house, and although
its features were partially obscured by a fairyland mantle of
snow, Lauren realized with a start it was Lake House.

"Why, this is Lake House!" she exclaimed.

"What?"

"In this picture of Mae Norman. This is Lake House
behind her, isn't it?"

"Sure is," said the girl.

Pleased that she had found something positive about the
house, she brought the postcard over to the counter. "Mae
Norman certainly was beautiful," she said, continuing to
admire the picture.

"Yes, she was," the girl said, and then added idly, "That
picture was taken just before the tragedy."

Lauren looked up abruptly. "What tragedy?"

Again the girl blinked at her with surprise. "A man was
murdered in the house during a party Mae Norman gave.
Apparently the scandal it caused is what ended her career."

Lauren's eyes widened as a look of horror spread across
her face. "There there have been two murders in the house?"
She tried to keep her voice down so Garrett wouldn't hear.

"You mean you didn't know any of this?" the girl asked
cautiously.

"No!" Lauren snapped, and the girl jumped. Feeling
foolish for losing her temper, she asked calmly, "How was
the man killed?"

The girl hesitated, afraid to go on. "Stabbed," she murmured falteringly.

"Did they catch the murderer this time?"

"They tried a man, but he was acquitted. No one ever really knew who did it. I guess that's why it ruined Mae Norman's career. There was no evidence she had committed the murder. But there was no evidence anyone else had done it either."

Lauren thought about everything she had been told for a moment and then looked at the girl pleadingly. "Have there been any other murders in the house you haven't told me about?"

"No, I don't think so," the girl said weakly, as she rang up Lauren's things.

"Thanks. Come on, Garrett," she said loudly. "Time to go."

When they arrived back at the house, Lauren told Garrett to go upstairs to his bedroom and then went looking for Stephen. She found him in the drawing room. "Look," he said jubilantly as he flicked a switch on the wall and all the lights in the room went on.

She was pleased by the display, but still too upset by what the shopgirl had told her about the house to show it.

"Stephen, did you know that two people were murdered in this house?"

Stephen's smile evaporated. "Who told you that?"

"A salesgirl at the Clearwater Lodge."

He stretched out his arm and bared the palm of his hand apologetically. "Listen, honey, it really doesn't matter."

She looked at him incredulously. "You mean you already know about it? You knew about it and you took the house anyway?"

"I didn't tell you because I didn't want to upset you. I knew it would probably bother you if you knew someone had been killed in the house. It all happened so long ago anyway I didn't see what real difference it made. I thought by not telling you I was just saving you from having to worry about it."

"Not just one," she corrected. "Two people. Two people were murdered in this house, and in neither instance was the murderer ever really found."

"So two people were murdered in the house!" he said, getting testy. "And so the murderers were never found. For God's sake, the two crimes took place over thirty years apart and the last one was committed more than sixty years ago! You sound like you think they might be connected."

Although she was angry, she knew he was right. She had been told about the two murders in such rapid succession she somehow assumed they might be connected, that in some strange way they presaged danger for them as well. But now she realized how ridiculous that was.

"Listen, if I'd known it was going to upset you so, I never would have kept the information from you. I thought I was doing the right thing."

His penitent air started to disperse her anger. "Well, for future reference, remember that I used to be an investigative reporter. I can't stand it when people keep important parts of a story from me."

"I'll remember."

She forced a smile. "Okay." She thought of something else. "By the way, when you told us about the house you said Sarah Balfram went crazy because she was jilted. You said that's why she built Lake House the way she did. But she wasn't jilted. Her fiancé was murdered. And not only that, but the shopgirl told me Sarah Balfram finished building Lake House before she even met her fiancé."

"So?"

"So, is there anything else you're not telling me?"

He raised both of his hands. "Honest, honey, all I know is she was crazy. I was hardly listening when the real estate

agent was telling me all these stupid old stories. I thought
he was just making them up because he thought I'd think
they were cool or something. I'm sorry."

"You don't know why she was crazy? The girl at Clearwater Lodge said something strange. She said Sarah Balfram was 'clever crazy.' The shopgirl said she used to give
lectures or something. Do you know anything about that?"

"No," he said firmly.

"Okay." She sighed, then paused in thought for a moment. "Oh, just out of curiosity, who did you hire to run
the generator?"

"An old guy. Mr. Foley. He's lived in the area for forty
years. He seemed the most dependable."

"Well, now that you've taken care of hiring someone
to run the generator, what do you say we all go on that
picnic? I bought a book of hiking trails through the Adirondacks." She withdrew the book from her bag.

Again Stephen became long-faced. "Gee, honey, this
hiring stuff took longer than I thought. I've got a dozen
phone calls I've gotta make. I know we came up here to
get away from everything, but some guy's just released a
single that's climbing the charts and *Rolling Stone* has called
him the next Stephen Ransom. Apparently he looks and
sounds just like me, even does the same sort of stuff I do.
I've gotta have a major powwow with Marty to figure out
what we're going to do."

She pursed her lips in a pout. "Okay."

He smiled and kissed her.

She watched him as he vanished toward the kitchen, and
then she turned and walked in the other direction. When
she reached the entrance hall, Garrett was bounding in the
front door excitedly. "I've got it," he cried.

"Got what?" she asked as he ran up to her.

"I know why Sarah Balfram made her house the way
she did."

She looked at him with apprehension. Although she was still convinced there was nothing to figure out, she did not like the look in his eye. "Why?"

"Do you remember the sentence that's written over the door?"

"Yes."

"Look at it again." He handed her a piece of paper on which he had copied down the words:

In girum imus nocte et consumimur igni.

She looked at it for a moment and then looked back at him. "Garrett, I don't read Latin."

"No, just look at the sentence again."

She looked at it again, but it remained inscrutable to her. "Garrett, I'm sorry, but I don't see anything."

"The letters in the words," he exclaimed. "They're the same forward as they are backward. When a sentence is written like that it's called a palindrome. It's a kind of puzzle."

She looked back at the paper and saw that he was right. "How neat!" she exclaimed. "What did you just call it?"

"A palindrome."

"Now, where on earth did you learn that?"

"In the puzzle section of one of my science magazines. There are lots of famous palindromes. 'A man, a plan, a canal, Panama.' That's a real well-known one. 'Tini saw drawer, a reward was in it,' is another."

She paused, nodding her head as she mentally spelled out each sentence in her mind. "You're right!" she exclaimed, but her exuberance was short-lived. "But those are in English. Have you figured out what this one means yet?"

"I don't know what the words mean, but I know *why* it's over the door." His eyes glowed with enthusiasm, but still she remained confused.

"Don't you see?" he continued. "She put a palindrome

over the door for a reason, as a sort of message. She's trying to tell us something. She's trying to tell us the house itself is some sort of giant puzzle."

A flutter of excitement passed through Lauren. Could he possibly be right? But after pondering the idea for a moment, she started to think of reasons to dismiss it. "I don't know, Garrett. I just asked Stephen whether there was anything else he hadn't told us about the house and he said no. If the house were some kind of giant puzzle I'm sure the real estate agent who rented him the place would have mentioned something about it."

"How do you know he would have mentioned it?"

"Because it would be pretty neat if the house was actually a puzzle or something, and he would have mentioned it to help rent the place."

"But maybe he didn't know," Garrett protested. "Maybe that's something Sarah Balfram, or whatever her name was, kept secret."

"Maybe," Lauren said, smiling. "But maybe not. Maybe instead you should start writing some of these wild ideas of yours down. With your imagination you could make a million."

Despite his mother's lack of interest, the idea that the house might be some kind of giant puzzle continued to fire Garrett's imagination, and later that afternoon he went walking through the first-floor rooms to see if he could find anything else that might support his theory. However, when he reached the Moorish-style billiard room he ran headlong into Stephen busily playing a solitaire game of pool.

"Hi, sport," Stephen said as he ran the pool cue through his crooked fingers and the balls broke explosively.

"Hi," Garrett mumbled. He wanted to turn and run, but he realized it would be too obviously rude.

Stephen sized up a ball and made another shot. Then he turned toward Garrett. "Hey, you wanna play pool with me?"

Garrett stiffened. Because he was so excited over his new theory, he most certainly did not want to play. "I don't know how to play," he said, trying to get out of the situation gracefully.

"Then I'll teach you," Stephen chirped.

"Well, I did play pool once. But I didn't like it."

"Maybe the reason you didn't like it is that you weren't that good at it yet. I can still teach you."

"No, I—" Garrett stammered. But then he noticed Stephen's eyes narrowing and realized it was pushing his luck to keep turning down his offers.

"Well, okay."

"Great! Then come over here and I'll show you how to set up a shot."

Garrett reluctantly approached the table, and Stephen handed him a cue. Then he stood behind Garrett and helped guide the cue into the proper position.

"Now, see that white ball? Try hitting it with the cue and getting it to knock that red ball into the pocket in the corner."

Garrett moved the cue back and forth between the crook in his fingers in a fashion so wobbly and palsied that he heard Stephen exhale loudly behind him.

"No, hold it more level, like this."

Stephen guided the cue into the correct position and then stepped back. Garrett rammed the cue forward and hit the white ball, but off center and with such force it went hopping wildly over the edge of the table and bounced onto the floor.

Stephen went and retrieved the ball from the floor. "Too hard. You don't have to ram the cue into the white ball. Try doing it more gently."

As Stephen walked back to the table Garrett looked at

him beseechingly, hoping he would perceive how little he was enjoying himself, but Stephen seemed not to notice. He set the balls in exactly the same position and stepped back. "Try it again."

Garrett returned his attention to the table and bit his lip with concentration. Under normal circumstances he hated such games. He saw no point in them. They didn't develop the intellect as chess did, and you didn't get anything out of them when they were over. There was no payoff, except to be able to say that someone won and someone lost. But to his astonishment, Stephen actually seemed to be trying for once, and he felt he had no choice but to reciprocate.

He slid the cue back and forth between his fingers, nervously trying to calculate just the right momentum. But once again, to his enormous chagrin, he hit the ball too hard and it bounced across the green baize of the table and onto the floor.

This time Stephen was less good-natured about it. "No, no, you used too much force. Pool is a game of precision and delicacy. You're not trying to annihilate the ball. You've got to be more gentle."

"I was more gentle this time."

"Well, you weren't gentle enough."

"Maybe I'm just not cut out to play pool."

Stephen remained determined. "No, try it again."

He set the balls up a third time and again Garrett slid the cue through his fingers, but this time he was so circumspect about what he was doing and tapped the ball so gently that it rolled only a few inches before stopping.

Stephen looked at him with hawk eyes. "Are you doing this just to annoy me?"

The accusation caused Garrett to flush. "No, I'm really trying."

Stephen continued to stare at him skeptically. "Then why aren't you doing it right? It isn't that difficult."

This angered Garrett, for although he was trying to do

what Stephen was telling him, he realized the reason he was failing was probably that his heart wasn't in it. "I told you I didn't want to play. I don't like pool."

Stephen seemed to have had about as much as he could take. "Do you know what would have happened if I had said something like that to my father?"

"Something like you didn't like pool?" Garrett asked with confusion.

"No, not if I didn't like pool. I mean what would have happened if my father was trying to teach me something and I told him I didn't want to learn it."

"No, what?" Garrett asked, fidgeting. Something strange had come into Stephen's demeanor, and it made Garrett nervous.

Stephen sat down slowly on the edge of the billiard table, the strange quality in his demeanor intensifying as he kept his gaze intently on Garrett. "Let me tell you a story. I'm not from New York originally. I bet you didn't know that. I grew up in a place called Charlevoix, Michigan. Do you have any idea where that is?"

Garrett shook his head in short, spasmodic movements.

Stephen held up his hand. "Well, Michigan's shaped like a mitten, and Charlevoix is way up here at the top. It's a lot different in Charlevoix than it is in New York. It's a place that's mainly just forest, kind of like here. The winters are cold, and the people have never heard of things like *gelato* or F.A.O. Schwarz.

"Well, in Charlevoix, when fall came, one thing that just about everyone would do was go out hunting. Every guy, at least."

He chalked the end of his billiard cue with a kind of lethal grace as he spoke.

"When I was little I used to long for the day when I was old enough to go off hunting with my dad. All during hunting season I'd get up at the crack of dawn when my dad got up. And I'd sit at the window for as many hours as it took for him to come home. When I got older he let me help clean his gun and practice shooting it. But he told me that I had to be at least twelve before he'd actually let me go with him.

"Well, finally the day came when I was old enough, and I dressed up in a red-and-black felt cap just like my dad wore, and a red jacket with a vest full of little pockets for the shotgun shells, and we went hunting together. It was great. There's just no other smell like the smell of a Michigan woods with a nip of frost in it. We had this old hunting dog named Spark, and she ran to and fro trying to flush out a rabbit or something. And finally my dad spotted a squirrel up in a tree. Only as soon as the squirrel saw us coming it ran to the other side of the tree where we couldn't see it. 'This is it, son,' my dad said. 'This one's yours.' Then he went to the other side of the tree and made a racket with Spark to scare the squirrel back over to my side.

Stephen exhaled wistfully. "Well, I took aim and fired and the squirrel fell out of the tree with a thud. And you know what happened?"

"No," Garrett said quietly. "What?"

"When I saw that squirrel with its eye popped out with a piece of rifle shot and blood oozing from a dozen other little holes in its body, I just went to pieces. I couldn't believe that I had actually killed the thing. I cried my eyes out. And you know what my dad did?" From the sparkle in Stephen's eye it was clear that whatever his dad had done, Stephen felt it was at least worthy of a "True-Life Accounts of Amazing People" piece in *Reader's Digest*.

"What?" Garrett asked, breathless with anticipation.

"He made me go on until I had shot another. And then another. In fact, from that day on until hunting season was over, he made me go hunting every day. And he made me skin the game I caught and clean it. Before winter came

I had bagged more small game than just about anyone else in the county. It didn't matter how unpleasant I thought it was. My dad just kept pushing me."

"But that's awful!"

"No, it wasn't, because, you see, my dad didn't allow me to fail. He made me become one of the best hunters in the county, and I'll always love him for that."

"But you felt bad when you shot the squirrel. It was mean of your dad to make you kill another."

"No! It would have been mean of my dad to not make me kill another. By making me go on, my dad taught me the importance of sticking with something, of not giving up until I had it conquered."

Garrett continued to blink at Stephen, the logic of Stephen's argument still eluding him. From the gleam in Stephen's eye, Garrett could not help but think that Stephen had made up the story just to punish him for how halfhearted he had been in his attempt to learn billiards. But he did not know. He only knew that Stephen's little story had left him more uncomfortable than he had been before.

After they finished dinner and were watching television on a portable set Stephen set up for them in the drawing room, Garrett's mood took a turn for the worse. At first Lauren was mystified, but when it came time for them to go to bed and his uneasiness peaked, she finally understood why.

"Garrett, are you afraid to go to bed because you think you're going to have another bad dream?" she asked as Stephen turned the television set off.

Garrett looked at her with wide, cautious eyes. "Maybe it wasn't a dream," he mumbled meekly.

"Well, whatever it was, is that why you're being so funny about going to bed?"

He looked down sheepishly at the floor and nodded.

Under other circumstances his stubborn insistence in the matter might have angered her, but given everything that had transpired during the day she found herself somewhat disconcerted.

She looked across the room at Stephen. "Well, maybe if it's all right with Stephen you can sleep in our room tonight."

"Honeeey," Stephen objected.

"Stephen, come on. It's scary being alone in this big house."

"But Garrett is almost a grown man now. Right, old buddy?"

Garrett merely gritted his teeth in silence. He particularly hated it when Stephen called him "old buddy." He certainly did not want Stephen to know that he was too scared to sleep in his own room, no matter how scared he really was. He was about to say he *wanted* to sleep in his own room when Stephen piped up again.

"Garrett's man enough not to let a bad dream get to him."

"It wasn't a dream!" Garrett snapped.

"So what are you trying to say—that the bogeyman really did come into your room?"

"Yes!"

"Well, if that's true, if it was some sort of being from the beyond, I don't see what the problem is. I mean, you're the one who said you'd like to make friends with a creature from another planet. Here's the next-best thing."

Lauren began to get truly annoyed with Stephen. Why was he egging on Garrett at a time like this?

For his part, Garrett once again thought he detected a hint of malice in Stephen's remarks, but the actual content of them reverberated through him like a thunderclap. For months he had dreamed of making contact with a being from another world, and yet he had been so frightened by his encounter with the thing, it had never occurred to him he might be letting just such an opportunity pass him by. He did not like admitting it, but Stephen was right. His own glib assertions about wanting to meet an alien life form meant nothing unless he was willing to back up his words with action. No matter how daunting a prospect it seemed, he had to sleep alone in his room.

Lauren's eyes were now steely. It was the first time Garrett had seen her actually annoyed with Stephen. "Stephen, there's a divan in our room. I think it's perfectly okay if Garrett wants to sleep there."

"It's all right, Mom," Garrett cut in.

She looked at him with surprise. "What?"

"It was silly of me to be afraid. I'll be okay."

"Are you sure?"

He nodded.

"Okay," she said.

But she was not appeased. Later, after tucking him in bed, she brought the matter up with Stephen again.

"I can't believe what you said to Garrett downstairs."

"Why not?" Stephen said with astonishment.

"Because he's only a little boy. And you were trying to make him ashamed of being frightened."

"Hey. He's gotta learn sometime not to be afraid of the dark."

"Maybe so. But when he's frightened you shouldn't be attacking him—you should be comforting him."

"I didn't attack him."

"You didn't comfort him. He's your son now, too."

"Look, I married you, not him. Just don't push me too far with this father act, okay?" He glowered.

His words shocked her deeply. Her primary reason for marrying Stephen had never been that he was ideal father material, but she had always expected that over time a genuine affection would develop between the two. All at once she realized that perhaps Garrett had not entirely imagined Stephen's animosity.

She stared at him in disbelief. "I can't believe you said that."

Perceiving her shock, he quickly tried to distance himself from the remark. "I didn't mean for that to come out the way it sounded." He put on a tired face and ran his fingers through his gorgeous mane of dark curls. "I'm sorry, okay? I spent four hours on the phone with Marty, and I'm just irritable and snappish. You know I think Garrett is a neat kid, and he and I are going to become very good pals."

He came up and took her by the shoulders. His bottomless green-gray eyes bored into hers. "The real reason I was so upset when you suggested he sleep in here is that I enjoy being alone with you so much." He tried to kiss her, but she turned her face away.

"Come on, isn't this better than fighting?" he coaxed as he nuzzled her ear.

She continued to resist, still stinging from his insensitivity, but he pulled her closer, kissing her and caressing her until she felt herself melting.

A part of her was still furious at him. But another part wanted nothing more than to be held and comforted, to feel the smooth expanse of his body against her once again.

"We have to talk about this some more."

"We will, we will," he said softly. With movements as carefully orchestrated as those of a cat closing in on its prey, he turned her around and kissed her and then carried her to the bed. Within minutes he was inside her, rocking, undulating in the slow saraband of his lovemaking.

But when they finished she lay awake and for the first time she started to wonder if there was something about Stephen she wasn't seeing.

She did not know how long it took her to fall asleep, but it seemed only minutes after she did that something woke her. At first she did not know what, and for several seconds she remained motionless. But then it came again, and she realized it had been a sound. Somewhere deep in the house there was a low creaking, like the mast of a ship swaying gently in the wind. Perplexed, she sat up in bed and listened, but as soon as she tried to focus in on the sound it ceased.

For a moment she was frightened. But then logic told her it was only natural for a house as old as Lake House to do some settling at night and creak and moan a bit. Still, something about the sound disturbed her, and she decided to look in on Garrett and make sure he was all right. Pulling her robe on, she strode toward the bedroom door. Once outside, she clicked the lights on and headed down the hall.

When she reached his door she opened it quietly. She did not want to wake him needlessly and was pleased when she saw he was fast asleep. But as she started back toward her room she realized she was thirsty, and, recalling that the water in the master bath was both tepid and a little rusty, she decided to go downstairs for some ice water.

When she reached the top of the stairs she turned on the entrance-hall lights, and she continued to turn on every light she came to, forging a blazing trail to the kitchen. After drinking her fill, she started back, but as she passed through the drawing room she noticed there was a full moon over the lake. She cupped her hands against the glass and saw that a mist had rolled in from the lake and covered everything in a gauzy blanket of fog. Even the lower limbs of the tamaracks were veiled in the ghostly pall, and in the soft bluish glow of the moonlight the forest seemed dreamlike.

Entranced, she continued to admire the scene for several seconds. Then suddenly an icy shiver ran up her spine. At first she was mystified, at a loss to explain why every nerve ending in her body was tingling with alarm. And then just as suddenly she realized. Although she did not know how, she knew without question she was being watched.

Panicking, she realized the only reason she was visible to someone outside was that she had turned so many lights on, and she quickly turned them off. But once again as she scanned the mist-enshrouded landscape, she could feel something staring at her, examining her with impunity, something watching her from the fog.

Not knowing what else to do, she ran upstairs, and when she reached the bedroom she flung herself under the covers. The force of her impact caused Stephen to grumble in his sleep, and she considered waking him. But then she realized she had no evidence to prove that her eerie sensation had been anything but nerves, and she decided against it. Still, it was some time before she drifted off to sleep again.

Several hours later, Garrett awoke uneasily too. However, he knew what had stirred him so rudely from his slumber. It was the thing. It was coming. Like a magnet to steel he felt its power as it coursed through the halls. When it neared his door he sat up in bed and told himself he was ready for it.

Only he was not. When his door burst open soundlessly, all the primeval fear that had gripped him the night before returned. Again he froze, unable to move. Only this time, because he was sitting he was able to see it more clearly. As it drifted toward him he saw its powerful arms and shoulders, but within its swirling depths he also discerned a heavily muscled torso and a pair of huge and sinewy hands. Once again it slowly circled the bed as if examining him for some unknown purpose, and when it turned he noticed it possessed the suggestion of a masculine profile. But still there was something paradoxical about its appearance, for everything that was massive about it was only occasionally given substance by its turbulent and vaporous form.

After it finished circling the bed it stopped, and again the unearthly tingle of its presence swept over him like a strange and silent wind. Suddenly, without warning, it spoke.

"Who are you?"

Its voice was deep and resonant, and hearing it made him tremble all the more. "I'm Garrett," he stammered. And then he added for good measure, "I'm a little boy."

It seemed to ponder this for a moment, a sudden eddy of darkness whirling up violently through its core.

"What are you doing in my house?" it demanded.

"I live here," he explained, but as soon as he uttered the words an even greater welling of darkness roiled up through it. Thinking he had angered it, he added quickly, "But I don't want to be here."

For a while it said nothing, and with each passing second a thousand different emotions reeled through him. Amazement. Terror. He could hardly believe he was talking to it, and suddenly his resolution to try to befriend it seemed completely beyond his capabilities. An eternity passed, and then another, and again he wondered if its silence meant he had offended it in some way. But then, just when he thought it was not going to reply, it spoke again.

"*Why* don't you want to be here?" it asked.

Because he did not yet know how it was reacting to what he had been saying to it, he hesitated and wondered how he should answer the question. But after considering several more evasive responses, he opted for the truth.

"Because this isn't my home. I really live in New York." He swallowed, trying to moisten his mouth enough so he could continue. "But then my mom married this guy, Stephen, and he decided we were going to come up here for the summer. Only I don't like Stephen. I mean, I don't think he likes me. But that's why I'm here."

After he finished, he paused, making sure the thing had not reacted adversely to anything he had said, and deciding that its lack of aggressive action was a good sign, he summoned up the courage to ask it a question.

"Who are you?"

"Who and what I am need not concern you!" it boomed, and the sound of its voice nearly sent him hurtling back under the covers. This time he was convinced it was going to attack him, but instead it just turned and started to leave. As it drifted toward the door he felt a mixture of relief and regret. It had not been easy for him to stand up to it as he had, and a part of him wished only for it to go and leave him unharmed. But another part, the part that always had to know, that could not leave any mystery unexplored, reminded him again of his decision to try to establish some sort of ongoing contact with it. His stomach knotted as he tried to figure out what to do. But finally, deciding it was clearly something alien and perhaps of profound importance—and deciding its behavior toward him indicated it was benign—he resolved to try to win its favor.

"Wait!" he cried.

It stopped and slowly turned around.

"I just . . ." he started, but the audacity of his request caused his fear to reassert itself. "I just wondered if . . . well . . . if you wanted to be friends."

He waited nervously for its response. It seemed so sure of itself, so arrogant and annoyed about his presence in the house, he felt certain it would scoff at the suggestion. But instead a farrago of strange shapes began to shift and move beneath its surface as if the idea intrigued it, and cast some new light on a situation it had almost overlooked.

"Friends?" it repeated with caution. "Why would you want to be friends with me, little boy?"

"Because I want to know who and what you are."

"But *why* do you want to know?"

The question left him momentarily stymied. "I don't know. I guess because you're—" He stopped abruptly, at a loss as to how best to refer to it.

"Because I'm what, boy?"

"Because you don't seem to be human and that makes me wonder what you are, that's all," he blurted out, hoping against hope the bluntness of his description would not provoke it.

Again it lapsed into lengthy rumination, but finally it seemed to waver. "I demand a lot from my friends," it warned portentously.

A ripple of excitement passed through him as he perceived the ray of hope the remark offered. "Like what?"

"If we were friends you would have to promise not to tell anyone about me or anything that takes place between us."

Obviously it would not want news of its existence to fall into the hands of individuals who might wish to do it harm, and, recalling that all of the aliens and friendly monsters in the movies he had seem always exacted similar promises, he agreed.

"Okay."

"Before we could be friends you would also have to do something to prove yourself to me, to show me I could trust you as a friend," it continued.

"Like what?" he asked again.

"I want you to find out someone's name for me. I would also like you to find out where this person lives."

The simplicity of the request relieved him. "That's all?"

"That's all."

"Who?"

"I would like you to find out the name of one of the men who applied for the job of running the generators today."

"You mean Mr. Foley, the man Stephen hired?"

"No, not that man. I'd like you to find out more about one of the men who didn't get the job. The man I want to know about arrived on foot. He had very pale skin. Do you know the man I'm talking about?"

Its desire to know the name of the man with pale skin perplexed him, but he nodded. "Yes."

"Do you think you could do that for me?"

"Yes," he said, realizing that Mr. Foley could probably provide him with the information.

A final maelstrom of darkness spiraled up through it, and although he did not know how, he sensed it was pleased.

"Good," it said.

And then, without further ado, it once again started toward the door.

"But how do I let you know what I find out?" he called after it.

"Tomorrow night after your parents are asleep I'll come to you again."

"And if I tell you the man's name and where he lives does that mean we're friends?"

"Yes," the thing answered as it glided into the darkness of the hallway. "It means we're friends."

After it departed, Garrett felt strangely light-headed because he had burned up so much adrenaline sustaining the courage to talk to it. But he was also ecstatic. Not only had he proved he had the mettle to act on his convictions, but he had at long last fulfilled his dream of making contact with another life form. He did not know what it was, a being from another planet or even from another dimension, but for the moment none of that mattered. All that mattered was that he had achieved his goal and in the process accomplished something extraordinary.

The next morning Garrett was still so excited he woke early. Too impatient to await breakfast, he dressed and was heading out his door when he ran into his mother in the hall. She looked at him with concern.

"Garrett, are you all right?"

"Yes, I'm all right," he said, barely hearing her question and trying to continue on around her.

"Are you sure?"

He looked at her with bewilderment. "Yes, I'm sure."

"Did you sleep all right? Did you have any more . . . well, any more dreams?"

At last he understood what she was angling for. He was going to have to lie to her, and this bothered him. He had never lied to her before, at least not about anything as important as this. It also occurred to him that in some strange way it meant he had to choose sides. If he decided not to tell his mother about the thing he was in a sense becoming its ally, and the finality of this made him uneasy.

Still, when he considered that the alternative meant never seeing the thing again, he knew he had no choice.

"No, no more dreams," he said.

For some reason she seemed to have trouble accepting this and continued to stare at him for several moments. But then she finally appeared to accept his answer. "Well, wherever you're going, don't be long. I'm going to start making breakfast soon."

He nodded and scampered on down the hall. When he reached the generator building, Mr. Foley was already sitting in a chair out in front. In his hands he held a jackknife, and he was in the process of whittling a most remarkable object, an interlocking chain connected to a box with a little ball rolling around inside it, all carved out of a single piece of wood.

"Hi," Garrett greeted. "What's that?"

"Hello, young fella," he said, glancing at the object in his hands. "Just one of my time-passers." He looked back at Garrett. "What brings you out here so early?"

Realizing that stating his purpose too openly might arouse unnecessary suspicions, he made up an excuse. "I thought I'd go for a walk in the woods," he muttered, entranced by how dexterously Mr. Foley was shaving off each small slice of wood.

"Does your mother know you're going for a walk?" the older man asked suspiciously.

"Yes," Garrett lied. "Why?"

"Because the woods are pretty big around here. Lots of dangerous things to watch out for. A boy your age shouldn't really go walking in them alone."

The older man's concern annoyed Garrett, not only because it was advice offered to keep him from doing something he had no intention of doing anyway, but also because it implied he wasn't old enough to do it if he wanted to. Still, his curiosity was aroused.

"What kind of dangerous things?" he asked.

"Well, there's a blackwater swamp only about twenty minutes in that direction." He pointed with the knife toward the forest. "It's probably where all those mosquitoes have been comin' from that are eatin' your mother."

"What's a blackwater swamp?" he inquired uneasily.

"Just a swamp where the water's all murky and black. But there could be hemlock bogs around it. You might get stuck in one. There could also be snappin' turtles. You get too close to a big snapper he could take one of your fingers right off." He glanced at Garrett casually as he shaved a large curl of wood off one of the links in the chain.

The blackwater swamp did sound threatening to Garrett, but it also intrigued him. "Are there any Swamp Things in the swamp?"

"What do you mean?"

"I've got a book upstairs called *Strange Creatures from the Beyond*, and it says there are different parts of the country where you're more apt to see a monster than in other parts. It says upstate New York is one of those parts and that around here things are seen in swamps, Loch Ness monsters and giant snakes and things. It calls them Swamp Things."

Mr. Foley glanced at the woods. His eyes sparkled. "Probably plenty of 'em."

"Any other dangers?" Garrett asked.

Mr. Foley scanned the woods for a moment longer and then looked back at Garrett. "Rattlesnakes," he said.

Garrett frowned. "I thought rattlesnakes only lived out West."

Mr. Foley smiled triumphantly. "Nah, lotsa rattlers in the woods. Saw one a couple of years ago."

"Is anyone ever bitten?"

"It's a possibility."

"Is there much Rocky Mountain spotted fever up here?" Garrett asked.

Mr. Foley's smile faded completely. "Haven't heard of any. Why?"

"Because there were a couple of cases of it in New York when we left. You get it from tick bites, you know. The day before we came up here I saw a news report that said one little boy was in a coma because of it. You can also get Lyme's disease from ticks, which is almost as bad. You can die from either of them. I bet there's plenty of ticks around here, too."

Mr. Foley examined the grass around his feet with apprehension.

"Can I ask you something else?" Garrett asked.

Mr. Foley eyed him warily. "What?"

"Do you remember the other guys who applied for this job?"

"Yeah," Mr. Foley said, his voice still cautious.

"Did you know all of them?"

"What d'ya mean?"

"I mean do you know their names? Are they from around here?"

"Yeah, they were all from around here. Why?"

"Because one of them looked like someone we used to know. I just wondered if you knew his name?"

A look of relief spread across Mr. Foley's face as his former good nature returned. "Where did you know him from?"

"Back in New York."

"Which one?"

Garrett described the man.

"Why, that's Elton Fugate. You couldn't have known him back in New York. He's lived here all his life. Besides, if you'd ever met him before you'd remember it."

"Why's that?"

"Because he's a bit odd. Lives all alone in a little cabin back in the woods. Usually makes his living as a trapper.

That way he doesn't have to deal with people much. I was surprised he even considered taking regular work."

Garrett thought about this for a moment. "Do you know where he lives?"

"When you were on your way to Clearwater Lodge, do you remember passing a little dirt road with a big 'Keep Out' sign on it?"

Garrett nodded.

"Well, if you were to follow that road up the mountain you'd come to Fugate's place. In fact, I think you might even be able to see his place from here." Mr. Foley put down his whittling and lifted Garrett up onto the chair. "Do you see that mountain over there?"

"Yes."

"Look up toward the top of it. Do you see that little patch of red in between the trees?"

Garrett scanned the mountain until he spotted a fleck of red amid the green. "Yes."

"That's it."

Mr. Foley went to lift him back down, but he jumped down quickly. It had embarrassed him that Mr. Foley had thought it necessary to lift him up in the first place.

"Thank you, Mr. Foley."

The older man smiled. "You're welcome, son."

"Well, I guess I'll go back inside now."

"Aren't you going to go on that walk?"

"No, I decided not to."

Mr. Foley's smile became even more expansive. "Oh, well, I think that's a fine idea. Come back and visit me again sometime. If you like, next time I'll show you how to whittle."

As Garrett walked back toward the house he felt a little disappointed that nothing Mr. Foley had said about Elton Fugate shed any light on why the being wanted to find out more about him. But at least he had accomplished his mission. It also occurred to him that perhaps part of the reason the house was designed to prevent anyone from venturing too deeply into its interior was to protect the being, or at least make it more difficult for anyone to blunder accidentally into its hiding place.

Realizing this, he decided that for the time being it might be wise to put his explorations of the house on hold and spend the day outside.

Still weighing heavily on Lauren's mind was the problem of what to do about Stephen's behavior the night before. From what he had said it was clear to her now he was not comfortable with Garrett. She had to turn the situation around.

When she reached the door she paused. She did not look forward to the task at hand and considered postponing it. But after realizing that the longer she waited the more difficult it would become, she opened the door. When she went inside she found Stephen not only had gotten out of bed and showered in her absence, but was nearly finished dressing.

"Good morning," he chirped.

"Good morning," she returned, a little stiffly.

"So what's for breakfast?"

She continued to look at him. "Let's talk first."

He looked at her confusedly. "About what?"

"I mean we have a problem on our hands and I think it's more important to try to solve it than to think about breakfast."

"What problem?"

She became even more annoyed. "It seems to me we're having some problems coming together as a family. I just wondered if you had given any thought to what we should do about that."

"I thought we settled all that last night."

"No, we got sidetracked last night."

He gave her a lascivious grin. "Well, not bad for side-tracking, eh?"

She folded her arms and frowned.

"Okay, okay," he said, threading a belt through his pants. "What do you want me to do?"

"I want you to be honest with me about how you feel about Garrett. Then I want us to put our heads together and figure out what we're going to do about it."

He stared down at the floor nervously. "Okay, I'm willing to do that, but you've got to promise me something in return."

"What?"

"If we're really going to put our cards on the table here, you've got to promise me you won't jump all over me if I say something you don't like. I mean, I just want you to know I haven't completely thought this thing out myself, so I think we should deal with this like a concept session."

"A concept session?"

"When we're trying to figure out how to market an album, Marty and I and a bunch of people from the record company all sit around a table and just say whatever comes into our minds. When we do, it's understood that if someone says something stupid no one else gets upset or holds it against him. The point is to try to solve the problem by letting everyone give his imagination free reign. Okay?"

The notion that family problems were somehow similar to the problems one encountered when trying to market a record album did not sit well with her, but she was willing to give just about anything a try. "Okay."

"Okay. Well, first, Garrett's a kid that takes some getting used to. I mean, when I was a kid I was into things like baseball and collecting record albums, but he's more like a little scientist. Even when I tried to talk to him about space like you suggested it was clear our points of view were polar opposites."

"You don't have to talk only about the things you're both into," she said.

"So what do we talk about?"

"Everybody has some sort of common ground. Talk to him about the weather. Ask him how he's feeling. If you look up and see an interesting cloud in the sky, point it out to him. I think part of the problem is that you're trying to make too big a deal out of relating to him. Kids aren't that difficult to win over."

He sighed. "Okay, maybe you're right, but let me ask you this. Would it really be that big a deal if we didn't get along?"

Lauren went completely white. "What do you mean?" she asked tonelessly.

"Well, for example, Marty and I are friends. In fact, he's been like a father to me. But I can't stand his wife. I think she's one of the most boring, imbecilic, and shrewish women I've ever met. But I don't let that interfere with my friendship with Marty. So, would it be that terrible if Garrett and I never became good buddies? I mean, I love you. Don't you think the three of us could . . . well, could peaceably coexist?"

Lauren was so shocked and hurt that before she could say anything he gestured for her to let him continue.

"Now listen, Lauren, you've got to understand, I'm just playing the game of 'what if' here. I mean, I told you I was worried about how good a father I was going to make. So I was thinking, what if after a couple of months it became clear Garrett and I just weren't destined to get along? What if you and I kept getting along fabulously, but Garrett and I just never clicked?" He turned toward the window and nervously busied himself with the last few buttons on his shirt.

"Yes?" she practically whispered.

"Well, I was just wondering, would you ever consider sending Garrett to some sort of boarding school?"

The question stunned her. "You've got to be kidding!"

He turned around quickly. "Now listen, I told you this was just a concept session. I'm just batting around some ideas."

She decided the best course was to be calm but firm. "Frankly I would never consider for one minute sending Garrett to boarding school. If it comes down to a choice between you and him, you'd better believe I'd choose my son." She paused a long moment for effect. "Now, I suggest we start spending some time together and actually start doing some things as a family. There are some cold cuts in the fridge downstairs. Why don't I make us some sandwiches and pull a bottle of Beaujolais out of the wine cellar and let's go on that picnic this afternoon."

After she delivered the lines he just stared at her, his eyes glittering with such hostility she thought he was going to explode. But then, miraculously, he seemed to have a change of heart.

"Okay, listen, I want you to know Marty and I still haven't finished figuring out what we're going to do about that singer I told you about and there are a dozen phone calls I should be making right now. But if you agree to do something for me, I'll put my business aside for the time being and we'll go on that picnic."

"What?" she asked warily.

"You've got to recognize that I meant what I said last night. Sometimes the reason I exclude Garrett is that I really do just want to be alone with you. So you've got to promise me that if I agree to start doing more things together as a family, you won't object on those occasions when I just want the two of us to be alone."

"I promise," she said weakly, as the accumulated tension drained from her body.

"Okay, then go and pack the lunch," he mumbled, his injured pride still keeping him from displaying a truly amicable expression.

She went into the hall and wondered if this confrontation, the first real one of their marriage, would solve the problem between Garrett and Stephen. But when she reached the stairs she felt a strange heaviness in the pit of her stomach. When she was working on a writing assignment she knew that the feeling was a kind of alarm, a warning signal that there was some important aspect of a story she was overlooking.

As she walked down the hall, her thoughts turned to the house. It had started to grate on her. Although she accepted that it was irrational to think that two murders committed in the distant past might bode any ill toward their own tenure there, she was still troubled by the curious anonymity of the place.

She disliked admitting it, but she was also beginning to wonder whether there was anything to Garrett's theory that the house was some sort of gigantic puzzle. She did not know why. Perhaps it was because she had been presented with so many surprises since arriving at the house that in some strange way she was beginning to expect them. Or perhaps it was simply Garrett's uncanny knack for being right when it came to odd and disconcerting facts. Whatever the case, she knew only that her curiosity was reasserting itself with a vengeance.

She decided there was at least one thing she could find out before they left for the picnic. When she reached the entrance hall, she went outside and copied down the inscription from over the door. Then she went into the coachmen's waiting room and dialed the number of *People Beat*. When the switchboard operator answered, she asked for Annie. Finally, after waiting about a minute, the familiar husky contralto answered.

"Hello?"

"Hi, Annie, it's me."

"Lauren, is that you? How's life among the leisure class?"

"Fine, Annie, how are you?"

"We're doing terrible without you, Lauren. If you ever want your job back."

"Thanks, Annie, you never know."

"So to what do I owe the honor of this call."

"I've got a small favor I want to ask you."

"Anything." She paused. "Well, almost anything. Shoot."

"You took Latin in college, right?"

The question clearly took her off guard. "Latin? Why on earth do you want to know that?" She coughed, the familiar smoker's cough.

"Come on, Annie, this is kind of important."

"Yes. Yes. Four years of it. For chrissakes, if I had been a man I probably would've joined the seminary."

Lauren smiled. It was just like Annie, Catholic to her core, to still be irreverent enough to use the term 'chrissakes.' "Well, this house where we're staying in the Adirondacks, it's got a Latin inscription over the door. I wonder if you could translate it for me."

"Sure. What's the line?"

She told her, and Annie was silent for a moment.

"Hmmm, that's strange."

"What?"

"Well, this word *girum*. It's not Latin. So I . . . wait a minute. Oh, I know what it is. It's the Latinized version of the Greek word *gyron*. It means 'around,' or to go in a circle. You know, as in the word 'gyroscope.' Only if I were translating it I think I would have kept the 'y' in it. Probably the work of some unlettered medieval scribe, if you'll pardon the pun." She coughed again.

"What about the rest?" But as she started to answer there was a crackle of static, and for a moment Lauren couldn't hear anything. "Wait, what did you say?"

"I said the rest is pretty simple. *Consumimur*, that's the

first person plural of the present indicative passive of *consumere*. It means 'we are consumed.' And *igni*, that means 'fire.' It's an ablative—"

"Annieee."

"Well, it's all pretty straightforward. Just figure it out. *Nocte* means 'by night.' *Et* means 'and.' *Imus* means 'we go.' "

"So what does it all mean put together?" she said eagerly.

"Well, I'd say it translates roughly as 'We circle in the night and are consumed by the fire.' "

After she recited the sentence they both went silent.

"Gee, that's an odd thing to have written over a door," Annie said mildly after a few seconds had elapsed.

For Lauren the ominousness of the remark made her wish for a moment she hadn't bothered to get the line translated. "Well, I guess at least some of the wording of the sentence was determined by the fact that it's a palindrome."

"It's a palindrome?" There was a pause as Annie studied the sentence again. "Hey, it is! Well, that's why whoever put this thing together changed the 'y' to an 'i.' It wouldn't be a palindrome if they hadn't."

"Well, thanks, Annie."

"Anytime, Lauren. Just call me." She paused. "So, Lauren, how are you doing really?"

Her repeating of the question perplexed Lauren. "I told you, fine, Annie. Why?"

She paused again. "Lauren, we've known each other a long time, and I hope you don't think I'm out of line with what I'm about to say. But I worry about you."

Lauren was mystified. "Why?"

"Because you're a smart lady. But for some reason—I don't know why—this marriage thing all seemed so sudden."

A mixture of anger and insecurity rippled through Lauren. She knew she had had some problems with men in the past, but she got the sense Annie was intimating there might be something about Stephen, and that was none of her business. "What are you getting at, Annie?" she asked with thinly veiled annoyance.

"Now, don't get me wrong," Annie said quickly. "All I'm saying is I've seen you go through some rough times before and sometimes it's taken you a while before you've asked for any help. And . . . well, Stephen has a reputation in the industry . . ." She stopped abruptly. "Well, I just don't want you to hesitate to call if you need anything. Okay?"

Lauren was still annoyed, but she knew Annie's concern was merely a sign of her affection. "Okay, Annie, but listen, we're fine. I mean, we've had a few bumps, but things are fine. But I'll call if I need anything, okay?"

"Okay."

"Well, thanks, Annie."

"You're welcome, Lauren." Annie coughed again. "Got to give these things up," she mumbled as she hung up the phone.

As Lauren left the coachmen's waiting room she thought again about Annie's concern. She also ran the sentence one more time through her mind. She had hoped translating it might help answer a few of her questions, but instead it only created more. What was the meaning of the enigmatic statement, and why had Sarah Balfram deemed it important enough to place over the front door? Lauren wished she had more time to delve into the matter, but remembering she had a picnic lunch to prepare, she forced herself to put it out of her mind and headed toward the kitchen.

To her great delight the picnic was a resounding success. Although Stephen started out a bit grumpy, after they reached a grassy area on the west side of the lake and were sipping wine in the sun, his mood took a definite turn for the better. He even made a number of amiable forays into conversation with Garrett and played them both a new song he was working on on his guitar. Garrett was no longer openly sullen toward Stephen and even made several passable attempts at sustaining his end of the conversation. By the time they returned to the house later that afternoon she was in such good spirits she wasn't even bothered when Stephen vanished into the coachmen's waiting room to embark on yet another marathon round of business calls.

For the first several minutes after they returned she busied herself in the kitchen putting away the picnic things. But as soon as she had time to slow down and relax a little, all of her questions about the house returned. Unable to endure her curiosity any longer, she decided it was time to explore some more of the house. She decided to ask Garrett to go with her.

She found him in one of the sun porches performing what at first appeared to be some kind of military march.

"What are you doing?" she asked.

At the sound of her voice he turned around, and something in his eyes made her realize he could not speak. She noticed also that his cheeks were puffed out and he appeared to be holding his breath. After tossing her a brief glance he resumed his quickstep, arms swinging to and fro. But before he could reach the end of the sun porch he exhaled loudly. His face fell. "Forty-one steps," he sighed.

She continued to look at him with bewilderment.

"I was seeing how far I could walk while holding my breath. I was able to go forty-one steps this time. I wanted to make it to the end of the room, but the room is fifty steps long."

"Why on earth would you want to practice holding your breath?"

"Because someday when I'm an adult I will probably travel into outer space, and when I do, it will probably be a good idea if I know how to hold my breath for long periods of time."

She knew she shouldn't ask, but she had to. "Why?"

"Because if there's an accident and all the air gets sucked out of the spaceship I'll be able to survive until I can get into a spacesuit."

"I see," she said. "Are you done practicing holding your breath?"

"I guess so. Why?"

"Because I thought I'd explore some more of the house and I wondered if you wanted to go with me."

For some reason the suggestion alarmed him. "I don't think you should do that."

"Why?"

He became oddly nervous. "I don't know. I just thought that maybe if the house is some sort of puzzle . . . well, maybe we should leave it alone."

Considering how insistent he had been when he first told her the house was a puzzle, his sudden lack of interest surprised her.

"Well, first of all, I'm not convinced that the house is a puzzle. But if it is, doesn't that mean we should try to solve it?"

"No," he said quickly.

"Why not?"

"Well—maybe the reason all the stairs and hallways keep leading back downstairs is that there are parts of the house we're not supposed to go into. Maybe the house is built that way to keep people out."

"Why, Garrett, if I didn't know better I might almost think there was something you didn't want me to see somewhere in the house," she said.

"No, it's not that," he said said quickly, and for a fraction of a second the rapidity with which he had answered made her think there was more to his denial than met the eye.

"Well, are you coming or not?" she said as she walked toward the door.

"No—*yes*," he sputtered, following behind.

When they reached the second-floor landing she paused. "So you say whichever way we turn, we'll always end up having to go back downstairs, right?"

He nodded hesitantly.

"Okay, then let's go this way," she said, and turned left. When they came to the small vestibule at the far end of the hall she opened one of the doors at random. Seeing what appeared to be an upstairs drawing room, she walked inside.

"Wait!" she heard Garrett call behind her, but it was too late. Before she knew what was happening she had become so dizzy she had to collapse on a nearby couch. Garrett inched up carefully beside her and told her about the room's asymmetries.

She sighed and shook her head. "Why anyone would want to do this to a house is beyond me." She stood and started through the room again, but again she felt the same horrible vertigo and was forced to lunge for the nearest door. Beyond was the trophy room, and after making sure Garrett was still following her she went through a door leading off it and found herself returned to the front entrance hall. It annoyed her that Garrett was evidently right about the house, and for a moment she refused to look him in the eye.

"See?" he said.

"That was just once," she protested. Unwilling to give up so easily, she tried again, but this time when she came to a stairway that seemed to lead back to the first floor, she refused to descend it and instead chose another route. However, they quickly got lost in a warren of interconnecting rooms and were forced to go down a flight of stairs.

"Okay, so what happens if we try to do something the house doesn't seem to want us to do?" she asked.

"What do you mean?"

"I mean, the drawing room upstairs seems to be designed to always make a person exit through the trophy room, but there are other ways out of the drawing room we haven't tried. What happens if we try to ignore the dizziness the room makes us feel and go through one of them instead?"

His eyes widened at the notion. But he also seemed intrigued by the idea. "I don't know."

"Well, come on, then."

They went upstairs to the drawing room, and Lauren stepped inside gingerly. Only this time instead of walking at a normal pace, she proceeded one step at a time as if walking a tightrope and paused between each step to see how she was feeling. To her delight, although the strange angles in the room still tugged dangerously at her sense of balance, the effect was so diminished that she could travel where she wanted to. After glancing behind her to make sure Garrett was doing the same, she made her way over to one of the doors.

Smiling triumphantly, she opened it, but to her dismay, beyond was a hallway even more warped than the drawing room. On one side of the sharply twisting corridor the wall was at least a foot taller than on the other side, and the planks of the floor were so buckled it looked as if the stress from such distortion might cause them to snap at any moment. She stepped inside.

"I don't think you should do that," Garrett said abruptly.

"For God's sake, Garrett, if it's that upsetting to you, just go back downstairs."

For several seconds after her reproof he just scowled at her, a mixture of resentment and hurt pride in his eyes. But again, for some reason he did not seem to want to let her continue on alone, and he quieted.

She walked boldly into the corridor. Because no attempt had been made to disguise its asymmetries, she had thought it would not have the same disorienting effect as the drawing room. But to her surprise, as soon as she started up the incline of the floor her head began to spin so rapidly she almost blacked out. In a desperate attempt to counteract the whirling of her senses she dropped to her knees and closed her eyes. Then she took several deep breaths.

"Mom!" Garrett cried, and she heard him run up beside her. She reached out to try to stop him, but it was too late. "Oh!" he exclaimed as he collided with her outstretched hand.

"Sit down and close your eyes!" she said as she guided him down with her hand. She heard him clunk beside her, and for a moment she thought he might have fainted. But then she reached out and felt that his head was still upright. "Take long deep breaths," she ordered. "And keep your eyes closed!"

They sat with their eyes closed for several minutes, and when she finally dared to open them she discovered than even when she was stationary on the floor the strange vertiginous effects of the hallway still pulled at her.

"How is it doing that?" Garrett asked as he looked at their surroundings through half-open eyes.

"I don't know."

"It doesn't seem to be built like the other room—"

"I know!" she interrupted. Scanning the passageway, she noticed that like every other hall in the house it possessed a number of doors. After noting their various locations, she put her hands on the floor and started to crawl forward.

"Come on," she said, beckoning for Garrett to follow. Since the disorienting effect of the drawing room appeared to be designed to keep people from going through certain doors, she reasoned that the twistings and turnings of the hallway were most likely intended to do the same. And since their dizzying influence was even more pronounced it seemed logical to assume they were drawing ever closer to whatever it was Sarah Balfram had gone to such great lengths to conceal.

As they moved forward, occasionally the swimming of her senses became so severe she had to stop and close her eyes for a moment. But always she paid careful attention to the parts of the hallway where the repulsive effect was the strongest, until finally it became clear it was centered around a doorway at the end of the hall.

Carefully she inched her way toward the door, and when she reached it, she paused and looked at Garrett again. Like her, he was using every ounce of his willpower to fight back the dizziness. Beads of perspiration had formed on his forehead. Although she hadn't realized it before she noticed that she too was damp with perspiration, and for a second she wondered whether she was doing the right thing. But then curiosity got the best of her and she reached out and opened the door.

When she did so a gush of cool, stale air rushed past them and a small flurry of dust flew into her eyes and caused her to squint. But when she opened them again she saw that beyond was another hallway, only it was a hallway unlike anything she had seen in the house so far. The first thing she noticed was that although it did not possess any windows, it was pervaded by a strange twilight, and it was a while before she realized the ghostly illumination appeared to be coming from a skylight at the top of a ventilation shaft high overhead.

She noticed also that the hallway was even more exaggeratedly out of proportion than the one they were standing in. So much so that at its far end what had started out to be walls and spindlework archways were now mere parodies of themselves, splays of wood and wainscoting gnarled and folded back on their original forms. They made the hallway seem less like part of a real house and more like a reflection caught and transfigured by a funhouse mirror.

A layer of cobwebs and dust covered everything. In

places the detritus was so thick that the floor and the walls were gray. The molding was so festooned with spiderwebs it all but vanished beneath the pall. Given the appearance of the place and the difficulty they had had in reaching it she was convinced they had stumbled on a part of the house no one had been in for a very long time.

Taking hold of the doorjambs, she cautiously lifted herself up and stepped inside. She was afraid the exaggerated angles of the hallway meant it would be even more disorienting than the one they were in, but to her surprise the mysterious vertigo appeared to let up a bit. However, as soon as she set foot inside, the floorboards creaked so mournfully she thought they might be unsafe. She stopped and tested them by bouncing up and down a little, and after deciding they seemed sturdy enough, she took another step. But again there came the sound of wood groaning against wood, only this time it seemed to spread out and extend even deeper into the corridor. There was a cobweb-encrusted door a short distance away, and she decided to risk the infirmity of the floor long enough to investigate.

"Stay here," she ordered, as she started forward, but before she could stop him Garrett had scrambled up beside her.

"No, I'm going with you," he said. She was about to snap at him, but after seeing how afraid he was, she reconsidered.

"Well, okay, but stay close to me."

As they crept forward the floor continued to creak and pop, but the thought of what might lie hidden behind the door drove her on. When they reached it she batted away the spiderwebs and then turned the knob. As it opened, dust wafted by them once again, but after it settled she saw that beyond was a spare and monkish little bedroom. Like the hallway they were standing in, it was entombed in a fine layer of dust and cobwebs. But what truly set it apart from all the other rooms in the house was that it possessed the belongings of its last inhabitant.

In a closet she could see clothes hanging, and on a night-stand next to the bed were a number of dusty medicine bottles and a sediment-encrusted drinking glass. Intrigued, she stepped a little farther into the room and made out other objects, a shawl draped over a chair, a hairbrush, a fountain pen, and a lap desk, all strewn carelessly about as if their owner had just left them, save that they were all in various states of decay and covered by the same gray patina of dust.

Mesmerized, she moved even deeper into the room, searching for some clue as to whom it once had belonged. And then she saw. On the lap desk was a piece of unused stationery dusty and mottled with age. Engraved across the top were the words: *Sarah Balfram.*

It had already occurred to her that this might be Sarah Balfram's room, but having her suspicions confirmed caused her to straighten with surprise. Why, with all of her wealth, had Sarah Balfram chosen to make her own bedroom so cramped and austere? And why, with so many far more splendid rooms throughout the house, had she chosen to situate it here?

She did not have time to contemplate these questions for long, for as she turned around something else caught her eye. Against the far wall was a narrow table draped with a rotting piece of linen, and on the table was an open book resting on an elaborately carved oak stand. She crossed over to it and saw that it was mildewed and yellowed and appeared to be very old. She noticed also that it was written in an archaic, almost biblical form of English, and although she was unable to wring much sense out of it, it appeared to be some kind of religious text.

As she stood staring at the book and the table she noticed something else. The floorboards in front of the table were worn as if someone had spent a great deal of time kneeling before the book, and then suddenly it hit her. The book and the table were some sort of altar.

She tilted the front of the book back with her knuckle so as to avoid touching its moldering surface. As she did so a sheath of spiderweb snapped free from the binding and wrapped around her wrist. She looked at the book and saw that embossed across its cover were the words: *The Book of the Secrets of Enoch.*

The title left her at a loss, but the import of the altar and the worn patches on the floor did not, and in a flash several disparate pieces of the puzzle suddenly clicked into place. When the shopgirl at Clearwater Lodge had said that Sarah Balfram was clever crazy, what she really meant—or, at least, what the original truth had probably been before it had trickled down through the great sieve of time and local tradition—was that Sarah Balfram had been some sort of religious fanatic.

At least religious fanaticism explained why an eccentric recluse like Sarah Balfram might have gone around and given the lectures the shopgirl had alluded to. It also explained why her bedroom was so ascetic. Indeed, as Lauren continued to gaze at the book she could not help but think that if she knew more about it and the specifics of Sarah Balfram's religious convictions, it might even explain why she had built the house the way she had. For a moment this thought caused her to consider taking the book with her. But then she decided it was too decayed and crumbling to risk touching.

No sooner had she made the decision than suddenly deep within the bowels the house there came another groaning of wood against wood, only this time longer and more sustained, like the baleful creaking of an ancient and abandoned ship listing in a storm.

"Come on," she said, afraid the sound indicated that the twisted and forgotten hallway could no longer endure the stress of their intrusion. But as she guided Garrett to the door, something else occurred to her. Although she had not realized it before, it struck her suddenly that the creaking, now so immediate and menacing, was the same sound which had awakened her the night before.

Given the creaking had started only after they had entered the hallway, she wondered if the previous night these sounds had also been caused by some sudden and unexpected stress. If this was the case, she wondered what had caused that stress. But again there came a groaning of timbers somewhere deep within the corridor and she realized they had already ventured too far, and they hastily retreated.

When they arrived back in the out-of-kilter drawing room her thoughts were in such tumult, she had to stop and collect herself. She was beginning to think Garrett was right. There was a method to Sarah Balfram's madness, and the house did seem to be some sort of gigantic puzzle. The real question was, what was the solution to that puzzle? Was the disused corridor all that the house concealed, or did it harbor something more? And if so, what?

The discovery of the derelict hallway and bedroom had filled her with such a sense of foreboding she felt she should not waste another second before telling Stephen about it.

When they arrived downstairs, she burst into the coachmen's waiting room, a thousand and one things ready to tumble from her mouth. But to her surprise, instead of finding Stephen, she found only a note taped to the receiver of the portable telephone:

Dear Lauren:

The telephone is acting up, so I decided to go to Clearwater Lodge to finish my calls. I will be back in a couple of hours.

Love,
Stephen

She crumpled the note in her hand. "Damn," she murmured. But when she turned back around she saw Garrett looking at her with concern.

"What is it?" he asked.

"Nothing," she said, feeling it might frighten him if he knew how upset she really was.

"Then why did you say 'damn'?"

"Because I wanted to talk to Stephen about something, and he's gone out on an errand."

"You mean about the part of the house we discovered?"

"No, I wanted to talk to him about what we should have for dinner tonight," she lied.

"Oh," he said. He started to walk away, but she stopped him.

"Garrett?"

"Yes, Mom?"

"You know the part of the house we were in just now?"

"Yes?"

"Well, I think it would be a good idea if you stayed away from it. I think it might be a little unsafe, and I don't want you getting hurt, okay?"

"Okay, Mom."

She breathed a sigh of relief, satisfied that she had made her point without making the forgotten hallway seem so forbidden that it became alluring to him. And after he walked away she went and sat out on the veranda to wait for Stephen.

She waited for over an hour, and when Stephen still hadn't shown up she decided to go inside and prepare dinner. However, it wasn't until after she and Garrett had eaten and night had fallen that she finally heard his car pull up in front of the house. She raced to the front door and opened it just as he was coming up the steps.

"My God, Stephen, where have you been?"

He looked at her quizzically. "At Clearwater Lodge. Didn't you get my note?"

"Yes, but I thought you'd be back by now. I was getting really worried."

He shook his head. "No, it's just that one call seemed to lead to another and I couldn't get away until now."

"Well, you won't believe what Garrett and I discovered—"

"Wait!" he said, stopping her in midsentence. "Before I do anything else, the first thing I've got to do is go for a swim."

At first she thought he was kidding. "But Stephen—"

He held up his hand. "No, listen, I've had a day like you wouldn't believe, and for the last two hours all I've thought about is coming home and relaxing by taking a dip in the lake." He started up the stairs, but then stopped. "So why don't you come with me?"

"But what about Garrett?" she asked.

"What about him?"

"He's in the drawing room watching television. Should I ask him if he wants to come with us?"

"Nah, let's just the two of us go."

She started to object, but he quickly intervened.

"Come on—you said that if I started agreeing to do more things as a family, you wouldn't complain on those occasions when I just want the two of us to be alone. Well, this is one of those times."

He gave her one of his beguilingly boyish smiles, and she sighed and gave in. "Okay."

They both went upstairs and changed into their swimming suits, and when they went outside she saw that the moon had formed a ribbon of light on the lake. Stephen charged full-speed into the water and then dove in.

"Aahhh," he said happily as he resurfaced about fifteen feet out and shook his mane of dark ringlets.

Lauren opted for a more tentative approach and started to immerse herself gingerly in the water. But then Stephen raced forward and began dragging her in.

"No, Stephen! No!" she shouted, but before she could stop him he had pulled her in. At first the water felt icy, but after she resurfaced and swam forward a few feet, it felt wonderful.

"That wasn't fair," she complained.

"Well, you can't enter a lake like this by taking little baby steps. You've got to do it all the way."

He disappeared under the water again and then reappeared still farther out in the lake. She was still anxious to tell him about her discovery of the forgotten hallway, and she realized she had no choice but to follow after him.

When she reached him she stopped and treaded water beside him. "Now can I tell you?"

"Well, I guess if even a moonlight swim hasn't made you forget about whatever it is, it must be important, so go ahead."

She told him everything, about the palindrome, about the existence of the disused hallway, and about the book they had found in Sarah Balfram's room, and when she finished she waited expectantly for his reaction.

"You mean you found a part of the house that hasn't been cleaned?"

"Yes."

"Well, that really pisses me off."

She didn't quite understand. "*What* pisses you off?"

"I told Marty I wanted the entire house cleaned before we moved in. I mean, I fucking paid for the entire house to be cleaned. But from what you're telling me it sounds like they didn't."

She gave a nervous and incredulous laugh. "Stephen, I can't believe that's all you're upset about."

"Why? What else should I be upset about?"

"Well, for starters I don't think the floor in that place was very safe. I mean, you should have heard how it creaked when we walked across it."

"Honey, the house is a hundred years old. I don't think a few creaking floors mean we necessarily have to hang a condemned sign on the door."

"But you should have seen the place. It looked like it was sculpted out of clay and then caught in a cyclone before it had a chance to dry."

"I don't see why that's such a surprise," he said, swimming another few feet. "I told you when we first moved in, the place is a bit strange here and there."

Somehow she felt she wasn't getting through to him.

"No, Stephen, it's *more* than strange. Don't you hear what I'm telling you? There's a subtle rhyme and reason to the way the house is laid out. It's a sort of labyrinth or something. Only I think there's more to the labyrinth than just madness. I think Sarah Balfram built the house the way she did for some very specific reason."

"Like what kind of reason?"

"I don't know. Like maybe she intended it to be some kind of giant puzzle or something," she said, feeling a little guilty about saying this after the way she had reacted when Garrett had first suggested the idea.

"Don't be ridiculous!"

"Why is that so ridiculous?"

"Because if the house were some kind of giant puzzle, Marty would have told me about it."

"But if he didn't even know about the existence of the secret hallway, what makes you think he would know about the house being a puzzle?"

"Because the broker who rented the house would have told him."

"Maybe the broker didn't know."

Her persistence in the matter nettled him. "Oh, come on, Lauren. Don't you think if Sarah Balfram had designed the house to be some sort of grand and imposing riddle, somewhere along the line someone would know about it and would have told us by now?"

"Maybe not," she said, also becoming a bit ruffled. "Maybe it's something that just isn't that commonly known. I mean, I wouldn't have figured it out if Garrett hadn't—"

"Garrett!" he cried. "So that's who's behind all of this. I should have known!"

"Listen," she said angrily, "that kid was the first to notice there was even an inscription over the door. *You* certainly didn't notice. And that kid was also the first to figure out it read the same forward as it did backward.

Neither you nor I caught that one. Given his track record so far, I don't think it's so absurd to listen to what else he has to say." She started to swim briskly toward the shore.

"Hey, wait a minute!" Stephen called after her. She heard him thrashing around vigorously in the water behind her, and before she knew it, he had swum up beside her. "Will you just wait a minute?" he soothed again as he reached out and playfully jiggled her shoulder with one hand. "I don't want to fight with you, Lauren. Jesus, it seems that all we've been doing lately is fighting about something."

His words caused a mingling of both astonishment and remorse to pass through her as she realized he was right. "I know," she said, looking down unhappily at the sparkling surface of the water between them.

"So look up at the stars," he murmured as he swam around behind her. "Look at how beautiful the night is. Do you really think we should be arguing with all this beauty around us?" He put his arms around her, and for a moment it felt as if the dark waters of the lake were engulfing her. But she felt unmistakably that some sort of wall had started to form between her and Stephen.

"Yes, it is a beautiful night," she said, hoping he did not detect the distance in her voice.

She pulled away from him and once again started toward the shore. Then suddenly she thought of something else. "Oh, by the way, did you and Marty figure out what to do about that singer you were worried about?"

"Yeah, we did."

"What?"

"We signed him to a six-year contract with this record company I own. Only he doesn't know I own it. He thinks we're going to give him the big push, but we're just going to let his career die on the vine. You know, talk him into recording songs we know are lousy. Send him on tour before he's ready. That sort of stuff. We had to offer him an awful lot of money to get him to sign so quickly, but it was worth it. At least this way I know he'll no longer be a threat." He nuzzled up against her. "Pretty clever of your main squeeze, huh?"

She drew back in horror. "But Stephen, that's terrible!"

"Why?" he asked with surprise.

"It's just so cold-blooded, so Machiavellian. I mean, when you told me about getting that junior exec fired, that was bad enough. But this is a person's life you're talking about. All his hopes and dreams. Is it really so easy for you to just snuff it out like that?"

"You're damn right it is!" he snarled. "What you just don't seem to realize is we're playing in the big leagues here. You got to do it to them before they do it to you. And besides, you know it's real easy for you to point out how cold and calculating and deplorable what I'm doing is, but I don't see you refusing any of the benefits that result from it. I mean, look around you, at this house, at the lake and the two hundred acres of land surrounding it. How the hell do you think I got it all, anyway?"

He shook his head as he calmed down a little. "Listen, I'm sorry, but it's just a bit much for me to work my ass off out there all day and then come back and have you criticize me for it. I've had too rough a day to stay out here and rag with you anymore. I'm going inside and going to bed. If you want to come in with me, fine."

And with that he turned around and swam back to the shore.

For several seconds she was too shocked by his outburst to do anything but tread water. She wanted more than anything just to stop fighting with Stephen, to run up to him and by dint of some magic have all of their mounting differences just go away. But she still thought what he had done was reprehensible, and although she could understand how he might view her disapproval as ingratitude, she had to say how she felt. The honeymoon is really over, she thought sadly.

As she walked out of the water she noticed the evening had grown so cool her damp skin actually gave off steam in the night air. Wrapping herself in a towel, she went inside and put Garrett to bed. Then she went back downstairs to the drawing room to just be alone for a while.

She did not know how long she had been sitting and staring out the window when she became aware of the sensation. She had been so deep in thought she hadn't even noticed that a mist had risen from the lake and had once again blanketed everything with fog. But as soon as she shifted the focus of her attention outward, she sensed it, the same uncanny feeling she was being watched.

Frightened, she went across the room and took a flashlight out of one of the desk drawers. Then she turned the lights off and returned to the window. The lake, the pines, all were as eerily still beneath the mantle of fog as if they had been captured in a picture postcard. And yet still, as she searched each break in the trees, each drift of shadow, she could feel the gaze of something boring down on her.

Her fear crescendoed into an almost mindless panic as she tried to figure out what to do. Should she get Stephen? Should she cry out? Finally, unable to bear the frustration of being victimized by something she could not see, she clicked the flashlight on and held it up to the window. At first as she passed the beam over the fog she saw nothing. But then suddenly in a swirl of mist at the far end of the lawn she saw what looked like the figure of a man. She could make out the outline of his head and the casual mien of his stance as he stood and watched her. But what made her blood run cold, what nearly caused her heart to stop, was the way his eyes caught the beam of the flashlight and reflected the light back at her. Only once before had she seen such a thing, when out West the eyes of a coyote glowed in the beam of her headlights. But even the coyote's eyes, glittering and green as emeralds, paled beside the fire that seemed to stream from the eyes of her mysterious intruder.

She glimpsed him for only a moment before he vanished back into the fog, but one glimpse was enough. Swept with terror, she ran to make sure the front door was locked and upstairs to the bedroom. But to her horror she found that Stephen was already fast asleep. She deliberated, wondering whether she should wake him. Remembering the tone of their conversation when they had parted, she nearly decided against it. But then fear got the better of her and she shook him by the shoulder.

He frowned, grumbling something as he shifted his position slightly, but he did not waken.

"No, Stephen, please," she begged as she jiggled him again, but still he remained unconscious.

Afraid to use any more aggressive action to wake him, she tiptoed over to the window and peeked through the curtain. This time when she surveyed the lawn, the sensation she was being watched did not occur. Concluding that the intruder had left, she undressed in the darkness and got into bed.

After he heard his mother retire, Garrett turned on a flashlight and opened one of his UFO books. But finding he was too fraught with anticipation to read, he turned the flashlight off and simply sat in his bed and waited. He was excited about meeting the thing again, but he was also worried. After their discovery of the forgotten hallway, he was even more convinced the house had been designed to protect the thing, and he hoped their intrusion had not disturbed or angered it.

Because he had had the day to think about it, he had also amassed quite a sizable list of questions he wanted to ask the thing, and he hoped his finding out of Fugate's name would please it enough to consent to answer a few of them. Not the least on his list was his desire to know precisely what it was. He was still convinced it was either an extraterrestrial or a being from another dimension— but he did not know which. Because of its misty appearance he was leaning toward the latter, but without anything further to go on, he could not be sure.

He was also dying to know what it was doing in the house. If the house had been designed to protect it, that suggested that the thing had been around at least since the house's construction, and that was a long time. In turn this made him wonder why it kept wandering the halls of Lake House. Why didn't it just leave?

After waiting for the thing for over an hour he began to worry it might not come at all. He got out of bed and took up his vigil by the door. Finally he felt the familiar ineffable magnetism that meant it was coming, and, not wanting to be too close to it when it entered, he tiptoed back to the edge of the bed and sat down.

Before long the door burst open and the thing drifted into the room. When it entered he still experienced a wave of fear, but he tried to ignore it.

"Hello," he stammered.

"Good evening," it returned. "Have you obtained the information I requested?"

"Yes," he said, beaming with pride. "The man's name is Elton Fugate."

It thought about this, but he could not tell whether the name held some special meaning for it, or if it was merely deciding what to do next.

"Did you find out where he lives?"

A flush of anxiety swept through him as he realized for the first time that although he knew where Fugate's house was visually, he had neglected to find out the name of the road he lived on or the precise address of the cabin.

"I don't know the name of the road, but I saw where he lived."

"What do you mean?"

He explained how Mr. Foley had stood him on a chair and pointed out Fugate's cabin to him.

"You mean his house is visible from here?"

"Yes," he returned, and on hearing his response the thing started to move through the room. As it did so, it folded its arms behind it, and he noticed that despite its vaporous appearance, its hands still rested on one another as if they were physical. It suddenly swung around and looked at the telescope gleaming in the moonlight.

"But this is some kind of seeing device, isn't it?"

"It's a telescope."

"But isn't it able to make distant objects look closer?"

"Yes."

"And if you looked through it wouldn't it be possible to see Fugate's house even better?"

The suggestion startled him, for although he had not thought about it before, he realized now that Fugate's house probably was within the purview of his telescope.

"If Mr. Fugate's house is visible from the window, yes, the telescope would allow us to see it much better."

"Then what are you waiting for?"

He looked at it incredulously, unable to believe it would suggest such a blatant act of spying so casually. But after seeing it was serious, the mischievousness of the idea began to appeal to him and he hopped off the bed. When he reached the telescope he opened one of the bay windows and scanned the distant mountain. It was quite some time before he finally found the yellow fleck of light that marked the spot where Fugate's house was located, and when he did and aimed the telescope at it, it took even longer to find it through the eyepiece.

To his astonishment he was able to see Fugate's house as clearly as if he were standing only about ten feet away.

Leaning against the outside of the cabin and shining dimly
in the moonlight he discerned a rake and several shovels,
and through a large window in the front of the cabin he
could see a shabby sofa, a dingy yellow lamp glowing on
a table, and a set of roughly hewn plank shelves leaning
against the wall. But what struck him most was how squalid
and unkempt the room was. Even at a distance he could
see that both the sofa and the lampshade were grimy beyond words, and scattered everywhere was a nearly impenetrable clutter of rags, dirty clothes, bottles, jars, food
wrappers, and other assorted debris.

He was just about to give the thing a run-down of what
he was seeing when suddenly a figure darted past the window. It moved so quickly it wasn't until it had gone by a
second time and then a third that Garrett realized it was
Fugate. Moreover, as Fugate continued his pacing he kept
waving his arms as if he were arguing with somebody.

"What is it?" the thing asked, sensing the sudden change
in Garrett's demeanor.

"It's Mr. Fugate," he said. "He seems to be upset about
something."

"How can you tell?"

"Because he's waving his arms and moving his mouth
as if he's yelling at somebody."

Garrett glanced briefly at the shadowy form towering
behind him and noticed from the sudden swirl of darkness
coursing up through it that the information seemed of
special interest to it.

"Can you see who he's yelling at?" it asked quickly.

"No."

"Then keep watching!"

He obeyed the command and continued to stare spellbound at the scene unfolding in the telescope's eyepiece. But as he watched, suddenly Fugate's behavior
changed. Instead of pacing he stopped and buried his face
in his hands as if racked by some torment he could no

longer endure. And then just as suddenly he reached out
and wildly pulled the person he was arguing with closer
to him.

Only it did not seem to be a person. At least, not really.
Although its general form was suggestive of something
human, it was leaning at such an awkward angle in relation
to Fugate that Garrett could not conceive how a human
being could hold such a position without falling. Indeed,
there was something so indefinably strange, so chillingly
enigmatic, about it that Garrett began to wonder if his eyes
were playing some sort of trick on him.

But before he could wring any sense out of what he was
seeing, Fugate lunged toward the figure, pushing it out of
sight, and for several seconds neither was visible. Garrett
watched breathlessly, expecting some terrible fight to erupt
at any moment, but instead Fugate finally stood and, ut-
tering some final acrimony at his downed opponent, calmly
turned out the light.

Garrett looked up frantically. "I can't see anymore. He's
turned the light off."

"But did you see who he was arguing with?"

"I don't know. It was strange. At first I thought it was
a person, but then he started to fight with it before I could
get a good look at it."

The patterns moving through the thing grew darker as
the news drove it into a near-frenzy of excitement. "You
mean he was fighting with something?

"Yes."

"But you could not see what it was?"

"No."

"Then I must know what that something is."

"But how?" Garrett asked.

It turned its dark and fathomless countenance toward
him as an even greater storm of darkness lashed up through
it. "You are going to have to go to Fugate's cabin and find
out for me."

"Me?" he asked incredulously.

"Yes, you must!" it snapped as if the answer were obvious.

"But why can't you go?" he argued, the idea of spying on Fugate at close range still filling him with terror.

"Because *you* must go!" it thundered, and although the intensity of its outburst caused him to jump he also detected a strange note of annoyance in its voice. At first this mystified him, and he wondered why his asking it why it couldn't go would strike such a nerve. But then in a flash it dawned on him. It couldn't go. Something, some unseen force or limitation, was confining it to the house. Indeed, he realized that its inability to travel also explained why it had wandered the hallways of Lake House for so long, even explained why it had not returned to wherever it had come from. It was something caught. Trapped. Perhaps as desirous to return to its own world, its own kind, as he was to return to his home in the city.

Following closely on the heels of this realization came another, even more startling. He did not know what he had seen taking place in Fugate's house, but he felt it was something eerie and inexplicably powerful. Suddenly it occurred to him that perhaps the reason the thing was so interested in finding out more about what was happening in Fugate's cabin was that it believed whatever was going on there held some clue or means of assisting it in its own return home. Indeed, as his mind continued to explode with one fantastic speculation after another it occurred to him that perhaps the thing Fugate was fighting with, the thing that was only like something human, was some kind of friend or relation to his own otherworldly companion.

He looked out the window at the mountain across the lake, longing to know what type of being it was and why Fugate was behaving so meanly toward it. He also knew that no matter how daunting an undertaking it seemed, he was going to have to do what it asked, because he did not want to lose the thing's friendship. And now that he thought he understood why it wanted him to go, he had even more reason to oblige its request. It needed his help, and given the precariousness of his own situation, he felt it possible that at some future time he might even need its help in return.

"But how will I go without my mother finding out?" he asked, and the tone of his voice communicated his acquiescence.

"You will have to wait until tomorrow night and sneak out after she thinks you have gone to bed," it said.

The idea of making his way to Fugate's house after dark frightened him even more, but the importance of his mission steeled him.

"And how will I let you know what I've found out?"

"Tomorrow night after you have returned to the house I will come to you again and you will tell me then."

"Okay."

It turned and started to leave.

"Wait!" he called after it.

It stopped and slowly pivoted.

"If I'm going to do this for you, will you at least tell me what your name is?"

It turned and once again started for the door, and for several seconds he thought it wasn't going to answer. But then, just before it vanished into the darkness of the hallway, it murmured its reply.

"I have no name."

The next morning Lauren was awakened by a sensation of movement, and when she opened her eyes she found Stephen nuzzling up against her and showing every indication of wanting to make love. Her first reaction was surprise at the ease with which he had apparently put their argument behind him. But before she had a chance to think about the matter any further, the memory of her experience from the night before came rushing back to her.

"Stephen, we've got to talk some more," she said, pulling away from him.

"Oh, do we have to?" He pouted boyishly as he reached for her again.

"Yes, we have to," she said, getting out of bed and putting on her robe.

"Okay." He sighed. "Now what is it?"

His prefacing of the question with the word "now" annoyed her, but she let it pass. "I saw someone outside the house last night."

He frowned. "You mean a prowler?"

"Yes, a prowler. Last night while I was sitting in the drawing room I suddenly had the feeling I was being watched, and when I got up and looked out the window I saw a man standing in the fog at the edge of the lake."

"Oh, honey, it was probably just Mr. Foley."

"Stephen, I shined a flashlight on the man, and it wasn't Mr. Foley."

"But you said it was foggy. How good a look could you get of him at that distance and in the fog?"

"Good enough to know it wasn't Mr. Foley."

"But how can you be so sure?"

"Because I—" She stopped in midsentence and looked at him angrily. "Oh, why is it that lately whenever I try to tell you about something I think we should both be concerned about, all you do is pooh-pooh me and treat me like some kind of overimaginative child?"

"Because lately you seem to think there's something menacing lurking in just about every shadow you look into," he shot back.

She became even more upset. "How can you say that? Why is it so difficult for you to believe that when I say something, it's because I've given it some thought and it's something I really do believe?"

He faltered, anguishing over whatever it was he wanted to say. "Because I think it's that kid!" he blurted out. "I think he's got you so spooked with all of his talk about monsters and things waking him up in the middle of the night, and green, splishy blood, you're ready to believe just about anything. I mean, if you would just stop and think about it for a moment you would realize how ludicrous this prowler business is."

His using Garrett as a scapegoat maddened her all the more.

"Why is it so ludicrous to believe there might have been a prowler outside the house?" she demanded hotly.

"Think about it, Lauren. We're in the middle of miles and miles of wilderness out here. It's obvious you didn't hear a car, or you would have mentioned it. That means your would-be prowler would have had to have walked here. But why would someone do that? People don't just stroll for hours down dark country roads just to stand in other people's yards."

An almost dazed feeling passed through her. The persuasiveness of his reasoning caused her to waver a little.

"But this man's eyes glowed when the beam of the flashlight hit them," she said in one last feeble effort to support the ominousness of her claim.

"So?"

His disinterest in this caused her to become completely engulfed by doubt. She suddenly wondered if she was just being stupid.

Suddenly another voice entered the conversation. "Human eyes don't glow like that when light hits them."

They turned with surprise to see Garrett standing in the bedroom doorway.

"What the hell are you doing, coming in here without knocking!" Stephen barked.

"I heard my mom shouting and I wanted to see what was wrong!" Garrett fired back, standing his ground.

"Well, you can just get the hell out before I—"

"Wait!" Lauren cried. She turned back toward her son. "What did you say, Garrett?"

"Oh, come on, Lauren, he—" Stephen started to protest.

"I want to hear what he said," she said in a voice that made him realize she meant business. She looked once again at Garrett.

"I said human eyes don't reflect light at night," he stated again.

"How do you know that?" she asked as Stephen grunted and shifted his weight behind her.

"I learned about it in a nature movie I saw at the Natural

History Museum. Only the eyes of things that hunt at night glow like that when a light is shined in them—you know, like predators and stuff. The reason is that animals that have to see at night have a layer of cells behind their retinas that acts like a mirror. It helps them see better in the dark. But human beings don't have it, only night things."

Lauren gaped at Stephen in triumphant anger, but before she could say anything he exploded. "Oh, Jesus! Great! This is all I need, the two of you wandering around this house thinking there is some guy with glowing eyes traipsing around out there after dark! For chrissakes, Lauren, will you just listen to yourself? You're beginning to sound like you belong in some kind of loony bin!"

"She does not!" Garrett shouted, stepping forward belligerently in his mother's defense.

His insolence was more than Stephen could handle. Wrapping the sheet clumsily around his waist, he stormed out of bed and jabbed his finger infuriatedly in Garrett's direction. "Listen, you little brat!" he roared. "I've had just about all I'm going to take out of you!" After he delivered the lines the air was so charged with tension that for several seconds time almost seemed to stand still. But then just as suddenly they all seemed to realize how dangerously out of hand things were becoming.

Stephen allowed his finger to drop as he shook. "Lauren, would you please send Garrett to his room. I'd like to talk to you alone."

Something in the tone of Stephen's voice told Lauren it was probably wise of her to comply.

"Garrett, go to your room. It'll be okay," she said as she took hold of his shoulders and gently aimed him toward the door. He looked at her entreatingly one last time, but she only shook her head and sent him on his way. She shut the door behind him.

Stephen looked at her calmly. "Lauren, I know you think you saw something out there. And you know I think it's hogwash. So I think all that's left for us to do on this one is agree to disagree."

She was still so tingling with anger that even his vaguely conciliatory suggestion left her unappeased. "Stephen, I think—"

"No, hear me out," he said, cutting her off, with a quaver of emotion in his voice. "Listen, Lauren, I'm going to tell you something I've never really told you before, no bullshit. I've had a lot of women. I mean, in my business it's just one of the occupational hazards. And I'm not going to lie to you, the truth is I'm not proud of the way I've treated some of the women that have been in my life. I guess . . . well . . . I guess some of them would probably say I was a real prick. But I think the problem has always been that I didn't love any of them. In fact, I didn't even think I could fall in love, until I met you." He stopped and shook his head as if it anguished him to have to admit what he was admitting. "I don't know. I know I don't say it that often, but I really do love you. We've got to stop this arguing."

He stared at her searchingly, something strangely beseeching mingling with the anger in his eyes.

"Oh. Stephen, I love you too, but I know what I saw, and I'm frightened. And if you won't take that seriously—"

"Look, honey. You know I'll protect you from whatever's out there."

He took her in his arms, and she started to cry softly. He rocked her and stroked her hair gently.

After their emotions had subsided, Stephen went down to check if the telephone was working. Lauren got dressed and went to prepare breakfast.

When the food was ready, she went to the entrance hall to get Stephen. As she got closer she heard his voice coming from the coachmen's waiting room. What struck her as odd was how softly he was speaking, almost as if he did not want anyone to overhear him. She crept up very quietly and stood just outside the door.

"Ah, you know how women are, Marty," he said under his breath.

Her curiosity was aroused, and she leaned even closer.

"Yeah, she finds something to be freaked out about pretty much every day now. This time I had to tell the bitch what a he-man I was before I could get her to calm down."

At first Lauren thought he was talking about someone else. These contemptuous and unfeeling remarks could not refer to her. But still the searing words continued.

"Yeah, of course it worked. She's a woman, isn't she?" He gave a dirty snicker, and the dark, queasy void opening inside her grew a little larger.

"No, getting her to agree to send the kid away to boarding school is going to take a little longer than I thought. . . . Yeah, she's dead set against the idea. . . . Naw, of course I'll get her to do it eventually. She's willful, but she's basically controllable."

A wave of sickly, almost suffocating horror passed through her as she realized with a jolt that she too had never been anything more to Stephen than just an object, another pawn in the tangle of his schemes and treacheries. She heard him mumble something else, but she no longer cared to listen and stalked into the room.

"Lauren," he gasped, looking up at her with surprise. "Marty, I'll call you back." He rattled the phone back into its receiver and gave her a nervous smile. "I didn't hear you come in."

"Obviously," she said very quietly.

He studied her face, searching for some clue as to how much she had overheard. And then, on the off chance she had heard nothing, he stood and nonchalantly slapped his hands against the sides of his legs.

"So, how's breakfast coming?"

"You piece of shit!" she said, rushing forward and trying to beat him with her fists.

"Oh, I guess you overheard?"

"Yes, I overheard!"

"Oh, come on, Lauren," he huffed, holding her hands to stop the blows. "Don't take any of what I said too seriously. I was just letting off a little steam."

But his words were lost on her.

"It's all just a game with you, isn't it? You've been treating me the same way you treated that junior exec and that singer you were worried about."

"Lauren, will you just give me a chance to explain—"

"It doesn't matter what lies you have to tell or how ruthless you have to be. All that matters is that you get your own way. You'll do anything just to get things your own way, won't you?"

"Goddammit, Lauren—"

"Won't you?"

"Yes!" he roared. "You're goddam fucking right! I don't want your fucking kid around. I never have. And yes, I will do whatever I goddam have to to have things exactly the way I want them in my life. And I'll tell you another thing. I don't see what's so fucking wrong about it. I mean, you seem to think playing by the rules is somehow better than playing by no rules. Well, it's time you woke up and smelled the coffee. It's survival of the fittest out there. It's the people who play by no rules who always end up on top." He pointed his finger up toward the heavens. "And if your little brat is right and there's anyone else out there, you can be goddam sure they don't play by any rules either."

After he finished his tirade he looked almost relieved, as if he had held the truth inside for so long it had begun to fester. But his words only anguished and infuriated her more. A thousand ways to challenge the logic of his argument rose up in her, followed closely by a thousand angry questions. But before she had a chance to ask any of them he stormed by her and toward the front door.

"Where are you going?" she demanded.

"I'm leaving!" he snapped.

Despite her anger toward him, the announcement sent a shock wave of panic through her. "What do you mean, leaving?"

"Splitting, going away!"

"But going where? For how long?"

"I don't know!" he shrieked as he ran down the front steps and got into the Porsche.

As he drove off a spray of gravel flew up toward the porch, and one of the tiny projectiles hit her in the ankle, causing it to bleed. But the pain of the wound was nothing compared to the pain she felt inside. As she went back into the house the tears started to flood her eyes.

Garrett came bounding down the stairs. Not wanting him to see how devastated she was, she tried to stifle her sobbing. But it was no use.

"Mom, what is it?" he gasped.

"Nothing," she said, the tears rolling down her cheeks.

"Then why are you crying?"

Unable to contain herself any longer, she sobbed openly. "Stephen and I had a fight."

"Oh," he said quietly. And then after a pause he asked, "Does that mean you guys are through?"

"No, of course it doesn't!" she shot back, but the words surprised even her. After everything Stephen had said she knew she could never go back to him, and she wondered why she would say such a thing.

"Is there anything you want me to do?" he asked softly.

His consideration touched her, and she cupped her hand affectionately over his cheek. "No, sweetie," she said, once again fighting back her tears and putting on a cheerful front. "Sometimes grown-ups fight. You know that. But I'll be all right. Why don't you just go in the kitchen and eat your breakfast."

He hesitated, and seeing he was still uncertain whether he should leave her, she forced herself to smile a little more broadly.

"Okay," he conceded. He started to walk away, but then stopped. "Oh, Mom?"

"Yes, Garrett?"

"You know that book you bought on hiking trails the other day?"

"Yes?"

"Could I borrow it?"

"Sure, it's in the drawing room. Come on and I'll get it for you."

They went into the drawing room and retrieved the book from the small occasional table where she had left it. But she wondered suddenly why he wanted it. "You're not planning on going on any hikes all by yourself, are you?"

"No, I just wanted to look at it."

"Okay," she said as she watched him take the book and go back upstairs.

After he left she abandoned herself to grief. At times her sobbing became so convulsive she felt dizzy and disoriented. But finally, after she had cried herself out, she began to assess her situation.

The first and most painful thing that surfaced out of the chaos of her thoughts was the horrible realization that she had done it to herself again. Throughout her relationship with Stephen she had caught glimpses of his duplicity and his manipulative nature, but she had ignored them, never imagining she too would become just one more victim. Annie was right. She did have a blind spot when it came to men. And once again she had fallen in love with a loser.

She knew her only choice was to leave him, but she realized why she had responded so viscerally when Garrett had asked her if she and Stephen were through. Although every ounce of her intellect told her she could not remain with Stephen, she realized that some other part of her, a deeper part, still could not face leaving him. The discovery filled her with revulsion. She madly searched for some reason why she should still feel such attachment to a man whose moral makeup she now despised.

She reached down deep inside herself to find it was not reason that caused her to retreat from the idea of leaving Stephen, but emotion, a dark and faceless bedrock of brute longing. She had two selves lurking inside her, one that knew her relationship with Stephen was over, and one, blind and ravenous, that still wanted him. This made her feel strangely debilitated. Like a person in a dream, she began to pace through the drawing room. She knew she should call Annie or make some other arrangements to leave the house, but she resisted and instead clung weakly to the hope that somehow everything would right itself, that if she only waited a little while longer, Stephen would return and somehow make amends for everything he had said and done.

She remained in a daze for the rest of the morning and as the afternoon slowly crept toward evening. After she fed Garrett his supper and put him to bed she returned to the drawing room and continued her fretting and her pacing. But as night began to settle over the lake and her memory of the man with glowing eyes reasserted itself, a flicker of her rational self returned. Racing to the window, she pulled the draperies shut, but even in her muddled state she knew that pulling the draperies would not thwart an intruder intent on doing some harm. In a panic she wondered what she should do next, but then she remembered Mr. Foley was within shouting distance.

She went outside and looked in the direction of the generator building. A faint mist was already beginning to rise off the lake, and somewhere in the distance a lone bullfrog croaked ominously. "Mr. Foley!" Lauren called, her voice cracking.

The windows of the generator building glowed brightly, but there was no answer.

"Mr. Foley!" she repeated, growing increasingly concerned. She was just about to race back into the house when the door to the generator building slowly creaked open.

Still seeing nothing, Lauren stepped back cautiously toward the house, but then finally she heard a familiar voice.

"That you, Mrs. Ransom? You want something?"

She heaved a sigh of relief as Mr. Foley stepped into the open. He ambled across the lawn and walked up the steps of the porch.

"What is it, Mrs. Ransom? Is something wrong?"

She racked her brain, trying to figure out what to tell him. "It's Mr. Ransom. I . . . well, you see, Mr. Ransom had to go away for the evening, and once it started to get dark I got a little worried, that's all."

"Worried? About what?"

Lauren glanced at the mist continuing to rise like steam off the lake. "Well, Garrett and I are going to be all alone here tonight. I just wanted to make sure you were here in case we needed anything."

Mr. Foley finally seemed to catch on. "Oh, you needn't worry, Mrs. Ransom. I'll be here if you need me. I'm not going anywhere."

The words made Lauren feel much better. "Thank you, Mr. Foley. And if there's anything I can get you in the house—a sandwich, anything—you let me know."

Mr. Foley smiled. "That's very kind of you, Mrs. Ransom. I've got my own little kitchen in the generator building, and it's pretty well stocked. But I appreciate the offer, and if I think of something I do need, I'll let you know."

He turned and started to walk away.

"Oh, by the way, Mr. Foley . . ."

"Yes, ma'am?"

"I was just wondering. Do you have a car? I didn't see one."

"No, ma'am, I don't own a car."

"But how do you get around? What do you do if you need groceries or something?"

"My daughter drives up once a week, and she takes me. You haven't seen her yet because she only comes on Sundays."

Lauren nodded, and once again Mr. Foley started to walk away.

"Oh, one more thing, Mr. Foley."

He stopped.

"Do you know if there are any taxi services in the area? I mean, if we should need to go somewhere before Stephen comes back, is there anyone I can call?"

Mr. Foley smiled apologetically. "No, ma'am, there's nothing like that around here. Everyone pretty much drives himself."

After his mother tucked him in, Garrett got out of bed and began to study the book of hiking trails, yet again. He had hoped they might reinforce his memory of where to turn off for Fugate's house, but instead he found its meandering routes indecipherable and realized he would have to rely on memory after all. After dressing and checking the flashlight to make sure it was working, he listened at the door and waited for his mother to go to bed. But it finally became apparent to him she was still too depressed over her fight with Stephen to sleep. He would have to try to sneak by her.

He crept downstairs, and when he reached the spindle-work archway leading to the drawing room, he peeked inside and saw that she was sitting in an armchair near the fireplace. She mostly just gazed into the fire, but occasionally she leaned her head back and emitted long despondent sighs. He waited until she was in the middle of one of these and then tiptoed quickly past. When he reached the front door he unlocked it gingerly and turned the knob. And after squeezing through the narrow gap he allowed himself, he shut the door quietly behind him.

Outside the night was cool and alive with the sounds of insects and bullfrogs, and once again the idea of making his way to Fugate's cabin in the pitchy darkness filled him with fear. But, recalling the importance of the task ahead of him, he marshaled his courage and started down the steps. Because he did not want to risk attracting his mother's attention he decided not to turn on his flashlight until he was far enough away from the house so that its beam would not be seen.

For the first several minutes as he followed the driveway around the lake he was still so apprehensive about being in the forest at night that every sound, every faint rustle and snap, nearly sent him running back to the house. But slowly, as his eyes adapted to the dark, his fear became tempered by a touch of fascination. He had never been alone in the woods after nightfall, and despite his unease, the newness of the experience bombarded him with a multitude of enthralling sensations.

First, he noticed that the night air was rich with a variety of smells. The most noticeable was the deep, resinous scent of the pines. But beneath this were others, the cool, watery smell of the lake, the green fragrance of the ferns and grasses, and occasionally even the rich, loamy smell of the earth itself.

But even more prominent were the sounds of the forest at night. Although at first he had heard only a cacophony of frogs and insects, just as his eyes had become accustomed to the dark, so too his ears became more attuned to various subtleties and shadings of sound. He began to discern the difference between the rhythmic stridulations of the tree crickets and the higher, shriller droning of the cicadas. He detected that the constant whispering of the wind through the pines actually possessed great peaks and lulls, as if, somewhere, it was being mysteriously orchestrated; and he noticed that occasionally, no matter how many rattles, murmurs, and furtive rustlings he could hear, the night was punctuated by great silences, silences so deep and eerily still that it seemed the world itself had stopped in its turning.

Thus he recognized also the mercurial nature of the woods at night, for just as he was beginning to feel comfortable, the forest would lapse into one of its unearthly hushes, causing his imagination to run wild. Indeed, by the time he reached the tunnel of pines that led down to the main highway, a silence of such duration had fallen over the land that he broke into a run. Once on the main road, he finally allowed himself to turn the flashlight on.

But to his dismay, he found that he did not feel that much better having the flashlight on than he did having it off. It was true that with it on he could see clearly whatever was in the beam's path, but suddenly what vague ability he possessed to see through the forest as a whole was completely canceled. It was as if he traded the ability to see everything just a little bit for the ability to see only a narrow strip completely, and he was not sure he had gotten the better part of the bargain. He also worried that if there was something in the forest he should be afraid of, with the flashlight on it was sure to notice his presence. But finally he concluded that the flashlight's advantages outweighed its disadvantages and decided to keep it on.

Fearing cars coming from behind might not see him, he continued on the shoulder of the road. But after walking for several miles and not seeing a single car pass by, he moved up to the smoother blacktop. Within about twenty minutes he had passed the first turnoff he and his mother had seen on their way to Clearwater Lodge, and shortly thereafter he passed another. But it was almost an hour before he finally reached the crudely painted keep-out sign and the winding dirt road that led up to Fugate's cabin.

He immediately turned the flashlight off so as not to telegraph his coming to Fugate. And then, taking a deep breath, he started up the drive. Although he had not noticed it before, the breeze had started to pick up a bit, causing little eddies of wind to rush through the upper branches of the pines, and in the moonlight it looked as if some heavy but invisible animal was making its way through the tops of the trees. Because his eyes had grown accustomed to the light of the flashlight, the shadows once again became deep troughs of darkness, and his inability to see more than a few feet in either direction added to his growing trepidation.

Finally, after walking up the steep and winding driveway for what seemed about a mile, he reached a clearing in the trees and spotted Fugate's cabin. It was strange being there in person, for everything, from the rakes and shovels leaning up against the outside to the large window in its front, looked exactly as it had through the telescope. Even the light was on, and as he stole quietly up to a clump of bushes near the cabin he could hear Fugate yelling inside.

After positioning himself behind the bushes he looked through the window and saw that once again Fugate was frantically pacing back and forth in the room and waving his arms as if arguing with somebody. A shot of excitement passed through Garrett as he realized that at last he was going to see who or what it was Fugate was arguing with. But to his great disappointment he discovered that even when he craned his neck the object of Fugate's wrath was still just out of range of his vision.

He listened carefully, hoping that if he could hear what Fugate was saying, it might provide him with some clue. He found that he was able to make out a phrase here and there.

". . . do this to me? . . . you're all the same! . . . can't take it . . . if you only knew . . . all the same . . ."

But what few snippets Garrett was able to pick up did not tell him much. A chill passed through him as he realized that much as he dreaded the idea, he was going to have to get closer.

After watching Fugate for several seconds and making sure he was not looking out the window, Garrett crouched down and ran up to the cabin itself. When he reached it he flattened his body up against the outer wall and listened for a moment just to make sure Fugate had not heard him. But detecting no change in the clip of Fugate's delivery, he slowly started to inch his way toward the window.

He had to advance carefully, for several times when he went to put his foot down he felt a twig start to crunch beneath his shoe. Several feet from the window he also encountered one of Fugate's rakes, and lifting it and gently placing it behind him proved to be an even more grueling and delicate process.

But finally he drew close to the very window itself, and as he did so Fugate's ranting became clearer.

". . . why?" he implored. "Why do you have to do this to me? . . . I don't want to . . . it's not me . . ."

Garrett leaned forward so he could see the room a little better. It was even more filthy and cluttered than it had appeared through the telescope. Here and there on the crumbling plasterboard walls were great swathes of dirt and grimy handprints, and there was such a thick accumulation of garbage and moldering refuse on the floor that Fugate had been forced to carve several trenches through it just so he could still walk through the room. There was also a smell, faint but gagging, like the stench of an animal den, save that it was disturbingly human, with traces of urine, sweat, and feces.

The smell revolted Garrett, but before he had time to think about what it meant, Fugate suddenly passed so close to the window Garrett was forced to jerk his head back to keep from being seen. Even so, as Fugate passed, Garrett caught a good enough glimpse of him to tell that he was just as dirty and unkempt as the cabin he lived in. His hair was greasy and matted, and his skin was white and beaded with perspiration. His eyes looked as though he had not slept in days. They were so reddened and desperate that Garrett was doubly convinced that the secret Fugate harbored was not of this earth.

Seeing that Fugate once again had his back toward him, he leaned forward again. But still Fugate's adversary remained just out of his sight. Finally, Fugate stopped and buried his face in his hands, apparently replaying precisely the same scene Garrett had witnessed through the telescope the night before. Garrett felt a thrill of anticipation, for he knew that any moment Fugate would begin to scuffle with his mysterious captive, and Garrett would see once and for all what sort of being or creature it was.

True to form, Fugate screamed and lunged, and wrestled his opponent into view. To Garrett's horror, Fugate was not only tussling with it, but strangling it, viciously, and Garrett's concern for the hapless creature nearly caused him to cry out. Until he saw what the thing was. For it was not a space being, or even something living, that Fugate was choking, but some sort of grotesque doll or manikin of a woman. The reason it had looked so awkward to him through the telescope was that it was completely rigid and appeared to be constructed out of vinyl and inflated like a beach ball. It was also naked and possessed a frowsy and garishly made-up face and had scruffy patches of lurid yellow hair on both its head and its pubic area.

A ring of grime had built up around the doll's neck, and it was clear from the layers of black fingerprints that Fugate had performed this bizarre strangulation in effigy countless times before.

The sight filled Garrett with such shock and disquiet that he stumbled backward and tripped over the rake behind him, causing it to fall and crash against the ground. In a flash, he pinned himself up against a pile of planks leaning against the cabin, hoping Fugate had not heard him.

"What the . . . ?" he heard the man exclaim inside.

Even at his distorted angle he could see Fugate pressing his face up against the glass and scanning the landscape to try to see what had made the sound. For several seconds Garrett remained motionless, hoping against hope that Fugate would just chalk up the sounds to some prowling animal. But suddenly Fugate's eyes met his, and his hopes were dashed.

Fugate let out a gravelly and gurgling scream of rage, and instantly Garrett broke into a run, charging back down the drive as fast as his legs would carry him.

To his horror he heard the door to the cabin burst open behind him, and he looked back briefly to see Fugate, still screaming like some crazed demon, bounding out into the darkness after him. Garrett ran as he had never run before, his feet hitting the ground with such force that every bone in his body felt as if it were being jarred out of its socket.

He had gotten a considerable head start on Fugate, but even as the cabin vanished in the distance behind him he could tell from the impact of Fugate's footsteps that he was closing on him. Blind with terror and not knowing what else to do, he turned off the drive and dashed into the forest. As he did so, memories of all the dangers Mr. Foley had warned him about—blackwater swamps, hemlock bogs, snakes, and other sundry menaces—all came rushing back to him. But he did not care, *could* not care, for even as he managed to negotiate an unusually dense and bramble-infested thicket, he could tell by the crashing sounds in the distance that Fugate had turned off the drive and was following him into the woods.

It was dark in the forest—the moonlight came through only in patches, and when it did it seemed abnormally bright and unearthly—but still Garrett pressed on. Calling on every instinct and sense of bearing he possessed, he tried to head in the direction of the highway. And finally, to his amazement and relief, he made it.

When he did, he stopped and listened carefully, but suddenly the night seemed eerily silent and portentous. He did not know if that meant Fugate was no longer following him, or if it meant instead that Fugate had only temporarily lost his bearings and had stopped to listen until he had once again determined Garrett's precise location. Terrorized by the notion that the latter might be the case, Garrett decided to remain hidden for a while until he was certain that he had actually lost Fugate. And although the highway ahead of him gleamed temptingly in the moonlight, he dropped to his haunches behind a clump of bushes at the edge of the road. And he listened and waited.

As the wind picked up, once again the house began to creak and moan, setting Lauren's already frazzled nerves even more on edge. In her unhinged state she decided that if she did not do something to try to get her mind off her worries she might snap completely. Having been reminded of her purchases at Clearwater Lodge by Garrett's request for the book on hiking trails, she went over to the occasional table and picked up the book on the great camps of the Adirondacks. So many things had happened since she had bought it that she hadn't even had a chance to look at it, and she hoped that it might provide some distraction.

She turned to the table of contents and saw that each chapter was devoted to a different great camp, and Clearwater Lodge was one of the names listed. She also noticed with surprise that there were more great camps in the Adirondacks than she had suspected. As she read down the list she marveled at the strangeness of some of their names: Cathead Hall, Gunga D'inn, The Willows, St. Regis Point. And Chapter 21 in the book covered none other than Lake House itself.

Flipping quickly through the pages, she located the section and began to read:

> Built between the years 1884 and 1890 by Sarah Balfram, the daughter of the industrialist and railroad tycoon Josiah Balfram, Lake House is believed to be the largest of the great camps in the

Adirondacks. Although no precise tally of its vital statistics exists, it is thought to contain at least 160 rooms, 1,010 doors, 129 staircases, 58 fireplaces, and over 9,500 windows and skylights.

She scanned quickly over the text, trying to determine if it contained anything she didn't already know:

> . . . one of the more intriguing features of the house is the peculiarity of its design . . . wildly Victorian . . . abounding with stairways that lead nowhere and miles of meandering hallways . . . Although no one knows what inspired Sarah Balfram to construct Lake House the way she did, it is assumed to have had something to do with her pronounced religious fanaticism.

Lauren paused, a rush of excitement passing through her at having her theory confirmed, and then she read on:

> But the strangest thing about Lake House is the extraordinary amount of bloodshed that has taken place within its walls. Only months after the house's completion, Sarah Balfram's fiancé, Viktor Oelrich, was shot to death in the house (presumably by Sarah's father, Josiah, although the latter subsequently disappeared and was never heard from again). In 1923, Hollywood director Desmond Hunt was stabbed to death during a party given at the house by silent-film star Mae Norman, an event which culminated in a scandal that ended Miss Norman's career. Since then a remarkable number of other murders have occurred at the house: the Krafft family massacre in 1929, the Ponzi murders in 1937 (as well as the subsequent murder of Duke Donovan, the

Pinkerton detective who investigated the Ponzi murders, also in 1937), the shooting of Ann and Marie Rouchard by an unknown assailant in 1952, the bludgeoning deaths of Wall Street commodities broker Sol Morgenthau and family in 1964, and the death by misadventure of a local teenager named Tom Pearson, who broke into the house in 1979 to do some exploring and apparently fell down a set of stairs.

Lauren read the litany with astonishment, each grisly entry only increasing her horror. When she finished, her thoughts were in such turmoil that whatever vestiges of rationality she had possessed were now completely gone. She threw the book savagely across the room, as if getting rid of it as quickly as possible might somehow defuse its shattering revelations. Absurdly, the first thing that surfaced in the jumble of her thoughts was anger at the fact that no one had told her the truth about Lake House before. And because she was already so upset with Stephen and did not know where he was, the main focus of her rancor became the shopgirl, Amy.

Storming into the coachmen's waiting room, she picked up the telephone and dialed Clearwater Lodge. At first, static clouded the line, but then it cleared and the line rang. When a male voice answered, she asked for Amy.

"I'm sorry, Amy's gone home for the day," the male voice returned amid a crackle of intense static. "Can I help you with something?"

"No!" Lauren shouted. "I need to speak to Amy!"

The voice on the other end of the line paused. "Well, could I take a message then and have Amy call you back tomorrow?"

Outside the wind picked up, and deep within the house there came the familiar long and baleful groaning of timbers.

"No!" Lauren gasped, now nearly whimpering. "It's

very important I speak to her now. Can't you give me her home phone number?"

"I'm sorry, we're not allowed to give employees' telephone numbers out to guests—"

"I'm not a guest!" she shrieked, and the desperation in her voice finally convinced him.

"Okay, okay, I'll give it to you." There was the sound of papers shuffling and then he came back on the telephone and gave her the number.

"Thank you," she said weakly and then hung up. But before she could dial the number there was another long crackle of static and she had to wait for almost a minute before it cleared. When it did, she dialed the number quickly, for she realized from the way the telephone was acting that it was definitely not reliable.

After waiting for half an hour and hearing nothing to indicate Fugate was anywhere nearby, Garrett decided to risk pushing on, and he crept quietly out from behind the bushes where he was hiding. When he reached the highway he stopped and listened again, just to make certain Fugate was not crashing out of the underbrush after him. But still hearing nothing, he tore off down the road as fast as he could run.

He ran until it felt as if his lungs were going to burst, and then he ran some more. At first as he ran he was still too gripped by fear to think about anything. But as he put more and more distance between himself and Fugate's cabin, he began to ponder the implications of what he had seen. Now he knew his theory about Fugate's harboring some sort of friend or ally to the thing was wrong, so he was again in the dark as to why it had been so anxious to learn what was going on in Fugate's cabin. Indeed, given how wrong he had been in his assessment of the situation, suddenly all of his assumptions were upset, and as his wits slowly returned to him, he was besieged by other questions. Had the thing suspected from the beginning that Fugate was unbalanced? And if so, what was it about Fugate's madness that it found so intriguing? And even more important, if it had suspected Fugate's insanity from the beginning, why hadn't it warned him to be careful?

These questions circled around and around in his head. A part of him resisted believing the thing had known about Fugate beforehand, but another part of him gave way increasingly to anger and the vague but growing feeling that somehow he had been betrayed. As his anger deepened, he began to confront the most difficult issue of all. Perhaps the thing was not an extraterrestrial or galactic castaway at all, but something far more inexplicable and sinister.

It seemed like an eternity before he finally reached the house, and when he did he was hyperventilating in great, hungry gulps. Fearful that the loudness of his breathing might attract his mother's attention, he used every ounce of his will to quell his gasping as he stealthily opened the front door.

Once inside he heard his mother talking animatedly on the telephone in the coachmen's waiting room. Locking the door quietly behind him, he tiptoed past and crept upstairs. When he reached his bedroom he once again allowed his lungs to continue their hungry gulping, but instead of going into his room he went past it until he came to the end of the hall. His mind was in such a ferment he felt he would explode if he did not get some answers to his questions, and rather than waiting for the thing to come to him, he decided to seek it out instead.

Turning left, he started down the hallway which ran along the eastern side of the house. Its right wall was dotted with windows, and its furnishings appeared ghostly blue in the moonlight. It also extended so far back into the house that its end seemed to vanish in the gloom, and for a moment he considered turning the lights on. But not wanting to do anything that might dissuade the thing from coming, he decided against the idea.

After walking far enough down the hallway that his mother could no longer hear him, he stopped, and then with a force and intensity of emotion that surprised even him, he shouted:

"Where are you?"

At first he sensed nothing, and he shouted again. But then, slowly, his skin began to prickle as he felt the thing approach.

Although he had experienced before what it was like to feel it approaching, for some reason standing in the hallway provided him with an even more vivid sense of its movements through the house. Indeed, as the tingling patterns moved and shifted over the surface of his skin, it was almost as if he could *see* it with his sense of touch, and like some strange sonar mechanism he tracked its progress in his mind's eye as it wended its way through the labyrinth of corridors. Nearer and nearer it came, traveling through the twists and turns of the house with the ease of a spider negotiating the treacheries of its web, until finally it appeared in the darkness at the far end of the hallway.

For a moment he nearly lost his nerve and wondered about the wisdom of challenging the thing on its own ground. But his anger and growing sense of urgency about learning the truth left him no choice but to remain.

The thing drifted forth out of the gloom at the far end of the hallway. Like a ship pulling a bank of fog in its wake, it seemed to bring some of the darkness with it, and to Garrett's astonishment, when it reached the first of the corridor's windows, the moonlight streaming through the panes suddenly winked out of existence. Despite the fact that it was actually several feet from the glass, the bluish shafts of light did not reappear until it had passed by, and when it reached the next window, the eclipse repeated. Garrett watched spellbound as it darkened each window in turn, soaking up the moonlight like some unearthly

sponge until finally, when it reached him, it was so awhirl
with darkness it seemed like something caught in a cyclone.

"What did you find out?" it asked quietly.

"Why did you send me there?" he shouted, unable to
contain himself any longer.

"Why? What happened?"

"I was nearly killed! That's what happened," he yelled, all
the while searching it for some clue in its behavior that would
either confirm or deny his suspicions that it had set him up.

"Why don't you start at the beginning and tell me what
happened?"

The question left him in a quandary, for if it had played
him for a fool, the last thing in the world he wanted to do was
cooperate with it further and provide it with any more information. But he knew from experience that it did not like
to be trifled with, and he feared what it might do if he refused.

Finally, he decided that if he told it, he at least might
be able to judge from its reactions how it felt about what
he had discovered and perhaps even why it had sent him.
Falteringly he began to tell it everything. The deeper he
got into his story the faster he spoke, as the memory of
his experience once again flooded his bloodstream with
adrenaline. But always as he proceeded with the account,
he watched every whorl of darkness within the thing, every
faint change in its demeanor.

Not once during his recitation did it offer him even the
slightest word of consolation for the ordeal he had been
through. Rather, it seemed interested only in the facts,
probing him carefully until it was satisfied that it had wrung
every last piece of information out of him.

But its interest was more than just clinical, for it slowly
became apparent that certain features of the story actually
excited it. At first Garrett tried to dismiss the thing's
arousal—for the idea that he might be alone and trapped
in a remote region of the house with something both evil
and unfathomably perverse was too appalling to accept.

But as he neared the end of his story, its fervor had become too obvious for him to ignore any longer.

"And you say from the markings on the doll's neck, it was clear that Fugate had choked it many times before?" it asked breathlessly.

"Yes," Garrett murmured, weak with dread at the situation he now found himself in.

"And you're sure you lost him before you reached the highway?"

But the truth finally pieced together in his mind, and instead of answering the question, he asked one himself.

"You're not a being from another planet at all, are you?"

It turned the void of its countenance toward him, and although he could not see its face, he sensed that it was somehow amused that he had made such a blunder.

"From another planet?" it asked perplexedly. It gave a low, guttural chuckle. "Whatever gave you that idea?"

But again Garrett scarcely even heard the question, for he was now too obsessed with his own. "What are you?" he asked feebly, imploringly.

For a moment he expected it to reply robotlike with its usual equivocal answer—who and what I am need not concern you—but instead it seemed to take pity on his foolishness and gave what it appeared to consider a more substantive reply.

"I am nothing you have ken of, boy."

The answer confused him. Was it a demon? A ghost? What was it that it was so convinced he could not comprehend it? "No, you've got to tell me!" he screamed at it, his desire to know its identity and intent suddenly overpowering his fear of angering it.

"Why?" it demanded coldly.

Whatever caution he had possessed became completely subsumed by outrage. "Because if you don't tell me, I won't keep my promise to keep your existence a secret!" he threatened. "I'll tell everyone about you!"

But before the sound of his voice had stopped ringing in the corridor, he was horrified at what he had said.

But it was too late.

Like a runaway locomotive, the thing came charging at him.

He screamed, stumbling backward, as it placed its massive arms on either side of him and pinned him against the wall. At such proximity the tingle of its presence was so powerful that it felt as if an electrical current were coursing through him. It leaned down and looked into his face, and he saw with astonishment that the vapory billows composing it actually possessed a complex and delicate cellular structure. In what he thought were the last milliseconds of his life, he became mesmerized by the microcosms of design contained within the thing, and was seized with wonder that something so insubstantial could possess what seemed to amount to a biological structure.

But then, just when he was certain the thing was going to kill him, it spoke instead. And more surprising, its voice was even and measured.

"I wouldn't do that if I were you."

The incongruously reasonable tone of its delivery baffled him.

"Why?" he asked, his cringing diminishing a fraction.

"Because something terrible is going to happen in this house, and if you keep your promise to me, I will protect you," it replied, continuing to speak in a slow, even-tempered manner.

This answer only added to his dismay and confusion. Was it telling him the truth, or was it only leading him on, baiting him with yet another layer of lies and deceptions so that it could continue to control him?

"Will you protect my mother also?" he asked, wondering what its answer would be.

"Yes."

"What is this terrible thing that's going to happen?"

"I can't tell you."

"Why?"

"Because I too am bound by a promise," it said enigmatically.

"And what happens if I do tell anyone about you?" he asked, half expecting it once again to fly into a rage.

"Then I could no longer promise you your safety," it returned simply. And then, without saying anything else, it moved away from him and started to drift back down the hall.

"Wait!" he yelled after it, his mind still swimming with questions.

But it ignored him.

"Will you please just wait a minute!" he entreated, but still it just glided on until it was swallowed once again by the gloom of the house.

But even before he had regained his composure, he realized it had left him in the worst of all possible positions, for now he was at a complete loss as to what to do. Every time he considered not telling his mother about it and keeping his promise, a voice in him told him he was falling for yet another of the thing's cunning tactics, and he should not waste another second before relating to her everything that he knew. But when he considered breaking his promise, he remembered the thing's warning and was once again haunted by the possibility that it was telling the truth, so if he betrayed its trust he was actually sealing not only his own doom, but his mother's as well. He was trapped in an insidious deadlock. As he returned to his room he prayed that somehow something would happen that would show him a way out of his impasse.

After the line rang four times, an elderly woman's voice sounded amid the static.

"Hello?"

"Hello," Lauren said. "Is Amy there?"

"Pardon me? I think we have a bad connection."

"Is Amy there?" she shouted again.

"Oh, just a moment, please."

After a thirty-second wait, Amy came on the phone. "Hello?"

"Hello, Amy, this is Lauren Montgomery." The phone crackled. "Can you hear me?"

"Yes, I can hear you."

"You may not remember me. I came into your shop a few days back. I'm the woman who moved into Lake House—"

"I remember," Amy chirped.

"Well, I've been doing some reading in this book I bought there, *Great Camps of the Adirondacks*, and according to it, it seems that Lake House has quite a reputation for murder and bloodshed."

There was a long silence on the other end of the phone, punctuated by still more static.

"Did you know anything about that?"

"Yes, I knew," Amy said sheepishly. "Just about everyone does."

Lauren could no longer control herself. "Well, why didn't you tell me?" she cried in a voice that was half accusation, half anguish.

Amy started to flounder. "Well, gee, seeing as how you just moved in and everything, and you got so upset when I told you about the murder of Sarah Balfram's fiancé and that guy when Mae Norman lived in the house, I just didn't want to make you any more upset."

The answer filled Lauren with rage. "Don't you realize what you've done to me now?"

Amy started to cry. "Why, what have I done?" she exclaimed in innocent dismay.

"You let us just continue to live here without warning us how dangerous it was!"

"I'm sorry," Amy blubbered, too cowed by Lauren's angry tone to question the legitimacy of the accusations.

"Well, is there anything else you haven't told me that I should know about the house?"

"No, nothing. I mean, I know there have been a lot of murders in the house, but I don't know the people's names. But I guess the book you have can tell you that."

Lauren still could not believe that the house's dire history could have been kept from her so completely.

"And you say that everyone around here knows about the house's reputation for bloodshed?"

Amy said something, but her voice was drowned out by the crackling.

"What?" Lauren said, "I couldn't hear you."

Again Amy spoke, but still her voice remained indecipherable.

"*What?*" Lauren shouted.

"Yes," Amy sobbed repentantly, her voice drifting in and out. "Everyone knows about Lake House. In fact, people have a saying around here. They say Lake House draws evil like a magnet."

And with that the phone went dead.

Outside in the darkness, Elton Fugate hid behind a large wisteria vine and gazed up at the windows of the house. He was quite proud of himself for the way he had hid in the woods until he heard the boy start down the highway, then followed the boy from only the sound of his footsteps against the blacktop, always hanging far enough behind so that he would not be seen. When he had seen the boy turn up the driveway to Lake House he had concluded that it was Stephen Ransom's son who had come spying on him. But he had wanted to actually see the boy go into the house, just to be sure.

The only thing that bothered him was whether or not the boy would tell his mother what he had seen. He noticed with satisfaction that Mr. Ransom's car was gone, that nice car, and that at least meant he didn't have to worry about whether Ransom knew.

But Mrs. Ransom, that was another thing.

He had half a mind to go in and take care of her right then and there. And the boy too. That would be the safest thing. He sure didn't want news of his little nightly ritual getting around to the locals—not after the way they had already treated him. But much as he disliked the idea, he knew he had to wait. It wasn't that he was afraid. Or even that he wasn't ready, for he knew he was ready. He had been practicing for over a year now, and he could almost taste it he was so ready.

What caused him to restrain his aching hands and turn around and start back down the driveway was that he knew he couldn't do anything until the Master gave the go-ahead.

It had been the Master who had started the transformation in him in the first place.

It had been the Master who had given him the power to believe.

And it would be the Master who would tell him when the time was right.

II

THE MASTER

And thy deep eyes amid the gloom
shine like jewels in a shroud.
—Longfellow

For Elton Fugate it had started when he was an infant.

His mother, Ada Fugate, had become pregnant when she was sixteen, and the thought of having her social life hampered by a swollen abdomen had made her hate Elton from the beginning. Had she known who Elton's father was she might have tried to get him to marry her, but because she had made herself available to any and all who wanted her since she was fourteen, she merely vented her wrath by hating Elton.

It was a family tradition.

Ada's mother had done the same thing to her, and indeed the entire Fugate family had a lengthy history of abuse and was bound by only the loosest of familial ties.

No one in the Fugate family had had more than a fourth-grade education. No one had ever come close to living above the poverty level. No one had ever gone to church, had ever gone hunting with the other locals, or had ever been part of the social fabric in any way. The only reason

Ada Fugate had had so much sex so early was that she was
available. But none of the boys ever asked her out to a
movie, or even consented to be seen in public with her.

She had started beating Elton almost from the moment
he was born. If he cried, she slapped him. If he laughed,
she slapped him. Sometimes she even made him hold hot
peppers in his mouth just to try to get him to cry so she
could hit him. But the cruelties did not end there. For
weeks on end she would feed him nothing but cold cereal.
Sometimes during the winter she would punish him by
making him sleep without blankets.

And sometimes she would vanish and leave him alone
for days in their little cabin—not the same cabin in which
he now lived, but one that was almost as much a hovel—
and although he remembered such times as frightening,
he counted them among the best times of his childhood.

For Elton, a turning point had come when he was seven.
Then a representative of the school board had come knocking at their door and insisted that Ada give Elton the
benefit of an education. And so the necessary paperwork
was done to allow Elton to enter Indian River Elementary
that fall. For Elton it was a both terrifying and glorious
proposition—terrifying because he had never known the
company of other children and had no idea what to expect;
glorious because the belief that there might be something
good about the human race had not yet been completely
extinguished in him. Thus he perceived going to school
as a ray of hope, an indication that perhaps his miserable
existence was at last about to take a turn for the better.

How wrong he had been.

For Elton, attending school proved to be almost as hel-
lish as staying at home. He had too many counts against
him, there were too many things that branded him immediately as an outcast and a pariah.

He was a head taller than all the other kindergartners.

He smelled of smoke because of the wood stove his mother used to heat their cabin.

His clothing was strange and raggedy.

His hair had a choppy look because of the crude and unmindful way his mother cut it.

Worst of all, he was dirty (his mother had never taken much stock in personal hygiene).

Any one of these blemishes was enough to place him at the bottom of the harsh pecking order of the childhood social hierarchy. Having all of them made Elton a virtual leper.

And no one can be crueler than children.

In class they complained when they were forced to sit near Elton.

During recess he was jeered at and taunted and some-times even punched or kicked—these last only when the teacher minding the recess turned a blind eye (which was not infrequent, because some of the teachers did not like Elton any more than his classmates did).

Every day after school, rain or shine, a group of boys would chase Elton home, and about half of the time, catch him and beat him to within an inch of his life.

Until whatever humanity was left in him was completely extinguished. He became something vacant. A shell. A mere simulacrum of a human being going through the motions of life and passively accepting whatever abuse and indignities were heaped upon him.

He continued in this state into adulthood, through a dozen menial and piss-ant jobs and even after his mother's death. But never did the storms brewing within him, the hatreds and the venoms, ever so much as produce a ripple outside his slavish and pain-benumbed consciousness.

Until he met the Master.

His first encounter with the Master had taken place en-tirely inside his head. It had started one morning when he awoke out of the blue with a bone-crushing headache. Nothing, not even a handful of aspirin and a half a bottle of Popov vodka, would get rid of it.

But soon the headaches evolved into a buzzing sensation. And the buzzing became a mumbling.

And then finally the mumbling became a voice, a voice that spoke to Elton both patiently and firmly.

The voice of the Master.

At first Elton was afraid of the voice and would run screaming and babbling through the woods in a frantic attempt to drown it out. No other voice he had ever heard in his life had had anything good to say, and he assumed this new voice inside his head would be no different.

But the voice always waited him out, was always there and ready to resume whenever he became too exhausted or too hoarse to continue his occlusive chatter, until slowly, inevitably, he was forced to listen to it.

When he did, he discovered to his great surprise that the voice—which called itself the Master—was offering him encouragement instead of criticism.

In rambling discourses that would sometimes go on for hours, the Master told him why his life had been so difficult. As the Master explained, Elton had only been undergoing a test, a rite of passage, to see if he was worthy. As for what it was that he was being determined worthy of, the Master told Elton it was the ability to perceive the beauty of hatred, the hidden but sublime exquisiteness of evil.

As the Master explained, most human beings labored under the delusion that hatred was wrong, and evil, something to shun. But it took a most extraordinary human being, one in a million like Elton, to have the strength and courage to recognize that quite the opposite was true.

Evil was beautiful.

It was the ruling force in the universe.

That was why evil was so pervasive in the world.

And that was why, no matter how strenuously the good tried to stamp out all things iniquitous and depraved, evil always rose again, like a phoenix.

The only problem was that this realization was too powerful a current to run through the filament of most mortal beings. Because most human beings were so paltry and weak, the awareness of evil's beauty burned them out, destroyed them before it had a chance to transform and empower them.

But Elton had not been destroyed. He had survived the searing winds of hatred. And that was why the Master had come to him, to groom and tutor him. To show him the way to allow the heady current of evil to course through him in full. As the Master explained to him, through his survival he had proved he was special and it was now his destiny to become the conquering Alexander of his day. Only instead of trampling geographical boundaries, he was to trample moral ones. And by bursting free from the restrictions of each social ethic in its turn, and recognizing how flimsy they all were, he was to experience fully the exuberance of iniquity.

And allow himself to become completely transformed by evil.

For Elton, it was a glorious revelation. At last his wretched existence made sense to him. All the questions, the blistering doubts and self-condemnations, that had haunted him over the years fell away like cataracts, and several times as he walked through the woods and listened as the Master told him how special he was, he actually whooped with joy.

But still he was skeptical. Not only had he had his hopes dashed before, but also, in the course of his schooling, he had done a little reading on schizophrenia. So he knew all too well the medical implications of hearing voices in one's head.

He proceeded with the utmost caution. He spent hours

questioning and challenging what the Master said, and when the Master told him to do something, such as move or speak in some new way, he did so with studious and scrupulous correctness—always paying close attention to what he was doing just to make sure the Master was not trying to dupe him in some way, or show him up for a fool.

Until slowly he became convinced of the Master's sincerity.

The old Elton died and a new one was born in his place.

And as he surrendered himself ever more to the Master's wishes, the Master became more real and his voice was no longer confined simply to the inside of Elton's head.

Sometimes as Elton stood in front of his cabin in the moonlight he would hear the Master speaking to him from his own shadow. As time went on, Elton began to hear the Master's voice coming from other shadows, the shadows of large rocks, and even from the shadowy and impenetrable gloom of the forest itself.

Until finally Elton actually began to see the Master as a misty figure standing in the darkness. And eventually as a seemingly solid presence who would occasionally accompany Elton on his midnight strolls.

It was the Master who had told Elton to purchase the doll and begin practicing on it. As the Master explained, it was important for Elton to acquire the *feel* of killing somebody before graduating to the real thing. The Master had also warned Elton that he would have to practice long and hard on the doll before he had acquired the purity of evil necessary to begin the final phase of his transformation. And even then, the Master warned Elton that he would have to wait for a sign.

But now, Elton was convinced the sign had come.

As he returned home after gazing up at the glowing yellow windows of Lake House, he gleefully counted up the auguries.

The boy had come to him.

The boy and his mother were alone and Mr. Ransom appeared to be away on business.

And most significant of all, it was Lake House, *Lake House*, the house that all along he had been drawn to, had wanted desperately to become employed by.

He had been bitter when he had not gotten the job of running the generators. But now he realized it had all been part of a plan. A first taste. A prelude to what lay ahead.

Now he knew that the time when he would graduate from dolls to actual flesh and blood was imminent.

All that remained was for the Master to come to him and tell him to begin.

For some reason the chilling succinctness of Amy's closing words finally snapped Lauren out of her stupor. She knew she and Garrett had to get away from the house as quickly as possible. But as she stared down at the dead telephone receiver in her hand, she realized the problem was how. She knew Mr. Foley did not have a car. She had come to her senses about Stephen and banished any illusion that he would be sensitive enough to fathom their plight and return to help them. Although a part of her still yearned for him and would probably not get over him for some time to come, she realized now that she had been playing the stupid and insipid girl for him; but that was over—any rescuing to be done in the situation was now completely up to her.

That left walking, a solution that was no solution, for as she recalled, driving at fifty miles an hour it had taken her the better part of half an hour to get to Clearwater

Lodge. Clearwater Lodge was twenty miles away, and that was a trek she couldn't imagine taking even in the daytime.

Going over and over the problem in her mind and bumping repeatedly into the same dead ends caused her again to become depressed. Only this time it was not a muddled and enfeebling depression, but an electrified one, stoked by the instinct to survive. She finally decided she had racked her brain enough for the evening and collapsed on one of the sofas in the drawing room to try to get some sleep. Tomorrow would have to be soon enough to cope.

When Lauren awoke, for a few brief and delightfully groggy seconds she remembered nothing of the day before. She gazed at the sunlight peeping in through the curtains, and it gave her a warm, glowing feeling inside. But as soon as she started to sit up she realized where she was and how uncomfortable she was from sleeping in her clothes, and both her memory and her troubled state of mind returned.

She remembered at once that she and Garrett had to get away from the house, and on the off chance the phone was once again working, she ran to the coachmen's waiting room. To her delight, when she lifted the receiver she discovered that, although faint, a trace of a dial tone could be heard. However, it was so covered over with white noise she found her dialing had no effect.

Realizing she had some difficult brainstorming ahead of her, she went to the kitchen to make herself a cup of coffee. When Garrett came downstairs she noticed that he too was unusually jumpy and ill at ease. Although his agitation puzzled her, she interpreted it as an empathic response to her own frazzled condition. Not wanting to upset him further, she decided to tell him about neither the entry on

Lake House in *Great Camps of the Adirondacks* or her decision that they should leave—at least until she had some
practical means of effecting their departure.

It was as she was watching Garrett finish up the last of
his breakfast that she heard a strange noise.

"Listen," she said, cocking her ear toward the front of
the house. "Do you hear that?"

Garrett stopped crunching on his shredded wheat and
listened. "So?" he murmured, at a loss as to why she found
the sound so mystifying.

"Do you know what it is?"

"It's the phone ringing," he said matter-of-factly.

Suddenly Lauren realized he was right and jumped up
from the table and raced into the coachmen's waiting room.
When she reached the telephone she muttered a silent prayer
as she picked up the receiver. As she did so she noticed
that Garrett had followed and was watching her curiously.

"Hello?"

The same scratchy white noise greeted her once again,
but in the background she heard a faint voice. "Hello?"

It was Marty, Stephen's manager.

"Yes, hello!" Lauren answered breathlessly. "Can you
hear me?"

"Hello?" Marty repeated, and from the tone of his voice
it was clear he had not heard her. "Hello? Hello?"

"Hello! Yes, I'm here!" Lauren shouted, panicking at
the thought of being tantalized by a call from the outside
world but not being able to communicate back. "Hello!
Oh, please, hello!"

Alarmed by her obvious anxiety, Garrett moved closer
to her.

"Lauren, is that you?" Marty said. "Listen, I think we've
got a bad connection. Hang up and let me call you back."

"No!" Lauren bellowed. "Marty, listen, something's
wrong with the phone! Don't hang up! I can hear you and
I'll just keep talking loud!"

Marty paused, but from his silence she realized he had heard her and was just processing the information. "Fine. If that's what you want to do."

"It's what I want to do!"

He paused again as if gathering the courage to tell her what he had to tell her. "Listen, Lauren, Stephen's told me about the blowup you two had."

She remained silent, but her grip on the telephone tightened.

Marty got right to the point. "He still loves you, Lauren. He'd like a reconciliation. But you've got to talk about the kid and a few other things. Stephen feels he gave it a fighting chance, but he's just not cut out to be a father."

Lauren glanced briefly down at Garrett. "Is he coming back up here?" she shouted without emotion, feeling very strange about having to scream out something that under other circumstances she would have delivered only in a half-voice.

"No," Marty returned simply.

In a way she was glad that Stephen had decided to abandon them and negotiate their marriage through his manager, for it eliminated even the slightest possibility of her weakening.

"What now?" she yelled impassively.

"Okay," Marty said in a voice more businesslike than emotional. "Stephen would like to know what *you* want to do. Do you want to stay on there for a while or come back to New York?"

"We want to get out right away!" she shouted. "Send someone for us right away!"

The static on the line intensified for a moment.

"What?" Marty asked, unable to hear her.

She began to panic again. "Marty, please, you've got to get us out of here as soon as possible!" she yelled frantically. "Could you please call a car service or something and get us out of here right away!"

"Hold on," Marty said, and she heard the telephone click amid another blitz of static as he put her on hold. But from the way he had spoken she had not been able to tell whether he had heard her or not.

"Oh, God!" she cried.

Her outburst caused Garrett to become even more frightened. "Mom, what is it?" he asked, tugging on her arm.

But she was too terrified that the connection, which she saw as their last remaining lifeline to the outside world, was going to become completely overwhelmed by static, and instead of answering she just put her arm around him and held him against her.

She remained on the line for what seemed like an eternity. As the seconds turned into minutes, and the minutes into vast pools of psychological time without dimension or boundary, she became increasingly gripped by the fear that she was no longer on hold at all. But then finally Marty came back on the line.

"Lauren?"

"Yes!"

"I've had my secretary call a couple of car services, but apparently they're pretty booked this time of year. We offered to pay them double their usual fare, but she says the earliest they can get someone up there to pick you up is tomorrow."

Lauren thought about what he had said for a moment. The idea of spending even one more evening in Lake House filled her with alarm. But she resolved to stay calm. What danger were they in, really?

"Okay, tomorrow then! Do you know about what time the car will be picking us up?"

She heard Marty asking his secretary in the background.

"The driver will leave here early tomorrow morning, so look for him sometime in the late afternoon, early evening."

"Okay, Marty. Please make sure he's here."

But the line was once again seized by interference, and she could not hear his response.

Although she was reconciled to the fact that she had gravely misjudged Stephen's character and had no choice but to leave him, the decision still left her feeling bereft. As she left the coachmen's waiting room it was all she could do to keep from crying.

Sensing her sadness, Garrett tagged along silently beside her as she went into the drawing room and sat down.

After some time had passed, he asked delicately: "Are you and Stephen going to get a divorce?"

Lauren took a deep breath as she fought back the tears. "Yes."

"Is it because of me?"

She smiled at him and ran her fingers through his hair affectionately. "No, sweetie. It's because of some things I found out about Stephen." She paused, trying to think of how best to explain the situation to him. "You see, you were right about Stephen all along. I found out that he wasn't the person I thought he was. In fact, I found out he's not really a very nice person at all."

He pondered the words solemnly.

"Is that why you were so anxious to get back to New York? Are you afraid of Stephen?"

"No, honey."

"Then why did you keep telling Marty that we've got to get out of here right away?"

She tried to think of some excuse to allay his concerns. "Because being here reminds me too much of Stephen. I would just prefer to be back in New York."

He appeared to accept the answer, but still he remained agitated about something.

"But we're not leaving until tomorrow?"

"No—apparently that's the earliest Marty can send a car for us."

He lapsed into a troubled silence. "Mom?" he asked after a long pause.

"Yes?" she returned, hoping he was finally going to reveal what was bothering him.

"How do you know when you should trust someone or not?"

Because Lauren did not know about the torment he was going through over whether or not to continue trusting the thing, she assumed he was referring to her own situation. The precociousness this suggested startled her.

"I don't know, Garrett," she said, gazing off into the distance and trying to figure out how to respond to a question whose answer she didn't know. "Sometimes it's obvious when you can trust someone. Like when you've known a person for a long time, you just know whether you can trust him or not. But sometimes it's not so easy. If you haven't known a person for a long time or if he really wants to fool you, all you can do is follow your instincts." She paused. "But even then you can be wrong about a person. Like the way I was wrong about Stephen."

Her mention of Stephen seemed first to jar him, and then to rouse in him a sudden passion. "But I tried to tell you about Stephen. Why didn't you listen to me?"

His chiding grated on her a little. "I don't know, Garrett. All I know is that when you told me, I just didn't see what you were talking about."

"But why didn't you see?"

"I don't know why." She sighed. "I just didn't. But one thing I do know is that someday when you're a little older you're going to find yourself in the same situation. For some reason or other you'll want to trust someone and someone you know is going to warn you not to, and you're going to find that it isn't always easy to know what to do in a situation like that. Things aren't always as black and white as the decision I had to make with Stephen may seem to you now. Life can be very complex."

"But what do you do when you *want* to trust someone, but you don't know whether you should or not?" he asked concernedly.

"Well, sometimes all you can do is take a blind stab and trust him."

"But what if that turns out to be completely the wrong thing to do? Wouldn't it be better not to trust him?"

She smiled softly. "I guess that's the age-old question. Should we go through our lives giving people the benefit of the doubt, or should we always be wary of them? Because we get burned now and then, should we stop trusting everyone? I guess my natural inclination has always been to trust people, to pick myself up after getting burned and take another stab at trusting someone else. I just wouldn't want to live in a world in which I felt I couldn't trust anyone, in which I had to live my life imprisoned in a fortress of cynicism and suspicion. I figure if you don't keep trying, you have no hope of ever winning." Her voice trailed off. "But maybe I'm just being a fool. I mean, it's obvious that my way doesn't work so well. I don't know."

She leaned her head against him and hugged him, but to her surprise he still felt tense and rigid.

"Is something wrong, Garrett?" she asked.

"No," he returned quickly.

"Are you sure?"

"I'm sure," he mumbled, and although she consciously accepted his answer, for the first time somewhere deep in the back of her mind, a part of her wondered fleetingly if he was keeping something from her.

After she had recovered from her conversation with Marty, Lauren spent the rest of the morning packing. Taking her clothes out of the closets and placing them in suitcases made her feel she was doing something to make their return to

New York more imminent. It helped her ignore the dread she felt about being forced to remain in the house for another day. Indeed, despite the brilliance of the morning sun, she turned on all the lights in every room she entered, and silly though the measure was, somehow that also made her feel better.

By late afternoon she and Garrett had finished packing, and to get his mind off things, she had sent him into the drawing room to watch television. When she tried the telephone for the umpteenth time—in hopes of contacting Annie and seeing if she could arrange for a car to pick them up sooner—she discovered that it was still gripped by a blizzard of static. Suddenly something happened which caused her heart to stop.

The lights in the entrance hall clicked off and then on again.

Lauren froze, wondering if she had actually seen what she had thought she had seen. But when the flickering was repeated a minute later, and then again thirty seconds after that, she knew her eyes had not been deceiving her.

Garrett ran in from the drawing room. "Mom, the electricity keeps going on and off."

"I know."

"Why?"

"I don't know. I think maybe we had better go and talk to Mr. Foley and find out."

Huddling together like two frightened children, they opened the door.

Outside the landscape looked as peaceful as always, but suddenly even the sunlight and the chirping of the birds seemed sinister to Lauren.

Together they walked briskly across the lawn, and when they reached the generator building she knocked on the door to Mr. Foley's living quarters.

"That's funny," Garrett said. "He doesn't usually shut this door during the day."

"I know," Lauren said nervously. She knocked on the door again, this time even louder, but still there was no reply.

She opened the door cautiously.

Inside, Mr. Foley's sparse living quarters looked as harmless and unthreatening as the mountain landscape surrounding them. His bed was unmade. There was a book lying open and facedown on a chair.

But there was no sign of Mr. Foley.

"Mr. Foley!" Lauren called. "Mr. Foley, are you here?"

Becoming more jittery by the moment, she crossed through the living quarters and opened the door to the room housing the generators. Inside was a row of gigantic diesel-guzzling, exhaust-belching contraptions that looked like something out of a World War I submarine. The myriad of levers, flywheels, and assorted gauges were mostly inscrutable to both of them, but about every thirty seconds or so a weathervane-like governor on one of the generators kept striking an adjacent pipe and shutting the entire system down.

Picking up a nearby rag, Lauren went over to the pipe and tried to bend it back away from the governor. However, it took all of her strength just to budge the pipe a little, and even then it showed every indication of wanting to inch back into the governor's path.

"I guess this is one of the things that needs constant attention," she said.

"What?"

"Nothing," she murmured. She placed her hands on her hips and turned around irritatedly. "Mr. Foley!" They both were silent for a moment. "Oh, where is that man?" she groused.

As she turned to leave, Garrett ran ahead of her, and when she reached Mr. Foley's living quarters he looked up at her with concern. "You know what? I think Mr. Foley's things are gone."

"What?"

"Look in the closet. He used to have his clothes in there, but now it's empty. And he always kept his whittling here on the dresser."

"His what?"

"His whittling. He used to whittle. But now that's gone too."

Garrett's words ricocheted in Lauren's skull. "But he couldn't. Why would he leave without telling us?"

Although she was completely mystified by Mr. Foley's rapid and unannounced departure, suddenly every instinct she possessed told her that it was imperative they return to the house as quickly as possible.

"Come on," she said, guiding Garrett brusquely out the door.

As they hastened back across the lawn, Lauren felt a nervous prickle move up her spine and across her cheeks, and although she did not know why, she could not shake the feeling that suddenly they were in some kind of danger.

Garrett seemed to share her premonition, and without a word spoken between them, their walking increased to a run.

Indeed, she was so convinced something was about to happen that she did not even know precisely when her fear turned into the awareness that she could hear the the snapping sounds of someone coming through the forest nearby.

But when she did, time dilated into that strange and dreamlike eternity that always typifies a state of panic.

And as she struggled to move through the slow-motion, thick-as-glass world of that eternity, the snapping turned into a thrashing sound.

And then suddenly the thrashing sound ended as a man burst out of the bushes before them.

Both Lauren and Garrett screamed—Garrett because he was convinced the man was Fugate and Lauren because she was convinced that the man, whoever he was, meant to do them harm.

But then Garrett stopped screaming when he saw the man was not Fugate.

And Lauren stopped when she realized the man was screaming also.

"Good God!" the man cried, placing his hand over his heart. "Who the hell are you?"

"Who the hell are you?" Lauren countered angrily, and then, because she was still not certain the man was harmless, she pulled Garrett up protectively against her.

"My name is Gordon, Harry Gordon, and I—" he started with terse indignation, but then he looked up at the house and back at them, and repeated the double take. "Hey, wait a minute. You don't live here or something, do you?"

"We most certainly do," Lauren returned with her own version of terse indignation. From the man's behavior thus far she half expected him to continue his aggressive questioning, but instead, on hearing her words his face became bright scarlet.

"Oh, God, I'm sorry. I didn't know anyone was living here." He started to back away. "Listen, I'm really sorry."

"Well, wait a minute," she said sharply. "What are you doing here, anyway?"

He stopped, and as he fidgeted with what seemed to be sincere embarrassment, she examined his features more closely. He appeared to be in his middle to late thirties and had sandy blond hair and soulful hazel eyes. She noticed also that he was pleasant-looking, although not exactly handsome, and his clothing was clean but rumpled in a way that seemed charmingly boyish. In fact, he reminded her a little of Gary Cooper.

"I just wanted to see the house," he explained. He shifted his weight nervously, and in spite of his earlier aggressiveness, she noticed that there was actually something quite gentle and unassuming about him. "You see, I'm a writer. A newspaper reporter, actually. I work for the *Albany Courier*. They sent me up here to do a story, and, well, I've read so much about Lake House over the years, since I was in the area I decided to come over and take a look at the place."

A wave of relief passed through her, but not wanting to seem too friendly, she tried to conceal how overjoyed she was at seeing another human being. "Well, you'll forgive me, Mr. Gordon, for being so short with you, but you really did give us quite a jolt."

Gordon began to loosen up a little also. "I'm really sorry. It really is all my fault."

"Oh, that's okay. We were a little jumpy anyway. You see, we've just discovered a little mystery. We've just found out that one of our workers has disappeared."

"Oh?"

"It's probably nothing. By the way, my name is Lauren Ransom." She extended her hand. "And this is my son, Garrett. We were just going to go up to the veranda to have some lemonade. Would you like to join us?" She had suddenly begun to perceive Mr. Gordon as a ray of hope, and the notion that he might leave as quickly as he had appeared began to alarm her.

"Oh, that's okay. I've really intruded on you much more than I should have already."

"Oh, it's no intrusion, really," she said, hoping her eagerness was not too apparent.

He stuck his hands in his trouser pockets, and for a moment she was convinced he was still going to decline. But then suddenly their eyes locked, and although the look that passed between them was not quite flirtatious—for Lauren was still far too shellshocked from her debacle with Stephen to even begin to muster the wherewithal to flirt with someone—it contained enough of a spark, a pop of emotional electricity, to tilt the balance and persuade him to accept.

"Sure. Why not?" he said.

"How did you get up here?" she asked. "We didn't hear a car drive up."

"Oh, I rode a bicycle," he returned, the sheepish Gary Cooper part of his personality coming out again as he pointed toward a clump of bushes in the distance. "I've got a car back at the lodge I'm staying at, but whenever I travel I always bring my bike along so I can get in some exercise. You don't get much exercise sitting at a typewriter all day."

Lauren looked and saw that leaning up against the clump of bushes was a blue Schwinn ten-speed. She also noticed for the first time that he was wearing a backpack and hiking boots.

"What lodge are you staying at?" she inquired as they walked up toward the house.

"Clearwater Lodge. Have you heard of it?"

She nodded.

Garrett, however, ignored the exchange. He was too captivated by Gordon's passing reference to a car, for he realized that it provided them with a possible way of avoiding staying even one more night at the house.

He waited until Gordon had ambled ahead of them a few feet and then tugged surreptitiously on Lauren's arm. "Let's ask Mr. Gordon if *he'll* give us a ride back to New York," he whispered.

Lauren shushed him with mock annoyance and then, fearing that Gordon might turn around and see them furtively conferring, quickly extracted herself from his grasp. However, Gordon's mention of owning a car had not passed by her unnoticed either. Unfortunately, she did not perceive it as the same solution to their problem as Garrett did. Not only was there the little matter of getting the three of them together in the same location as the car—with a bicycle as the only current mode of transportation—but even if she did come up with the courage to forsake all semblance of social etiquette and ask Gordon to drop whatever he was doing and volunteer to be their car service, she was not sure she wanted to. Despite what she had said to Garrett earlier about trusting people, she discovered that, for the time being at least, she really wasn't ready to trust anyone. And although Gordon had not given them even the slightest reason to doubt his character, she would not feel comfortable asking for his help until she knew a little more about him.

When they reached the veranda, Lauren gestured for Gordon to have a seat and then went into the kitchen to get them some lemonade.

"Your son tells me that you write for *People Beat*," Gordon commented when she returned.

"I used to," she said, serving them and then sitting down.

"Boy, I wish I could write for a publication like that."

"Why, aren't you happy writing for the *Albany Courier*?"

"Oh, sure, but when you work for a regional publication like the *Courier*, working for a national publication just seems more exciting."

"Only because the grass is always greener on the other side. Believe me, I know lots of writers at *People Beat* who sit around and dream about moving out of Manhattan and working for some less hectic regional publication. I mean, look at me. I'm not writing for anyone right now, but I left."

"I guess you're right," he said, smiling, and again she noticed that despite his ease at making conversation, he still seemed a bit nervous around her. This pleased her, for she had been feeling rather ugly as of late and it reconfirmed for her that she had not lost her touch and was still attractive to men.

She took a sip of her lemonade. "You said the *Courier*

sent you up to this area to do a story. Do you mind if I ask about what?"

Again he blushed. "Oh, I always feel a little funny talking about what I write about."

"Why?"

"Because my area of specialty is a bit strange. You see, I write about weird phenomena: haunted houses, people who claim to have been abducted by UFOs, that kind of stuff. But when I talk about it, sometimes people get a little uneasy. You know, they think that if you're into that, you must be some kind of a nut."

Garrett looked as if someone had just given him a B-12 shot. "Cool!" he squealed.

But Lauren was somewhat less than thrilled. "And are you?" she asked.

"Am I what?"

"Some kind of nut?" she finished, offering the question in as light and nonchalant a voice as she could muster. But the revelation had ruffled her a little.

For the first time a bit of fire flashed through Gordon's eyes. "No, I'm not a nut. Believe me, I'm a pretty average and normal guy in just about every other way. I drink Budweiser. I love my mother. It's just that I think there are some pretty strange things going on in this world that haven't been explained yet, and I happen to believe it's important we try to understand them."

"Right!" Garrett agreed, nodding seriously.

Gordon instantly reverted to his more soft-spoken self. "Looks like your son here might be into a few of the things I'm talking about," he said to Lauren, tossing Garrett a smile.

"I am," Garrett said in the most thoughtful and adult voice he could affect.

But Lauren scarcely noticed. "So what was the story the *Courier* sent you up here to cover?" she asked with a trace of dread in her voice.

"Are you sure you want to know?" Gordon asked gently.

"Yes," she said unconvincingly.

He shifted in his chair. "Well, please understand that I don't necessarily endorse what I'm about to tell you. I mean, I've talked to a few people who allege to have seen it, but I still don't know quite what to think about it."

"Think about what?" she pressed impatiently.

"Apparently people have been seeing something pretty strange on the highways up here lately. We keep getting reports from drivers who say they've passed a hitchhiker on the road at night. Only the weird thing is, when they pass this guy, they say his eyes glow in the beams of their headlights. You know, glow like the eyes of an animal."

Lauren's blood ran cold.

"Hey, my mom saw something like that!" Garrett exclaimed.

Gordon's head jerked abruptly in Lauren's direction. "You mean you've passed this guy also?"

"Not exactly," she stammered.

"She didn't see him on the road. She saw him out here in the yard!" Garrett announced.

The news seemed to disconcert even Gordon. "Is this true, Mrs. Ransom?"

Lauren nodded, but was still too busy assimilating the information to speak.

"Well, you know, it's very strange for a human being's eyes to glow like that. Usually, only animals that hunt at night have eyes that glow in reflected light. That's because things with night vision have—"

"—an extra layer of cells behind their retinas to help them collect more light," Garrett said, speaking simultaneously with Gordon and using almost exactly the same words. This caused each to look at the other with the jubilation of a kindred spirit.

"I know, I know!" Lauren shot back testily.

Seeing how edgy she was becoming, Gordon instantly backed down.

"Listen, we don't have to talk about this if you don't want to."

"No, it's okay," she said, calming down a little.

Gordon looked down nervously into his lemonade. "Do you think you might tell me a little more about exactly what it was that you saw? It would help me immensely with the story I'm putting together."

"You can't use anything I tell you," she interjected quickly. "I mean, you can use it, but please don't identify either me or the house."

"No, that's fine," he said, reaching down into his backpack and pulling out a pad and pencil.

She told him everything she remembered about the figure she had seen standing in the fog, and after she finished, he fell into a long and meditative silence.

"Well, what do you think it was I saw out here the other night?" she asked.

He hesitated.

"Mr. Gordon, please, I've got to know."

"This is just my opinion, but to be quite honest with you, Mrs. Ransom, I think you probably saw what I call an Incomprehensible," he said solemnly. "By Incomprehensible, I mean a creature or being that cannot be explained by our current scientific understanding."

"You mean you think I saw something supernatural?"

"Quite possibly."

"Come *on*."

He took hold of both ends of his pencil and twirled it between his fingers as he leaned back in his chair. "Listen, there are some very strange things roaming the surface of this planet, things that our common sense tells us just aren't possible. But they're there nonetheless. Have you ever heard of Spring-Heeled Jack?"

She shook her head.

"Spring-Heeled Jack was a very famous Incomprehensible sighted frequently roaming the moonlit streets of London throughout the nineteenth century. The first account we have of him is from the 1830s when a young woman rushed into a police station one night and reported that she had been attacked by a man whose eyes glowed like balls of fire. As she described it, her bizarre assailant was also wearing some kind of helmet and a tight-fitting costume made out of oilskin, and in addition to his volcanic eyes, he was hideously ugly, had fingers that ended in claws, and spat blue-and-white fire.

"Needless to say, her story was greeted with skepticism until the man attacked another person, and then another. In the years that followed he was seen by dozens of different people, sometimes even by large groups of people. But whenever his astonished onlookers tried to run him down and corner him, he would laugh and escape by leaping over whatever building he happened to be nearest to, which is of course why he came to be dubbed Spring-Heeled Jack. His physical strength was so extraordinary and he terrorized London for so long that in the 1870s Queen Victoria even ordered the army to roam the streets at night and try to capture him. But it was to no avail. Reports of encounters with Spring-Heeled Jack continued to roll in until 1904, almost seventy years after his initial sighting. But then, for reasons unknown, the sightings stopped, and Spring-Heeled Jack was never heard from again."

By the end of the story Garrett had become so enthralled by what Gordon was saying that he was barely even blinking. Lauren, however, was only disturbed.

After a long paused she said: "But things like that don't happen today."

"Sure they do," Gordon replied, now so swept up with his subject that he no longer seemed to notice her anxiety. "Take, for example, West Virginia's Mothman. In the late

1960s two couples were out driving late one night when they saw a strange-looking creature standing by the road and watching them. The thing was nearly seven feet tall, was winged, and had two huge red eyes that looked like automobile reflectors. At first they thought it might be some weirdo in some sort of Halloween getup or something, but then the thing lifted into the air and started flying after them. Even when they pushed the accelerator all the way to the floor, it kept up with them effortlessly, flying just a few feet behind the car and grinning at them like a demon through their rear window all the way into town.

"From that day on, sightings of the thing started to pour in, and when the police were called in to investigate it even chased the patrol cars. Over the next several years literally hundreds of reputable witnesses saw the Mothman. And then, in the early 1970s, the reports just trickled to a stop."

"But this just can't be," Lauren argued. "If these things were really happening, we would know about them. Scientists would be investigating them."

He shook his head. "But that's just it. Science doesn't investigate these things. What you've got to understand is that science doesn't like things that don't fit neatly into its theories, things that defy its accepted logic. It just sweeps this kind of stuff under the rug. But it's not for lack of evidence that something very strange is going on on this planet. I mean, when you start to delve into the subject you find that the history books are filled with accounts of human encounters with Incomprehensibles. According to Arab texts, in the latter part of the eighth century a veritable army of gigantic and unearthly doglike creatures, with bristles along their backs and huge batlike ears, appeared out of nowhere and ravaged villages throughout the Middle East for several decades. Then there's the well-known Beast of Gevaudan, a huge, wolflike creature with cloven feet that stalked the French countryside for several years during the eighteenth century. Despite the Beast of

Gevaudan's short reign it still brutally murdered three dozen people and seriously wounded over a hundred others before a company of cavalry dispatched by King Louis XV hunted it down and killed it. But believe me, these are only a few examples. There are many more. I could go on for hours."

"But where do these things come from?" Lauren asked.

"That's one of the most interesting aspects of the phenomenon," Gordon replied. "You see, when you go back through the history books and really start to delve into the old accounts you quickly discover that there are certain areas around the world where these things have popped up again and again. Haunted places. In fact, if you find a place where someone has had a really extraordinary encounter with an Incomprehensible, you can be pretty sure that if you dig back twenty or thirty years you'll find that someone else had a similar encounter in roughly the same geographic area. It may have been a different kind of Incomprehensible, a doglike creature instead of a manlike creature, but it will be something inexplicable and out of the ordinary. Researchers who study this sort of thing call these places 'window' areas, and although no one knows exactly what they are, many believe that they're some kind of coordinate point, a weak spot or doorway between different dimensions. In fact, although you may not be aware of it, the Adirondack Mountains themselves are quite a well-known window area and have quite a rich history of UFO sightings, lake monsters, encounters with Bigfoot, and a host of other assorted oddities. That's why I wasn't so surprised when this man with glowing eyes popped up. Even the Indians knew that this part of upper New York was a haunted place." He waved his hand at the lake. "In fact, even the name of this lake, Lake Ketcimanitowa, means 'place of great supernatural power' in Algonquin."

"I knew about this being a place where you see a lot of

strange things!" Garrett exclaimed excitedly. "I've got a book upstairs that talks about that."

By now Lauren was so riveted she had no choice but to go on. "So what you're saying is that these things are somehow popping in from other dimensions?"

"It seems that at least some of them are."

"What are the rest of them doing?"

"The fact that most of these things are sighted in window areas doesn't necessarily mean they originated in the window area. Maybe they've been wandering around for years, centuries even, and are just drawn to window areas. I mean, maybe the reason they are sighted most frequently in these window areas is that that's where they congregate."

"But why would they congregate in window areas?"

He shrugged as he balanced the pencil between his finger and the table. "Who knows? Maybe they derive some power out of being in window areas. Or maybe even they themselves don't know. Maybe they're just drawn to window areas in the same way that night-flying insects are drawn to certain colors of light."

"But why are they here?" she asked. "*What* are they?"

"Well, as you can imagine, there are a lot of different theories that attempt to explain that. Some people believe they're from other planets. Others think that they're some kind of nightmarish projection of the collective human unconscious. But I don't really believe either of those explanations."

"What do you believe?"

The uneasy Gary Cooper part of his personality came out again. "Well, you've got to understand, this isn't exactly a theory I would stake my life on. It's just something I muse about from time to time. But I think there might be something to it."

"I understand!" she snapped impatiently.

He settled back in his chair as if pleased that someone was at last providing him a forum in which to air his beliefs. "Well, virtually all of the world's most ancient religious texts speak of a time when both man and supernatural being walked the earth together. According to these ancient traditions, this free intermingling of mortal and supernatural beings ended when a great war broke out between the forces of light and darkness. The powers of light won and the supernatural and mortal realms were separated, but on occasion things supernatural and evil return to walk the earth once more, and in some strange way the war between light and darkness still goes on, unseen but ever raging."

"What ancient texts?" Lauren asked.

"Probably the most explicit description of the war between the powers of light and darkness comes from an ancient pre-Christian work known as *The Book of the Secrets of Enoch*."

"Oh, my God." Lauren froze with shock.

"Is something wrong?"

"We found a room in the house that we think was Sarah Balfram's bedroom, and in it was a copy of *The Book of the Secrets of Enoch*."

"Well, there's nothing really that strange about that. The book is well known to anyone who has a serious interest in Christianity. In fact, parts of the Bible are actually more like term papers compiled from bits and pieces of other books, and *Enoch* is one of books from which the Bible was taken. Entire passages from the Old Testament book of Genesis are lifted straight from it."

"But Sarah Balfram didn't have a copy of the Bible in her room, or even a copy of the Old Testament. The only book she had a copy of was *The Book of the Secrets of Enoch*, and she apparently revered it so much she even had it mounted on a little altar."

"Well, that is strange," Gordon murmured. "I've never

really heard of anyone worshiping *The Book of the Secrets of Enoch* as his sole scripture." He lapsed into concentration, and after a few moments he suddenly started to get excited. "You know, I just thought of something. The reason that Enoch, the pre-Christian prophet who wrote the book, was able to describe what had happened during the great war between light and darkness was, he said, that two angels appeared to him one day and took him on a trip through heaven. He said that during this trip through heaven he was given a series of visions that told him all about the war between good and evil, the fall of the angels, and everything else that he wrote about. Those were the 'secrets' he mentions in the title of the book.

"Well, I believe the story about Sarah Balfram goes that when she was a little girl she had a series of visions. I've never really been able to find out what her visions were about, but maybe the reason she was so drawn to *The Book of the Secrets of Enoch* is that she thought her experiences and Enoch's were somehow similar."

The idea galvanized Lauren. "You think maybe she believed there was still some kind of war between good and evil going on?"

"Maybe. I don't know."

"Do you think her beliefs had something to do with why she built her house the way she did?"

"I don't know."

"Is there anything in the book that sheds any light on why she had such kooky architectural ideas?"

He shrugged and sighed. "No, there's not really anything that talks about houses or designs for buildings or anything like that." He paused. "But you know, there is something in the book that stuck out when I read it. I mean, I can't imagine how it could be tied in with any of this, but I've always thought that it meant something, or at least meant more than a simple reading of the book makes one realize."

"What's that?"

"According to Enoch, in addition to the powers of light and darkness there is a third force at work on this planet, a class of entities he calls 'Watcher Angels.' As he explains, when the great war between light and darkness broke out, some of the forces of good actually went over to the side of evil. These are the dark angelic forces the Bible now refers to as fallen angels. But some of these fallen angels, it seems, did not really surrender themselves completely to evil, and after the war was over they were caught, trapped, left behind on the earth and frozen in a strange limbo somewhere in between the powers of light and darkness. These are the third class of entities Enoch refers to as the Watchers."

Garrett had been hypnotized by everything Gordon was telling them, but the mention of the Watchers caused him to sit forward with a jolt. Although he did not know quite how, he knew with abrupt and intransigent certainty that the being in the house, the thing whose identity he had puzzled over for so long, was a Watcher.

"But are the Watcher Angels good or bad?" he asked.

Gordon looked perplexed at Garrett's question. "That's just it. Enoch doesn't say. That's why I've always found them so intriguing. Enoch goes to such great lengths to describe where the Watcher Angels came from and what they're called, but he never explains whether they're good or evil."

Lauren looked up at the walls of Lake House. "Well, it doesn't really tell us anything about the house, does it?"

"I guess not. For some reason I just thought I should mention it." He glanced again at Garrett, and for a moment something in his gaze made Garrett think that Gordon suspected something. But then whatever mote of awareness was in his eyes vanished.

"Well," he said, draining the last swallow of his lemonade, "I've already taken up more of your time than I should have."

"Oh, it's okay," Lauren said perfunctorily, but too preoccupied with everything Gordon had said to be fully alert to the significance of his leaving.

For Garrett, however, Gordon's announcement had quite a different effect. Despite the enthusiasm with which he had greeted Gordon's macabre litany of anecdotes, he was more frightened than ever at the idea of remaining in the house for another night. From the way his mother had responded to his suggestion of asking Gordon to drive back and pick them up, he knew he would be making a mistake if he brought the matter up again in front of Gordon. But he was desperate to get her to consider the option again.

To his delight, his opportunity came when Gordon suddenly jumped up and descended the steps. When he did so, Garrett quickly leaned over in his mother's direction.

"Are you going to ask him if he'll go get his car and come pick us up?" he whispered.

But to his dismay his mother still screwed up her face. "Garrett, I can't ask him to drive us all the way to New York."

"Then ask him if he'll drive us wherever he's going. Then we can get a ride to New York from there."

But still Lauren resisted the idea.

"Mommmm," he pleaded in a hush.

"Garrett, please! Take this inside," she said tersely and loud enough that Gordon turned around to see what was going on.

Garrett reluctantly took the tray with the lemonade and glasses back into the house, and Lauren went to the top of the steps. "It was very nice meeting you, Mr. Gordon," she said politely.

Her reluctance to ask Gordon for assistance was not because the idea didn't appeal to her. Nor was it due even to any lingering mistrust of Gordon, for during the course of their conversation she had become quite impressed with his overall character, had even perceived in the flashes of personality that he had allowed to shine through his shy and reserved exterior that he was probably a pretty nice guy.

"It certainly was," Gordon said, searching her eyes briefly as if he sensed her uncertainty. "Thanks for the lemonade."

"You're welcome," Lauren returned, but even as she uttered the words she found herself walking down the steps. "I'll walk you to your bike," she said, formulating the explanation as much for herself as for him.

When they reached the bushes where Gordon's bicycle was parked, he slipped his arms into the straps of his backpack and hoisted it up onto his back.

But as he readied to depart and she noticed how long the shadows were becoming, she wondered if she was making a mistake. As she did so, a storm of doubt and uncertainty rose up in her, and once again she considered broaching the subject of a ride with him.

But still something stopped her, some unconquerable hesitancy, and she found herself trapped in silence.

He was just about to get on his bicycle when suddenly he stopped and stared intently into the distance.

"I'm not sure, but I think there's someone standing in the bushes over there," he said unexpectedly.

Alarmed, Lauren looked in the direction in which he was staring. "Where?" she asked nervously. "I don't see anything."

"Over there," Gordon said, pointing.

But before she had a chance to say anything further, he called out. "Hey, you! What are you doing in there? We can see you, so you might as well come out!"

To Lauren's surprise, although she still saw nothing, suddenly the bushes started to move and a man stepped out into the drive.

As he walked slowly toward them she felt a tide of gooseflesh move up her arms and across the back of her neck. But when he got near enough for her to see who it was, she breathed a sigh of relief.

"Oh, it's you," she said, realizing it was one of the men who had applied for the job of running the generators. "Have you come to replace Mr. Foley? He seems to have disappeared and left us without anyone to run the generators."

"I . . ." Elton Fugate stammered. "Yeah . . . I've come to replace him." For a moment he appeared almost nonplussed, but then a strange sort of astonished amusement seemed to creep into his expression.

"You know this man?" Gordon asked sharply.

"Yes," Lauren said, nodding. "He's one of the men my husband interviewed to work here." She looked back sternly at Fugate. "So where is Mr. Foley, anyway? Why did he leave us in the lurch like this?"

Fugate's amusement was once again replaced by nervousness. "He had to leave," he said without elaboration. "He asked me to come."

"Well, I assume my husband showed you where everything is?" she said in a businesslike voice.

"Yup." He gave a twitch and then smiled.

"Then you might as well go on up. The generators are already acting up, and I think you'd better get to work on them right away."

He gave a funny, jerky little nod of compliance and then shuffled by them.

As he ambled past, Lauren noticed that Gordon was still watching him intently, and for a second she almost thought that he perceived something in the man's manner or appearance that troubled him. But then he appeared to dismiss whatever it was and looked back at her.

"It's going to be dark soon. I guess I'd better get going."

His mention of the impending darkness brought another

question to her mind. "You're going to ride your bicycle in the dark? Isn't that a little dangerous?"

"I've got a light," he said, pointing to a little flashlight thing he had strapped on his leg. "Besides, there really aren't that many cars on these roads. You're pretty isolated up here. In fact, I'll be surprised if I see any."

He got up onto his bike. "Well, nice meeting you. So long."

"So long," she said, waving after him as he started down the drive.

As she walked back up toward the house, she still felt a good deal of regret at Gordon's departure, but all of his talk about strange beings and men with glowing eyes had spooked her somewhat, and she was relieved that she did not have to hear any more of it. She took solace in the unexpected arrival of the man to run the generators. (What was his name? She realized suddenly that she had forgotten to ask.) At least that potential nightmare had worked itself out.

Indeed, for a time, the idea that they might have to spend their last night in the house without electricity had outweighed all her other fears. As she headed back toward the house, she dared to think that perhaps things were going to be all right after all.

Her good spirits were short-lived. Once she was back inside the house, back inside the somber and all-embracing aura of its power, the dark and tingling depression that had gripped her earlier in the day started to return.

Fearful of succumbing once again to its debilitating power, she resolved that perhaps just being in the company of another human being might help her maintain a more even keel, and she decided to look for Garrett.

She found him in the drawing room. Although the television was on, he was gazing despairingly off into space.

"Garrett, what is it?" she asked.

"Why didn't you ask him to go get his car and come pick us up?" he rasped.

"I just didn't feel right about it, Garrett. I—"

"Well you should have!" he retorted angrily, his mood taking a precipitous turn for the worse. "I don't understand why you didn't!"

Her first impulse was to reprimand him for his rudeness,

but then, realizing that the last twenty-four hours had no doubt been hard on him as well, she controlled her anger and reached out to try to comfort him.

But he only darted away.

"Garrett!"

She followed him through the entrance hall and into the wicker-furnished sun porch, and when she caught up with him she grabbed him by the shoulders. "Garrett, listen to me. It's going to be all right. The car is coming for us tomorrow."

"But you should have asked him," he whined, on the verge of tears.

For a moment she remained mystified. But then it finally hit her. He was upset about more than just her not asking Gordon for a ride. Something else was bothering him.

"Garrett, what is it?" she demanded. "What's really the matter?"

From the evasive look in his eyes she knew she was right, but still he refused to confide in her. "Nothing," he said.

"Come on, Garrett, you can tell me. Now what is it?"

She saw his eyes dart back and forth as he searched every curve and hollow of her face, could almost feel how badly he wanted to tell her. But still he kept whatever it was inside him.

"It's nothing," he repeated weakly. "There's nothing else bothering me." But from the sudden solemnity of his manner she realized that instead of telling her he had decided merely to keep whatever it was to himself. He pulled away from her listlessly.

"Garrett, I know it's something. Won't you please just tell me?"

"No, you don't know," he said, but something about the way he phrased the sentence made her realize that it was more than just a denial. From the oddly tortured and belligerent mien he had assumed she realized also that whatever chance she had had of prying the secret out of him had now passed. She knew from experience that when he made up his mind to hold something in, nothing, not even the threat of punishment, could get him to open up.

Feeling too weak to pursue the matter any further, she collapsed onto one of the wicker sofas. As she stared at him in frustration, he once again began to practice holding his breath while he paced out the length of the sun porch. And as she watched him sublimate his panic by indulging in this strange, hyperactive ritual, she herself began to pace, only mentally. Deeper and deeper she sank into an endless vortex of tracking back over everything Gordon had told them, and then every conceivable reason she could come up with to explain Garrett's perturbed silence.

As she did so, she felt herself falling. To pull herself back to reality she decided to attempt cooking them some dinner. She got up and was just about to start for the kitchen when she thought of yet another trivial domestic chore she could do to help keep herself anchored to sanity.

"Garrett, I left the plate with the cookies out on the veranda. Do you think you could get them for me? I'm going to do the dishes."

Without saying a word, he marched off toward the front of the house to do as she requested.

Lauren left the sun porch and went down a hallway leading into the kitchen. When she reached it, she immediately clicked on all the lights and went over to the sink. Glancing out the window, she saw that the first faint strains of twilight had tinged the sky, and an evening breeze had started to rustle through the pines.

She turned on the faucets and filled the sink with a thundering stream of water. However, it wasn't until she had finished washing the breakfast dishes that Garrett finally came in with the plate of cookies. And when he did she noticed instantly that his moodiness had been replaced by a new look, an expression of sudden and total bewilderment.

"Garrett, what is it?"

He looked up at her, and she noticed that he seemed less frightened and more uncertain, as if he wasn't sure whether whatever it was that had happened to him during the fetching of the cookies was even worth mentioning.

"I went to get the cookies like you asked," he started.

"Yes?"

"Well, when I went outside I decided to see how far around the house I could get while holding my breath."

"And?"

He shifted his weight hesitantly. "When I went by the outside of the part of the house where the sun porch is I found that I could hold my breath all the way across."

He stopped as if he had just conveyed something of profound importance to her.

"So?" she asked, confused.

"So, I can't do that inside the house. Inside the house I can't make it all the way across."

A strange flutter came in the pit of her stomach, but her intellect still lagged behind.

"I don't understand, Garrett. So what are you trying to tell me?"

"Mommm," he groused impatiently, "don't you see? The sun porch is longer on the inside than it is on the outside. I even counted out the paces just to make sure. On the inside it takes fifty paces to get from one end to the other, but on the outside it takes only forty-one."

The import of what he was saying finally started to seep through to her, but she refused to believe it. "Oh, come on, Garrett, that's impossible."

"Mommm. I paced it out twice just to make sure."

She felt almost giddy as she tumbled what he was saying around in her mind. "Then you must have made a mistake!" she said, still unable to accept it. "Come on and I'll show you."

She tramped out of the room, and when they reached the sun porch she counted out loud as she paced it out briskly.

"Thirty-six," she announced when she reached the end. "I guess that's because my steps are longer than yours."

They went outside.

But even when she neared the end of the sun porch's outer wall and tried desperately to ration her strides and make them equal the figure she had obtained on the inside, she realized she was not going to make it.

"Twenty-eight," she mumbled disconcertedly.

"See?" Garrett said.

"Oh, come on, Garrett. I must have done something wrong." She pivoted around and stubbornly paced out the length of the exterior wall again. "Ah ha! Twenty-nine!" she declared, convinced that the slightly larger figure indicated that she was gaining ground on the discrepancy.

They rushed back in and she repaced the length of the porch's interior, but as she neared the end of the room, her frown returned. "Thirty-five," she muttered with queasy disbelief.

In a vain attempt to stave off the panic growing within her, she considered going through the entire process yet a third time. But then slowly, reluctantly, she looked up at the house and faced the implications of the disparity in measurements.

The sun porch was larger on the inside than it was on the outside.

The house creaked somewhere deep inside.

"What does it mean?" Garrett entreated.

"I don't know!" Lauren said testily as the enormity of the discovery continued to reel through her.

But she did know. Or at least she knew partially.

For if the sun porch was larger on the inside than it was on the outside it meant that the house was also larger, that despite the impossibility of such a state of affairs, it possessed more space on the inside, more volume, than its external dimensions could account for.

And that meant that the strange bent of its architecture, the often dizzying twists and turns of its design, were more than just surface flourishes. It meant that there was actually some sort of spatial distortion taking place within the house, that somehow space was being warped within its confines.

But how? she wondered. And why?

And then suddenly, like a series of silent explosions, the pieces fell together in her mind and she knew.

"Garrett, I don't think this means anything," she lied.

"But Mom, you just—"

"I know, but you know what I think is happening here?"

His attention remained glued on her.

"I think this is just another one of the house's tricks. You know, like the rooms upstairs that are designed to make you feel dizzy when you walk through them. I think somehow we're just being fooled again." She paused to see how completely he had bought the fabrication, and after noting that he seemed to accept it, she went on.

"Listen, I think I have something in my bedroom upstairs that will enable us to decide whether I'm right or not. Why don't you go into the drawing room and watch some TV and I'll go up and get it."

"No, I want to go with you."

"No, honey, I'm going to change my clothes while I'm at it. I'll be right down."

"But I—"

But before he could argue with her any further she scooted him in the direction of the drawing room.

Then she went upstairs.

When she reached her bedroom she went in only long

enough to retrieve a flashlight and then left and started back down the hall in the direction from which she had come.

"Your secret's remained hidden long enough, Sarah Balfram," she mumbled to herself.

Through the upstairs drawing room she went, and then through the even more warped hallway, crawling and groping her way blindly where she had to, until she reached the forgotten corridor in which Sarah Balfram's bedroom was located. And once there, she clicked on the powerful beam of the flashlight.

However, the bedroom was not her destination.

She was heading for something else.

Although she still had a residue of fear about the solidity of the floor, somehow she knew that it was safe, that the creaking was due less to deterioration than to stress caused by the spatial distortions taking place within the house.

She stepped onto the ancient floor.

As she expected, the beams and struts of the corridor creaked balefully and somewhere deep in the house came a longer and more abiding groaning of timbers—the sound that had reminded her earlier of an abandoned ship listing in a storm.

Intrepidly, she took another step, and then another, and each seemed to evoke a more portentous chorus of creaking than the last. But still she moved on until she had traveled the full length of the corridor and had reached an absurdly distorted doorway at the end. From the warps and bends in its surface and the convoluted way it fit into its frame, she feared she might not even be able to open it. But when she turned the handle she discovered that with her full weight she was able to open it wide.

Directing the beam of the flashlight inside, she saw that beyond was another hallway. Only this one was even larger and was only slightly bent. And despite the attempt that had been made to make it fit in with the decor of the house by papering it in a rich brocade, now mildewed and faded, and covering its length with an oriental carpet, now worn and rotting, it was clear that it was no normal hallway. Aside from its enormous size, she detected that the pilasters lining its walls were actually massive wooden beams, like railroad ties, albeit painted to disguise their true identity; and the ceiling was also ribbed and buttressed with balks, making the entire place look more like some unearthly mine shaft than a corridor in a house.

But the feature which riveted her was the door at the far end of the hall, for it was at least twelve feet tall and eight feet wide, and seemed to be hewn out of beams that were every bit as massive as the buttresses of the hallway. Even more striking was the size of the iron braces which held them together and the rusty but gargantuan latch and deadbolt sealing the door in place.

Frightened, but too obsessed to turn back, she crept up to the door, and when she reached it she stopped and held her breath and listened.

So consumed by fantastic imaginings was she that she half expected to hear something shuffling about on the other side, something ancient yearning to get out.

But instead all she heard was what sounded like wind howling, only distantly.

And the occasional swaying and creaking of the house.

Still wary, she banged on the door with her fist. "Hello!" she yelled, a part of her almost laughing at the ludicrousness of thinking there would be anything alive behind the door.

But still all she heard was a faint susurration, the faraway rushing of air.

Hearing nothing which indicated any immediate danger or menace, she placed the flashlight between her arm and her side and grabbed the deadbolt with both hands.

And then she slid it back and slowly pulled open the door.

As soon as she did she discovered that what had sounded like a rushing of air was indeed a wind. Moreover, it was a wind whose power she had underestimated because of the muffling effect of the door, and even before the door was completely open she could hear it whistling and feel the icy lashes of its touch.

She gasped, for even though she had had a vague sense of what she might find beyond, actually having her suspicions confirmed left her speechless.

For beyond the door was only darkness. Not the darkness of an empty room, or even the eerie, sound-hungry darkness of a very large enclosure, a vacant auditorium or gymnasium. But a much vaster darkness than that.

Beyond the door was an infinite darkness, an ocean of blackness so vast that when she pointed the flashlight into it, the beam seemed to extend forever before it waned and was swallowed by the gloom. Impossible as the existence of the cavern of infinity was, it was there, sequestered deep within the confines of the house, and she, Lauren Ransom, was standing at its precipice and being buffeted by its wind.

And even while there remained many things about the darkness that she did not know, she knew one thing: it was not a mere void, a chasm of emptiness without reason or purpose. She knew that it was a passageway—for an epiphany had blazed through her after her discovery that a spatial distortion existed within the house. She had realized then that it was not the Adirondacks that were the window area, the place of great supernatural power. It was the house and the lake, themselves. Here was the doorway between this dimension . . .

And some other.

As she struggled to absorb the implications of this, other realizations came to her, through faculties she had never even dreamed she possessed. By some means unknown to her she sensed suddenly that the darkness was not empty. There was something in it. Something alive. It was not close. But it was there. *They* were there, for she sensed also that it was legion, a vast, fomenting sea of things, things whose cries were so distant, or so faint, that they had long since become one with the howling wind.

And as quickly as this entered her thoughts, she noticed something else. She noticed that the threshold of the doorway was worn, deeply worn. The forgotten hallway was perhaps not as forgotten as she had imagined. Things had used it, had used the door also. There were scuffs and pits in its threshold, and scratches and worn areas on its surface.

What manner of creature had passed through the doorway and gone into the darkness?

What had come out?

She slammed the door shut and engaged the bolt. As she ran back down the hallway and groped her way through the twisted passageways beyond, she no longer cared. She now had only one thought on her mind. Even if they had to walk all the way to Clearwater Lodge in the dark, they were getting out of the house.

When she reached her bedroom she stopped only long enough to get her coat, and then she went to Garrett's room and got him a jacket. She knew that it could get quite chilly at night in the mountains, and she wanted them to be prepared for the long hike ahead of them.

Then she ran down the stairs and into the drawing room.

"Come on! We're leaving!" she shouted at Garrett. She pulled him up by the arm and hurled him unceremoniously into his jacket. She left the television blaring.

"Why? What is it?" he gasped.

"We've got to get out of here now!" she shot back.

Perceiving her agitation, he too started to panic as he followed her quickly into the entrance hall.

But when she flung the door open and started to barrel through, she ran headlong into the man who had come to run the generators.

"Oh!" she cried, frightened by his unexpected presence. As she reclaimed her senses, her shock turned into anger.

"What are you doing hovering outside the door like that?" she demanded truculently. "Why aren't you down tending to the generators?"

Behind her Garrett let out a cry of horror, but given the unexpectedness of the man's presence outside their door, she did not think it at all strange.

"Because I don't want to be down there," Fugate said, leering at her oddly. "I want to be up here with you."

"Well, you can't be up here with us," she stated flatly, growing increasingly vexed at his insolence.

And then she saw the glint of the straight razor in his hand.

Screaming, she tried to slam the door on him, but he quickly blocked its closing with his foot. Jerking Garrett by the arm, she raced toward one of the spindlework archways on the other side of the entrance hall, but Fugate lunged and grabbed hold of Garrett's leg, causing him to tumble to the floor.

No longer fearing for her own safety, she turned around, but before she could reach Garrett, Fugate had pulled him up against him and was holding the straight razor at his neck.

"I'll cut him!"

She froze. "No! Please, don't!" She noticed that the fall had bloodied one of Garrett's lips and saw the panic in his eyes. "Please, I'll do whatever you want."

Fugate started to calm down. "You won't try to run?"

"No," she said in as convincing a voice as she could manage.

"You'll do whatever I want?"

The words shot through her like a lightning bolt, sparking into flames every dark fear and nightmarish worry she had ever possessed, but she knew she had no choice. "Anything," she said, swallowing.

Fugate loosened his grip on Garrett, but only a little.
"Then let's go into the kitchen." He pointed with his el-
bow. "You lead."

An innocuous suggestion on the surface, but she read
into it the most ominous meanings. As she led them to
the kitchen she tried desperately to think of what she could
do. But with him still holding the straight razor at Garrett's
throat, she knew she dared not attempt anything.

"You come sit at the table with me, bud," he said to
Garrett when they reached the kitchen. Without saying a
word, Garrett did as he was told and followed Fugate over
to the kitchen table.

"And now you make me some dinner," he told Lauren.

The idea of trying to bustle around the kitchen and put
together a meal while a psychopath was sitting only a few
feet away holding a straight razor at her son's throat made
Lauren almost dizzy with horror.

"Okay," she said, forcing a flicker of a smile. "What
would you like?"

"Whadya got?"

To her dismay she felt a tear trickle down her cheek,
and she quickly brushed it off with her upper arm. "Peas,"
she said, feeling suddenly that it was the most meaningless
and stupid sounding word in the world. "Lamb chops—
they're frozen. Frozen hamburger patties. Eggs. Coffee
cake. Instant mashed potatoes."

"I like instant mashed potatoes."

"Okay," she said agreeably. "Would you like anything
else?"

He instantly purpled and exploded in a fit of rage. "You
think I only eat potatoes?"

She jumped. "No, of course not," she apologized,
growing increasingly aware of just how mad he was. She
paused, terrified to go on. "Do you want me to keep listing
things?" she asked falteringly.

"Yes!" he growled.

"All kinds of cheeses. Croissants."

"Kra-whats?"

Her mind raced as she carefully tried to formulate an answer that would not incur his wrath. "They're a kind of roll."

"Do you have bread?"

"Yes."

"Can you make French toast?"

She nodded.

His eyes lit up like a child's. "Instant mashed potatoes and French toast!" he announced as he swelled his chest and settled back into his chair.

She tried to tabulate what she would need for the requested meal, but with each passing second the gravity of their situation dragged her down more. She could not believe it was actually happening to them. It was the sort of thing one read about in the papers. He was a killer. They might be killed. They were *going* to be killed.

The thoughts moved through her mind with such dizzying speed that she started to feel faint, and realizing that they had hope only if she was able to keep her wits about her, she forced herself to calm down.

Instant mashed potatoes, she thought. Salt. Potato flakes. Water. She took a pan down from the rack above the stove and filled it with water. She placed it on one of the burners and turned on the gas. She started mechanically for the pantry and then stopped dead in her tracks.

She looked at him fearfully. "Some of the ingredients I need are in the other room. How should I get them?"

"Just go," Fugate said with a smile as he dangled the straight razor in front of Garrett's face like a charm. "I trust you."

Clenching her teeth to control her hatred for him, she went into the pantry. Then she quickly gathered the things she needed and raced back into the kitchen.

Suddenly Fugate shifted in his seat. "By the way, have you guys eaten?"

"Yes," Lauren lied.

He seemed to detect her evasion. "What did you have?"

"Cheese sandwiches and cream of tomato soup," she rattled.

He frowned. "Well, you're going to eat again, so make enough for all of us."

"No, really, we—"

He slammed his fist down violently on the table. "Make enough for all!" And then, just as suddenly as his outburst had come, he calmed and seemed almost penitent. "If we're going to be a family, we're all going to have to eat together from now on," he said earnestly.

The words sent a chill up her spine, and she looked at him awestruck.

"Mommm?" Garrett implored, looking to her desperately for some sort of denial to Fugate's remark.

"Shut up!" Fugate shouted as he lashed out and grazed Garrett's cheek with the straight razor. Lauren let out a guttural scream of rage and started to lunge for him, but with lightning speed he yanked Garrett down by the hair and held the razor once again at his neck threateningly.

She froze while at the same time Fugate launched into a strange and feverish tirade. "Children should be quiet! Children are brats! Children are worthless! Children should shut up! Children are no good!"

Garrett started to cry, a little trickle of blood starting to stream down from the cut in his face.

"Shut up!" Fugate shrieked.

Garrett sniffled, trying to stop.

"*Shattup!*" Fugate shrilled even louder.

Garrett suppressed his crying.

But the sight of him bleeding, and the helpless, mindless furor she felt at seeing another human being, a reeking, filthy, disheveled, ugly stranger reach out and willfully harm her child, *cut* her child, filled her with more rage

21921921921921921921921921921921921921921921921921921922192192121921921921921921921921921921921921921921921921921922192192192192192192192192192192192192219219219219219219219219219219219219219221921921921921921921921921922192192192192192192192219219219219221921

than she had ever experienced before in her life. And it was at that moment that something clicked in Lauren. Her state of half-crazed, adrenaline-filled terror became even more finely honed with hatred, and she knew that even if she died in the process she had to do something to stop Fugate and to keep him from harming Garrett any further.

Fugate seemed to sense the sudden leap of intensity her fury had taken.

He shook his head with self-righteous indignation. "None of this is my idea. I didn't want to come up here and do any of this."

The announcement took her completely off-guard. "Whose idea was it?"

"The Master's."

She turned the words over desperately in her mind, trying to wring some sense out of them: "Who's the Master?"

Puffing with self-importance, Fugate told them everything, about how the Master had first appeared in the form of headaches, and then as a voice at the back of his thoughts, and then finally as an external presence whose purpose it was to change him, to guide and nurture him toward his true destiny of pursuing ultimate evil.

But as chilling as his revelation was, it only steeled Lauren.

When Fugate finished his tale, no one said anything for several seconds, and then suddenly in the distance the house emitted another one of its long, unpropitious creaks.

"What was that?" Fugate asked.

"Just the house settling," she replied, but suddenly she remembered the doorway. She had been so preoccupied by the immediacy of Fugate's threat that she had forgotten about it. But now as her memory came flooding back to her she wondered what she should do about the information. Should she tell him about it, tell him the danger they were all in? Or would it only incite him further?

"Hey, how's the food coming?" Fugate interjected.

"Fine," she said, pouring some of the potato flakes into a measuring cup.

And then she looked into the boiling water and saw their salvation.

She looked back at Fugate. He was sitting only inches away from Garrett, and from the way he was holding the straight razor she knew that he could slice Garrett to ribbons within a fraction of a second. But if she aimed carefully, waited until his head was turned, and hit him full in the face while he was looking away from Garrett, she felt she might be able to knock him out of commission. It was a long shot. But it was their only hope.

Not wanting to arouse suspicion, she continued cooking. She cracked open an egg and emptied it into a flat-bottomed bowl and then sprinkled in some nutmeg.

And then she got a brainstorm.

"The secret of good instant mashed potatoes is to mix the potato flakes in rapidly," she said loudly. And then, on seeing that she had Fugate's attention, she lifted the cup of potato flakes up and started to pour them while she vigorously stirred the water. Only instead of pouring them into the pan, she poured them behind the pan and at an angle she hoped would keep Fugate from seeing where they were really going.

As she did so a few of the flakes spilled into the burner and crackled. She looked quickly at Fugate, hoping he did not detect her deception.

But from the way he was licking his lips she realized he had not.

"There," she said, stirring the water slower and slower so as to complete the illusion that there were actually potatoes thickening in the pan. "Now . . . see if these are thick enough."

She lifted the pan off the stove and started across the

kitchen, and when she had approached within a few feet
of the table she swiftly tilted it back and flung the boiling
water in Fugate's direction.

Only at the last second, Fugate realized what she was
doing and dove away from the table. Although the water
caught his arm and the back of his head it did not truly
incapacitate him.

"Run!" she shouted at Garrett as Fugate screamed in
agony.

Dashing away from the table, Garrett ran out of the
kitchen, and Lauren followed after him. But as they tore
through the hallway she heard Fugate bellow with rage
behind them.

He was following.

Like animals trying to escape from a tiger, they thrashed
through the ruby-red dining room, through another in-
tervening hallway, and toward the front of the house. But
by the time they had reached the entrance hall, Fugate was
right behind them, swinging the razor in wild, crazy arcs
and frothing at the mouth like a rabid beast.

Screaming, Lauren tried to propel Garrett even faster to
the door, but in her haste she caused him to stumble, and
both of them crashed loudly to the floor. Before they could
get up again, Fugate was on top of them.

Grabbing Garrett by the hair, he pulled him back and
held the razor high up over him. But then, just as he was
about to deliver the final blow, someone knocked on the
front door.

Fugate looked at the door with alarm.

"Please—" Lauren started to cry, but before she could
finish her request for help, Fugate had silenced her by
threateningly holding the razor a little higher.

"Answer it," he whispered, yanking Garrett to his feet
and dragging him around to the back of the door. "Tell
whoever it is to go away."

Composing herself as best she could, she got up and slowly opened the door. To her surprise, standing on the other side was Harry Gordon.

As soon as he saw her, he blushed uneasily. "Listen, I'm really sorry for bothering you again and I know this probably sounds really stupid, but while we were talking I got this funny feeling something might be the matter here." He looked at her penetratingly. "Please, I swear this isn't a line, but I got so worried I had to come back and make sure you and your son were all right."

"Of course we're all right," she returned quickly, too quickly, and then to try to cover for her blunder she forced a smile. "But it was awfully nice of you to pedal all the way back here just to check."

Gordon noticed her agitation and became troubled. "Are you sure nothing's the matter?"

"Yes, of course I'm sure," she said in the most nonchalant voice she could summon. Inside she was screaming, dying to think of some way to communicate to him how desperately they needed help, but out of the corner of her eye she could see Fugate holding the straight razor against the bare skin of Garrett's throat, and she did not dare breathe a word.

Gordon looked unconvinced. "Well, listen, I know this is really presumptuous of me, but I've got a sleeping bag rolled up in my backpack. Do you think it might be all right if I spread it out down by the lake and spent the night here? It's getting kind of late, and—"

"No!" Lauren interrupted quickly. "I mean . . . I'd prefer that you didn't."

"Oh . . ." Gordon said, flushing with embarassment, and then suddenly the strangest look came over his face and she saw him staring at something out of the corner of his eyes. For a moment she was at a loss as to what had transfixed him. But then she realized. He could see Fugate holding Garrett hostage through the crack between the door and its frame.

Recognizing the danger he was in—they were all in—he started to back off the porch, and Lauren felt a rush of excitement at the realization that now at least he would be able to help them. But with the uncanny perceptivity of a true psychopath, Fugate sensed immediately what was happening and jumped out from his hiding place with Garrett still in tow.

"Stop! Stop now or I'll kill him!"

Gordon saw the straight razor and froze.

Fugate grunted. "Okay, you come in too. Now I have a real family. A wife, a son, and a guest. You're the guest."

Gordon reluctantly walked into the entrance hall, and Fugate kicked the door shut with his foot.

For the first time Lauren noticed that some of the boiling water had hit him in the face—his cheek as well as his arm was beet-red.

"So, thought you would stop me, did you?" he crowed. "Well, now we'll see. Now we'll see." He nodded with his head for them to go into the drawing room. "Go in there."

Lauren couldn't take it any more and began to cry. "Why? What are you going to do?"

"We're going to be a family!" he snapped as if the answer were annoyingly obvious. "And what do good American families do? They watch TV. We're going to watch TV."

She was beginning to feel that with every passing second their chances of getting away from Fugate were diminishing exponentially.

"I'm sorry," she mumbled apologetically to Gordon.

"It's okay," he returned, glaring at Fugate with an intensity that suddenly proved wrong everything that she had assumed about his character. "It's not your fault."

"Shut up!" Fugate roared. And then, just as they were

about to walk through the spindlework archway leading to the drawing room, he cried: "No, wait! Stop! Where's the telephone?"

"In there," she said, pointing at the coachmen's waiting room.

"Okay, everyone in there."

Lauren and Gordon walked obediently into the coachmen's waiting room while Fugate stood with Garrett at the door.

He looked at the telephone and then at Gordon. "Smash it."

Gordon looked worriedly at Lauren. "It's okay," she said. "It's broken anyway."

"Ha! Nice try," Fugate sneered. He looked back at Gordon. "Smash it!"

Gordon picked up a nearby lamp and, using its base as a bludgeon, smashed the telephone to bits.

Fugate eyed a roll of twine hanging on a hook in the corner. "Bring that also," he ordered Gordon. He backed away, allowing Lauren and Gordon to walk ahead of him. "Okay, now we watch TV."

He herded them all into the drawing room and ordered Lauren to sit in a chair. To her horror, he tied her feet to the legs of the chair and bound her hands uncomfortably behind her back.

Then he backhanded her savagely across the face. Outraged, Garrett tried to rush to her protection, but Gordon restrained him.

"That's for scalding me, you fucking bitch!" Fugate screamed.

He backhanded her again with even more force, and this time it was Gordon's turn to give a start as if he were going to rush forward. But still he held himself back, smoldering with hatred.

"And that's for not having my dinner ready when I got home," Fugate finished.

He turned back to Garrett and Gordon. "And you . . . you two sit down on that sofa there."

They carefully complied.

Content that he had things the way he wanted, Fugate pulled a chair up beside Lauren's and clicked the TV on with the remote control. Then he started to punch through the channels.

Although his blows had profoundly demoralized her, she realized that perhaps their only chance of overcoming him was in regaining his trust. After they had watched television for about twenty minutes she once again summoned the courage to try to engage him in conversation. But Fugate would hear none of it and only screamed at her to shut up. Perceiving what she was up to, Gordon also tried to draw him into conversation, and although he was able to find out Fugate's name, Fugate rebuked him into silence as well. The three of them could only play Fugate's macabre game and wait nervously to see what happened next.

On and on they waited while Fugate alternately chortled or cursed at one television show after another, until finally, toward the end of the evening, Gordon dared to speak again.

"Are you going to keep us here all night?"

Fugate jerked his head in Gordon's direction and regarded him with suspicion. "Why do you ask?"

Gordon formulated his words carefully. "Because it's getting rather late. I thought maybe you'd allow me to make a suggestion."

Fugate's eyes narrowed. "Like what?"

"Well, it's obvious Garrett here is getting pretty sleepy. It's also obvious that you have a clear view of the main staircase and could certainly see whether we went up or down. I thought maybe you'd let Garrett and me go upstairs and get some sleep."

"There are other stairs you could come down!" Fugate snapped mistrustfully.

Gordon offered him a placating smile. "But look, you've got the boy's mother. There are also no doorways behind you, so we wouldn't be able to sneak up on you. Do you think we're going to try anything while you're still sitting there with her tied in that chair and that straight razor in your hand?"

Fugate looked at Lauren and then back at Gordon, and from the doubtful expression on his face it was clear he was still not convinced.

"Besides," Gordon said, adding the *coup de grâce*, "I've never really ever met anyone quite as amazing as you. Sitting here with you like this I think I've started to see why you're doing this. You're really very special. An extraordinary human being. I've really started to respect you for what you're doing."

Fugate sat up with regal erectness, his face still eerily lit by the multicolored glow of the television. "You think so?" he asked with the tone of one who knew it was true, but wanted to hear it again.

"I know it's so."

Fugate looked at the main staircase in the distance. "You're only going upstairs to get some sleep?"

"Just to sleep."

"You promise you won't try anything?"

"I promise."

He thought about it for a moment longer. "Well, okay. But you've got to come back downstairs when I call for you."

"Fine," Gordon said, taking Garrett firmly by the hand and leading him toward the door. He stopped. "Oh, by the way."

Fugate looked at him attentively.

"You're not planning on doing anything to Mrs. Ransom while we're gone, are you? I'd kind of like to be present if you decide to do something."

"Oh, I'm not going to do anything while you're gone," Fugate returned earnestly. "We're watching TV."

Gordon smiled and continued leading Garrett out of the drawing room.

When they reached the stairs, Garrett suddenly went rigid. "Why did you say those things?" he demanded in a hush.

"I was lying," Gordon whispered back, continuing to pull him up the stairs. When they reached the landing and were out of sight, Gordon relaxed a little. "I was just telling him what he wanted to hear so he would trust us enough to let us come up."

"Are we really going to sleep?"

"No."

"What did we come up here for?"

"Let's get a little farther away from the stairs and then I'll tell you."

But as Gordon continued to lead him down the hallway and in the direction of the bedrooms, suddenly all the lights in the house went out.

"Dammit!" Gordon exclaimed. "What's he up to now?"

A few seconds later the lights came back on.

"I don't think it's him," Garrett returned. "It's the generators. When no one is watching them they start to do this."

Gordon frowned at the light fixtures over their heads, waiting for them to click off again, but for the moment they remained lit. When he reached the master bedroom he opened the door and went inside. Then he tossed his backpack onto the floor.

"Okay," Garrett repeated after he had followed Gordon inside. "So why did we come up here?"

Gordon knelt down in front of him so he was looking directly into Garrett's eyes. "Okay, listen, Garrett. I want to tell you something." He paused as if choosing his words carefully. "I've read a lot about this house, and I've been studying it for a long time. And I think I know enough to say that it's no normal house. I mean, even if you put aside all the weird things about its architecture, I think there's more to the house than just that."

"Like what?" Garrett asked warily.

"You remember how we were talking about window areas and the Adirondacks being a place where a lot of unusual things happen?"

Garrett nodded.

"As I said earlier today, even the Indians knew that the land around this lake was an especially powerful place." Gordon looked up toward the ceiling. "Well, I don't think it was any coincidence that Sarah Balfram chose this place as the spot to build her house. I think that the house is some kind of focuser of the energy that exists in this place. I think it's some kind of power point."

"So?" Garrett asked.

Gordon looked at him searchingly. "Well, earlier today when we were talking about the house I got the distinct impression that you knew more than you were saying. I think something's happened to you in this house, something you haven't told anyone about." Gordon paused. "And although I'm not quite sure how, I think if you told me about it it might provide us with some means of overcoming Fugate. It might be the ace in the hole that we need to get out of this situation."

Garrett went stiff. With horror, he suddenly realized he was in precisely the situation his mother had prophesied. How had his mother put it? *Someday you'll want to trust someone and someone you know is going to warn you not to, and you're going to find that it isn't always easy to know what to do.* He remembered what the thing had told him: how something terrible was going to happen in the house and how it would protect him and his mother if he did not reveal the secret of its existence. But now, with Gordon prodding him in the other direction and trying to get him to break his pact of secrecy with the thing, he was at a loss as to what to do. He remembered Gordon's earlier description of the Watcher Angels, and how he had instantly been convinced that the thing was a Watcher. But were the Watchers good or evil? No one knew, according to Gordon.

He prided himself on being a person who kept his word, and it was true—the thing had never in any way harmed him. Still, he never expected to find himself in a situation this grave. His mother was downstairs, tied to a chair by a lunatic who might kill her at any moment. He feared that if he did not tell Gordon what he knew, he might be giving up their only hope of getting out of the house alive.

Finally, he started to cry, and he decided to divulge his terrible secret. "Yes, something did happen to me," he said between sobs, his body racked with chills.

He proceeded to tell Gordon everything, and halfway through his account the lights flickered off and on once again. When Garrett finished, Gordon sat down on the bed and laced his fingers into a church as he contemplated Garrett's story.

"Is that all you know about the thing?" he pressed.

Garrett nodded.

Gordon looked at him sharply. "And this thing, it didn't tell you anything about the house itself? It didn't give you any clue about what the house's true purpose was?"

"No, it got angry whenever I asked it anything."

Gordon got up from the bed and began to pace. Finally, he stopped. "Then you and I have got to try to find out what this house really is."

"But how?"

"We've just got to do some exploring." He started for the door, and Garrett followed. When they reached the hall the lights went off and on again.

"Shouldn't we take a flashlight?" Garrett suggested.

"Yeah, maybe you're right," Gordon returned. "I've got one in my backpack." He started back toward the bedroom, but Garrett raced ahead of him.

"I'll get it!"

For a moment Garrett almost got the sense that Gordon was going to try to stop him, but then he apparently decided against the idea as Garrett lifted the flap of the bag and rifled through its contents. He quickly found the flashlight Gordon had been using as a bicycle light, and when he did he took it out and clicked it on. But just as he was about to stand he noticed something else in the bag, something that at first confused him.

It was a chain attached to a box containing a little ball, all carved out of a single piece of wood. It was Mr. Foley's whittling.

He looked back at Gordon, the ramifications of the discovery too numbing, too utterly terrifying, for him to fully absorb. The lights went off again, and on instinct he jumped away from the bag and pointed the flashlight back at Gordon.

And when he did, Gordon's eyes lit up like flaming embers, *glittering and emerald-green.*

Panicking, Garrett tried to run, but Gordon caught him at once and twisted his arm behind his back. Then he guided him brusquely downstairs. When they reached the drawing room, he pushed Garrett rudely inside, and Lauren looked up with alarm.

"The jig's up, Elton," Gordon hissed. "The boy knows."

"Knows what?" Lauren asked confusedly, looking first at Garrett and then back at Gordon.

But as she watched, Gordon underwent a strange transformation. Like a man who had held his stomach in for the duration of an important meeting, he seemed to relax somehow, and with a strange little suspiration the stress and tension seemed to drain from his body. And as they did, his body changed. The smooth skin of his face and hands instantly became covered by a fine web of wrinkles—not the pronounced, deeply hewn wrinkles of someone who has spent a lot of time in the sun, but a much finer, more delicate kind. These made him appear both youthful and oddly ancient at one and the same time.

Even more dramatic changes followed. With a creaking sound, his fingers grew longer, as did his nails, which curled and became sharper as they clouded over with a sickly grayish-yellow cast. His flesh began to bulge slightly in places and became concave in others until it had rearranged itself into a physique that was gaunt and grotesque. Like seedlings in some monstrously growing rain forest, his teeth became longer and stretched into rapierlike points.

But the most remarkable change took place in his eyes, for as his body shifted and sculpted itself into its true shape, they started to emit a greenish light—not just any light, but a lurid, otherworldly candescence that seemed to grow stronger with each tremor that passed through him. The brighter they became, the emptier they seemed, until they had become unspeakably terrifying voids.

Lauren knew instantly that these were the eyes she had seen watching her from the fog. But still she did not understand what was happening and why Gordon and Fugate suddenly seemed so familiar.

"What's going on?" she implored. "What are you?"

As she asked the question, Fugate began to prance around and clap his hands gleefully like an ecstatic and depraved Rumpelstiltskin.

But Gordon only smiled unctuously, threateningly. "But Mrs. Ransom, I thought you would have figured it out by now. I'm the one Elton as been telling you about. I'm the Master."

III

THE PURPOSE

And there appeared to me two men very tall, such as I have never seen on earth. And these men said to me: "Be of good cheer, Enoch, be not afraid; the everlasting God hath sent us to thee, and, lo! today thou shalt ascend with us into heaven." And it came to pass that these men took me on their wings and placed me on the clouds. And lo! the clouds moved. And then I looked and saw many things, what has happened before on the earth and what has been left behind. I have seen forces unimaginable to man, and other things . . . the treasuries of the snow and ice and the angels who guard the terrible store-places.

—The Book of the Secrets of Enoch

She shook her head slowly, unable to believe what her eyes were telling her. "But I thought . . ."

By now Gordon's transformation was complete, and in his full glory he was so horrible that Garrett ran over to his mother's side.

A trace of a smile played over Gordon's pale and vampirish face. "You thought the Master was only a madman's delusion?"

Although Lauren said nothing, from her expression it was clear that he had anticipated her question correctly.

"No, I'm quite real. You see, I was very far away from here when I first sensed Elton's presence, sensed how special he was."

Fugate beamed like a proud disciple.

The Master stalked a little deeper into the room, his long and powerful arms now held in a strangely insectlike pose at his sides. "But because I sensed that he had the potential to be even more special, to understand the meaning of true

evil, I reached out with my mind, insinuated myself into
his thoughts, until I could travel the thousands of miles
that separated us."

The Master sat down slowly on the couch and smiled
at Fugate affectionately. "But at first he resisted me and
perceived my communications only as headaches. Until
finally I won his trust and was able to hold on to him and
make my way here."

"What are you?" Lauren asked.

"I am just one of the things that walks the earth."

"But what kind of thing?"

"Careful," the Master purred. "I have feelings too, you
know. And I take offense easily."

Lauren swallowed hard as a chill passed through her,
but still she was driven to find out more. "Where do you
come from?"

The Master looked almost wistful. "That's the kicker.
I don't know. You see, my memory is fitful. I tend to
remember the peaks, the moments in my life when I have
been truly exalted by evil, but everything else . . . well,
fades. I know that I am ancient. I remember when the
Romans destroyed Carthage." His eyes glowed a little
brighter. "I have never seen so much blood, and for so
long." He paused. "I think I remember Ashurnaṣirpal. At
least I remember a place long ago, a desert, and a lot of
carnage that seems of his style. And, of course, I remember
quite a few of my disciples, I think, the various men and
women I have encountered throughout my wanderings
and whom I have deemed promising enough to take under
my tutelage." He again looked fondly at Fugate. "But I
don't remember my birth, my actual origin, any more than
you do yours, although I think it likely that I was somehow
a product of that great war we talked about."

"But what do you want with us? Why are you here?"

"Well, it's this house, isn't it?" the Master said, standing
and looking at the oak baulks of the vaulted ceiling over-

head. "As I was telling your son earlier, I don't think it's any coincidence that Sarah Balfram chose one of the most powerful and ancient spots in the country—this lake—on which to erect her house. It's clear from the way the house is built and that enticing palindrome over the door that the house is some kind of puzzle, a gauntlet thrown down at the feet of any who are discerning enough to perceive it. But I think it's more than just a puzzle."

"I know," Lauren said resignedly. "It's some kind of window, a passageway between dimensions."

"Well, not a passageway really," the Master returned unexpectedly. "At least, not in the sense that it was intended to allow free concourse back and forth between the two dimensions."

"Then what?"

He strolled through the room, still looking up at the baulks of the ceiling. "More of a vault, I should think. A means of concealing something."

"Concealing what?"

"Ah, that's the question."

"I'm sure you have an answer."

"Oh, I do, I do." He held one of his bony fingers aloft. "At least I have a theory. You see, the Watcher Angels are not the only thing Enoch mentions without fully explaining. After the angels finished taking him on a tour of heaven and showing him visions of the great war, he says they took him and showed him something else. From the way he wrote about it it's obvious he knew he was being shown something of extreme importance. But for some reason, perhaps because he was sworn to secrecy, when he wrote down his experiences, he decided to describe what he had seen in only one brief and very cryptic line. He said only that the angels had shown him 'the treasuries of the snow and ice and the angels who guard the terrible store-places.' "

The words made another shiver pass up through Lauren's spine. "And what do *you* think he was talking about? What are the terrible store-places?"

"Well, think about it," the Master countered. "Enoch had just been shown a vision of the great war and had learned that the powers of light had won and expunged the forces of darkness from the earth. And immediately thereafter he was shown a series of places where something terrible is stored. I think what he was shown was where the losers of that great war were imprisoned. I think the terrible store-places were where the powers of darkness that had been defeated in that war were locked away."

"But this house was only built in the nineteenth century. How could it be one of the terrible store-places?"

"Technically speaking, it's not the house that is the store-place. It's the window area, the dimensional weak spot that has existed in this region since time immemorial. The house is only the doorway, the porthole as it were, that has allowed this world to connect with that other."

"But how did Sarah Balfram know how to design a house that would do that? And how did she go about building such a house? I mean, what did she say to the workmen who put this place together—'Here's a dimensional doorway; build me a house around it'?"

The Master shook his head wearily as if the answers to her questions were so manifest they almost weren't worth the effort of a reply. "First of all, it's obvious from the fact that she had visions as a child that something came to her and told her how to build the house. And as for how the house managed to punch through to the terrible store-place that existed here, I suspect it accomplished that feat by virtue of its shape."

She looked at him perplexedly.

"There are many ancient systems that talk about the sacredness of geometry and how different shapes are supposed to change and alter the space within and around them. I think the house is the ultimate product of one of those ancient and sacred geometries, a mathematical lens that by virtue of the twistings and turnings of its architecture has managed to open up a doorway between dimensions. Indeed, I imagine that hole punched between dimensions—which no doubt lies hidden somewhere deep in the heart of the house—did not even exist until the house was completed. Like a lens constructed in piecemeal fashion, it was probably not able to perform its function as a focuser until it existed in its whole and proper shape."

Lauren knew from what she had already discovered about the house that he was almost certainly correct. But that left one important question. "Why was Sarah Balfram instructed to build the house? What purpose does it serve now?"

The Master laced his fingers together as he paced through the room. "Now we come to the meat of the matter."

Fugate shifted his weight excitedly, and the Master continued. "You are no doubt unaware of this fact, but to those of us who have recognized the beauty of evil, who have surrendered our hearts completely to the unutterable darkness, the house has a voice. It calls to us, beckons us, pulls us. Elton here has heard the house calling. I have heard it, felt its tugging, and that is why I am here." A tremor passed through him as he suddenly pulsed with energy. "You see, thoughout my life, my long, long life, I have wondered why I was here, why I was one of the few of my kind to survive only to be doomed to wander endlessly on this darkness-forsaken world of petty, chirping souls. I knew that part of my purpose was to teach, to pass on my wisdom to receptive students like Elton, but still I knew there had to be more. It wasn't until I discovered this house and came to realize that it led to the terrible store-place that I comprehended what my destiny was. You see, I think it was the forces of darkness who came to Sarah Balfram and told her to build this house here. I think that by using her as an instrument they man-

aged to place a kind of sword in the stone here, a Gordian
knot to be stumbled upon by a warrior powerful enough
for the cause. Then it is to be cleaved, to allow all those
things imprisoned here to be released upon the world once
again."

His eyes were now glowing so fierily that Lauren and
Garrett could scarcely bear to look him in the face.

"I think that is why the house as been drawing things
evil to it lo these many years. It's been searching for exactly the right leader to launch this new offensive, panning
through the dross for the gold." He raised his clenched
hand to the ceiling. "Well, it has found its leader now.
I can feel it, feel it in my bones. This house is my destiny.
I know it. I am the one it has been searching for all
along."

Outside, the wind picked up, and the house creaked
again.

"But if you figured that out a while ago, why didn't
you come into the house then? Why wait until we came?"

The Master looked at her archly. "I have not survived
for so long by being a fool. I wanted you to test the waters
first, make sure there were no preliminary pitfalls or booby
traps."

The lights went out and remained off. Nevertheless, the
room was illuminated by the powerful green beams of the
Master's eyes.

"But once you knew that, why did you then go through
the charade of pretending to be a reporter? Why not just
barge in and overpower us to begin with?"

The Master snorted. "Because I had hoped to gain your
assistance in helping me find the doorway and avoiding
the traps without your knowing my real purpose. I felt it
was the easiest route to take." He looked at Garrett. "Besides, I had reason to believe that at least one of you had
been sworn to secrecy about the house, and as it turns out
my suspicions were quite correct."

Lauren looked confusedly at Garrett and then back at the Master. "What do you mean?"

The Master took a step closer to Garrett, training his glowing eyes on him. "You may be interested to know, Mrs. Ransom, that there's a Watcher Angel somewhere in this house. You may be even more interested to learn that it has been keeping company with your son here, using your son to help it get the information it needs."

She looked at Garrett with alarm. "Is this true, Garrett?"

He squirmed nervously.

"But what does it want? Why is it here?"

The Master smiled, but his eyes narrowed. "That's the problem. None of us seems to know."

Garrett looked up at the Master with surprise and spoke for the first time. "*You* don't know?"

The Master's eyes became mere slits. "No, I don't." He looked up with irritation at the house. "Oh, I've sensed its presence here. I sense it even now. I'm not quite sure where it is, but I can feel that it's somewhere in the labyrinth of the house. Lurking. Waiting for something. But its energy is too ambivalent for me to tell whether it's good or evil. I can sense that it was once evil, extraordinarily evil. But it also has yearnings toward the good." He shook his head. "But I have no idea which side of it is the strongest. They are too evenly mixed for me to tell. I think that's why it's here. It's the wild card in all of this. It may be that its purpose is to assist in the opening of the doorway, or to ensure that only the most suitable candidate succeeds in unleashing the store-place. Or it may have been placed here by the forces of light to protect the store-place, to do battle with anyone who tries to release its contents. I don't know."

His expression filled with venom. "But one thing I do know: the time for talk has ended. Now it's time for action." He nodded at Fugate, and Fugate moved closer to Lauren, the straight razor poised in his hand.

As he did so, the Master went and jerked Garrett over to his side. "Now, boy, you're going to tell me where that doorway is."

Garrett looked at him aghast. "But I don't know!"

The Master loomed closer to him. "No! There'll be no more excuses. If you don't tell me I'm going to have Elton here cut off all your mother's fingers." He tossed Fugate a smile. "He'll start with her little finger."

Reaching behind the chair, Fugate untied Lauren's hands, and then he forced her to place her right hand on the arm of the chair and held the straight razor over her little finger.

"One by one," the Master repeated calmly.

Garrett started to cry as he searched the Master's face beseechingly. "But I don't know! Really I don't!"

The Master remained unmoved. "Okay, Elton, cut off her pinky."

As Fugate started to lower the straight razor over her little finger, Lauren shut her eyes. She knew that Garrett didn't know the location of the doorway. *She* knew. But she knew also that no matter what they did to her she could never be a party to the releasing of what was inside.

She felt the straight razor cut through the top layer of her skin, and Garrett started to scream.

"No, please! Please! I don't know! Don't hurt my mother!"

Lauren's every instinct was to pull her hand away, but she knew it was no use. She was tied to the chair. If she jerked away she would only be prolonging the ordeal. With a cool, oddly painless tingle she felt the surgically sharp razor slice into her skin.

Garrett went wild and tried to wrench away from the Master's viselike grip. *"I don't know! I don't know!"*

"Wait a minute, Elton," the Master said placidly.

With great reluctance Fugate stopped, but Lauren was too terrified to open her eyes and see how deeply her finger had been sliced. Finally, she mustered the courage to look and saw that although her hand was bleeding profusely, the cut did not seem to have done any irreparable damage. She twitched her pinky and was relieved that she could still move it.

"Why?" Fugate groused.

"Because I think Garrett here might be telling us the truth." With lightning speed he pushed Garrett stomach-down on the couch and pinned him against the cushions. "Let's cut off his fingers and see what Mrs. Ransom has to tell us."

As Fugate let go of her and started toward Garrett, she felt a sinking feeling, for she knew that she did not have the willpower to sit by and allow them to harm her child. No matter how terrible the consequences she knew she had to tell the Master where the door was located.

"No, wait!" she said just as Fugate was lowering the straight razor over Garrett's hand. "I'll tell you where it is."

"Ohhh," Fugate groaned.

But the Master smiled. "Very impressive, Mrs. Ransom. You withstood all that pain just to keep your secret from me? You are a woman of much more substance than I suspected. Untie her, Elton."

Fugate did as he was told. "Next time I'm going to be quicker," he grumbled as he cut the twine away from her ankles.

Garrett ran to his mother's side.

"All right," the Master continued. "Now, before we begin, I wonder if there is a large silver serving tray in the house. It must be round and it must be made of silver."

Recalling the large collection of Georgian silver in the butler's pantry, she nodded. "But why on earth—?"

"Just show us where it is," the Master said, stopping her in midsentence.

She took them to the butler's pantry and searched through the cupboards until she found a tray that fit his specifications.

"Yes, this will do nicely," he said, admiring the heavy silver tray. The lights blinked several times in succession.

"If there are any flashlights within reaching distance you might want to get those also," he added.

She retrieved several flashlights from a closet just outside the butler's pantry, and after taking one for herself and giving both Garrett and Fugate one, she offered the Master one.

He smiled at her patronizingly. "You forget, I see quite well in the dark without such things. Just lead on."

She took them back through the drawing room and up the stairs. Then she led them through the series of ever more treacherously distorted rooms and corridors and into the forgotten hallway. When they reached it she felt another surge of guilt and horror at the consequences of what she was doing, but she could not endure seeing Garrett tortured, and knew she had no choice.

She opened the twisted door at the end of the forgotten hallway and showed the Master the passage leading to the store-place. "In there," she said.

"You first," he countered.

She stepped inside, and when they reached the massive and heavily bolted door the Master seemed almost in ecstasy.

The house creaked and rattled around them.

"So long," he murmured, raising both his skeletal hands as if in prayer. "I've waited so long for this."

He leaned the silver tray up against the wall and then turned to Fugate. "Give me the razor."

Lauren went rigid as Fugate obliged, fearing some fiendish sacrifice was about to take place.

But instead of harming them he reached out and drew the blade quickly across Fugate's arm, cutting deep.

Fugate let out a yelp. "Why did you do that?" he roared.

"Shut up!" the Master returned. "You'll be all right. It's blood for the cause." He pulled Fugate's bleeding arm closer to him and collected a palmful of the trickling blood. He handed the straight razor back to Fugate. "Now tie something around that and keep an eye on them."

Next the Master knelt in front of the silver tray and, using his finger as a paintbrush, quickly sketched a series of cryptic symbols around its surface; and as soon as he finished the last one a sudden strange calm fell over the house. It did not stop creaking. The sense of awesome and foreboding power that pervaded the large and heavily reinforced hallway did not vanish. But something changed. The quality or aura of the house was different. Quieter.

"What's happened?" Lauren asked nervously.

"I've just done something that has nullified the power of our friend the Watcher," the Master replied. "Now it no longer has any power to move or operate anywhere in the house."

"Where did you learn to do that?" she gasped.

He looked at her tiredly. "I'm old, Mrs. Ransom. I've got powers you've never dreamed of."

And then he turned away from her.

"Hold them back there," he instructed, wafting his hand at Fugate.

He stepped forward and slowly opened the door. The wind and the distant howling swept through the corridor, and for several rapt moments the Master just stood at the precipice of darkness and waited.

But then finally his exaltation faded. "Nothing's happening," he complained. "They should be coming."

"Nothing came out when I opened the door before," Lauren interjected.

He looked at her unbelievingly. "You opened the door before?"

She became frightened all over again for what she had done. "Y-yes," she stuttered.

"And nothing came out then either?"

She shook her head.

"Maybe we need the Watcher to help us after all," Fugate offered. "Maybe it knows how to release them."

The wind continued to whistle. "Maybe," he said. "But I don't want to risk it. At least, not yet."

Fugate frowned. "Then what are we going to do in the meantime?"

"We're going to have to find out what's keeping our friends from coming out."

"But how?"

"Someone's going to have to go in there."

An uneasy silence fell over the room as the Master surveyed their faces.

"You," he said to Lauren, and her face turned to chalk.

"But how am I going to go in there? It's nothing but empty space."

"There's a staircase."

"I didn't see a staircase."

"Believe me. I can see in the darkness much better than you can. There's a drop of about ten feet to reach it, but it's there."

The thought of entering the seemingly endless darkness made her half-crazed with fear. "No, I can't, really. *Please.*"

"You must, Mrs. Ransom. There's no other way. And besides, if you don't . . ." He glanced at Garrett.

Her heart sank, but she knew she had no choice. She crept up to the threshold of the doorway and aimed her flashlight down. To her surprise she saw that there was a staircase, an ancient staircase made of stone, and as she traced the beam of the flashlight over it she saw that it seemed to descend forever into the gloom.

Her knees started to weaken underneath her, but before she knew what was happening the Master picked her up by the arms and with superhuman strength lowered her into the darkness.

About four feet down she hit the surface of the stone.

"Mom!" she heard Garrett call overhead.

She froze, afraid to move even so much as an inch in the total darkness, and then suddenly she realized that when he had grabbed her she had dropped the flashlight on the floor of the hallway.

"Please, give me the flashlight!" she said to the Master. He held the flashlight out through the open rectangle above her, and she grabbed it with both hands. Then she quickly shined it around her feet to get a better grasp of her surroundings.

The landing she was standing on was about fifteen feet square, and like the stone of the door's threshold it was scuffed and pitted. The steps themselves were extremely wide, but because there were no railings on either side, their steepness made her head swim, and for a moment she thought she was going to faint. Positioning herself as squarely in the middle of the staircase as possible, she inched her way toward the first step.

"Go on!" the Master ordered. "You're going to have to move faster than that if you expect to make any progress."

She looked up and saw that to goad her on he had brought Garrett up to the doorway and was making him standing dangerously close to the edge.

Breathing deeply, she started down the steps.

Occasionally as she descended she crept to within a foot or two of the edge of the stairs and pointed the flashlight into the Stygian darkness. But invariably she saw what appeared to be a limitless drop.

On and on she went, and the farther she traveled the stronger the wind became. Five minutes passed, and then ten, until she noticed that the doorway had dwindled into a point of light and vanished. Still she pressed on.

As she advanced, the air became colder, icier, and acquired an odd wintery smell. Even stranger, the darkness started to become brighter. At first the difference was so subtle it was almost imperceptible, but slowly the gloom became suffused with a faint twilight glow.

Finally, as the unearthly twilight became brighter, she realized with a jolt she had only about a hundred steps to go. Even more startling, in the bluish half-light that now pervaded everything she saw that she was once again approaching solid ground.

But it was not familiar ground. Spreading out in all directions from the base of the stairs was a vast and seemingly endless frozen waste. In appearance, it might have been a scene from the Arctic, save that the slabs and escarpments of ice that covered it were far too smooth and regular to have been carved by natural forces. From the helter-skelter way they were piled against one another it was clear that at some point in the distant past they had been formed by some enormous and violent upheaval. But whatever the cataclysm had been, it was now echoed only in their shape, and they seemed more like tombstones, funerary monoliths disturbed only by the snow and the wind.

As she stared at the alien landscape spreading out before her she realized something else. The strange, almost lunar terrain was also the source of the faint but vast pulsation of life she had sensed when she had first opened the doorway. Despite its barren appearance, there was something alive in this godforsaken netherworld.

Frightened, she turned to leave, but as soon as she started up the stairs, she heard a voice.

"Not yet, Mrs. Ransom. I must see more."

It was the Master, and she swung around, trying to figure out how he had accompanied her without her knowledge.

But then she realized with horror that she had not heard him with her ears, but with her mind itself. His voice had come from inside her head.

"No!" she screamed, cupping her hands over her ears, but as soon as she resisted, her head was racked with pain.

"Stop!" the Master shouted, and the words echoed in the background of her thoughts. "Stop resisting me and it won't hurt."

But the realization that he had entrenched himself in her mind made her feel more violated than she had ever felt in her life.

Like something reptilian and primeval she felt him wriggling around inside her thoughts, felt the tendrils of his influence struggling madly to access her senses.

She resisted, and the searing pain intensified.

Fearing she was going to black out and fall and hurt herself, she gave in.

"There," the Master said, sighing mentally. "Now continue until you've reached the bottom of the stairs. I must see more."

Reluctantly, she turned around, and as she descended into the midst of the icy monoliths, the feeling that she was drawing close to something alive increased. Indeed, by the time she reached the bottom of the steps, the sensation had grown so powerful that her flesh was prickling. She frantically pointed the flashlight all around her, half expecting to see some giant shape looming up next to her. But still, there was no sign of activity, and the only movement remained the occasional eddying of the snow in the wind.

"*Keep going,*" the Master prodded.

Realizing she had no choice, she crept forward. By now, the prickling of her flesh had become very powerful, and she realized that whatever the legion of things were that inhabited the place, they were close, very close. But it wasn't until she shined the flashlight on the face of one of the slabs of ice that she saw. Entombed beneath its surface, and frozen in various bizarre and tormented postures, was a phantasmagoria of the most grotesque creatures she had ever seen. Griffins, harpies, monkeylike demons, and fierce winged dogs. Basilisks, devils of all shapes and sizes with taloned hands and huge leathery wings, flying serpents, and dwarfs with gigantic blood-red eyes.

As she moved the flashlight quickly from one block of ice to the next she saw that each seemed to contain more creatures than the last. Some, like the numerous devils, were recognizable to her. But others were so ghastly and foreign that she gasped: strange ogreish creatures with shapeless lumps of flesh for faces, gauzy sylphlike beings with hollow sunken eyes, imps no larger than mice, things that looked burned and faceless save for their razor-sharp teeth, locusts wearing what looked like little suits of armor, and hordes of other insectlike creatures that distantly resembled houseflies, wasps, and bees, but possessed additional horrific features which clearly betrayed their demonic nature.

The monstrous appearance of the creatures terrified Lauren, but what frightened her all the more was how mysteriously familiar they all seemed. It was as if some unconscious, ancient, and perhaps even prehuman part of her recognized them, recognized what they had represented to her genetic forebears, and although she did not know them consciously, their appearance still tugged at her, still plucked at some deep and primordial part of her being.

Suddenly, and to her great astonishment, her terror became mingled with joy. For a moment she was baffled, wondering why she was experiencing such an inappropriate response. But then she realized. It was not her joy, but *his*. She was feeling the Master's elation.

"All right," he told her telepathically, "I've seen enough. You can come back."

She spun around and started up the stairs, and as soon as she did it seemed to her she could almost hear the keening of the things in the ice reaching out to her, trying to call her back. With each passing step, the siren song grew more desperate and beckoning. And its meaning was clear. Despite their dormant appearance, the things wanted out. They did not want her to leave.

It taxed her endurance to the limit, but she did not stop running until she reached the top landing. When she did the Master hauled her up the last few feet and she collapsed on the floor in exhaustion.

"Mom!" Garrett cried, rushing over to comfort her.

But the Master ignored her, and just continued to stare into the darkness.

"So I was right!" he exclaimed.

"But if they're frozen in ice, how are we going to get them out?" Fugate asked. "Build a fire?"

"Don't be ridiculous," the Master said, looking at him as if it were the stupidest thing he had ever heard. "We would never be able to cart enough wood down there to melt all that ice." He returned his attention to the darkness. "No. It was magic that put them there. And it will be magic that will set them free."

Realizing another display of the Master's power was in the offing, Fugate placed the palms of his hands together excitedly and stepped back to watch.

The Master closed his eyes and took several long deep breaths. Then he raised his arms wide like a king addressing his subjects and began to chant: "*Ayperos naberrs adiram glassyalabolas. Chameron hayras ador cabuvodium.*" As he intoned the words a breeze began to rustle through the hallway and the house creaked.

"*Lhavala casmiel beldor forneus. Asmoday octinimoes abravor tah!*"

As soon as he finished the incantation a great rushing of air swept past them, and Lauren held on to Garrett tightly. Like an invisible locomotive the magical wind roared down the stairs, and as it collided with the various winds and air currents it met in the darkness it made a strange thrashing sound like a piece of canvas flapping in a storm.

Lauren froze as the Master flexed his fingers and gazed excitedly into the darkness, waiting for the sound of his brethren being released.

But instead there was only silence.

"So what's happening?" Fugate asked nervously.

"I don't know!" the Master snapped, peeved that his magic had not seemed to work.

"But you said you had the power to—"

"I do!" the Master cut him off. "It's just going to take a little experimenting. I've just got to find the right way." He stroked his chin thoughtfully. "Maybe something that's a little older, a Babylonian spell . . ."

He once again raised his hands up toward the darkness. "*Nabu apla il apna sha. Ik iddina shaki shalu. Nabu apla il apna mardok. Shabu ish, ishali shak, sha ik ik kali sharri.*" As soon as he finished the words there was a brilliant flash of blue light, followed by a piercing whistling sound.

But again, after the first flourish of the spell subsided, nothing seemed to happen.

Fugate became even more distressed. "What are we going to do?" he whined.

"Shut up!" the Master snarled, beginning to lose his temper. "There's got to be some incantation that will work. If they were placed there by magic, then magic can release them. I know there's an incantation. I can feel it in my bones."

"But you've already tried twice. Don't you think it's time we try asking the Watcher for help?"

The Master looked at him with thinly veiled fury. "I told you, I don't want to risk releasing the Watcher unless we know a little more about why it is here. We still don't know whether it was placed here to help us or to stop us, and unless we can figure that out, I just don't want to risk it. Besides, I know I have the power to do this. I know I do."

The Master turned back toward the doorway and once

again began to marshal his concentration, but Fugate remained unappeased. He continued to wring his hands together and hop about nervously at the Master's side.

"But what if you—"

"Will you just *shut up!*" the Master shouted as he backhanded Fugate and sent him hurling against the wall. Outraged, Fugate charged back at him, swinging the straight razor in wild erratic arcs, but with preterhuman speed, the Master grabbed his wrist and violently flung him back again. This time Fugate fell, and when he did he crashed into the silver tray, sending it rolling straight toward Garrett.

The tray hit Garrett's feet and stopped, and for several seconds everyone froze. As Garrett stared down at the tray, he understood all too well what it meant to have it fall into his hands, and he realized he was faced with yet another situation in which he had to decide whether to trust or not to trust.

Should he quickly wipe the symbols off, and thus release the Watcher Angel?

Or would such a move only help the Master and make their own situation worse?

Realizing he had only a fraction of a second to decide, he quickly turned everything he knew about the Watcher over in his mind. But still he could find no firm answer, no slight preponderance of fact to indicate which of the two choices was the right one to make.

The Watcher *was* a wild card.

It was a lady-or-the-tiger situation.

Finally, he realized he had no choice but to trust, and he reached out and rapidly wiped several of the symbols off the silver tray with his sleeve.

The Master started forward. "No!"

But it was too late.

The odd stillness that had overtaken the house vanished. And within seconds the Watcher appeared at the end of the corridor. It quickly assessed the situation, looking first at the open doorway and then at each person in turn. Then, after apparently discerning that the Master was the main person responsible for what was happening, it drifted over to him and stopped only a few feet in front of him.

The Master stood his ground and stared back at the Watcher probingly. His emerald eyes narrowed.

"So now comes the moment of reckoning," he murmured calmly. "Which is it? Are you on their side? Or are you on ours?"

The Watcher gazed at him for a moment longer, and then suddenly it reached up into the air, and in a flash of light so brilliant it nearly blinded them, it plucked a massive sword out of the nothingness. From the dazzling way the sword sparkled it appeared to be constructed out of pure energy, and the sight of it caused the Master to step back cautiously.

"So now we know. You are on the side of light, aren't you? Well, I warn you, you have never contended with the likes of me before." After he finished the words, the Master held his arms out and prepared to do battle.

Lauren grabbed Garrett by the arm and tried to head for the door, but Fugate stopped them. "Wh-what should I do?" he stammered, frightened, and looking to the Master for direction.

"Keep them there!" the Master said, sizing the situation up out of the corner of his eye. "We may still need them—"

But the words had scarcely left his lips when suddenly the Watcher lunged for him. It crashed the glistening sword down, intending to cleave him in the shoulder, but the Master dove out of the way. The Watcher rushed forward, swinging the sword at him again, but again with supernatural swiftness the Master avoided the coruscating blade. Then he leaped to his feet and, gesturing magically with his hand in the air, hurtled a sizzling blue fireball straight at the Watcher.

The Watcher sidestepped it deftly, but was visibly startled, and the fireball crashed into the wall behind it and exploded in a shower of sparks.

"Didn't think I could do that, did you?" the Master gloated. He quickly shot another fireball at the Watcher, and then another, and although the Watcher dealt with each of them capably, they provided the Master with enough time to try another incantation. "*In hep nehebka, neb mahotep mene ra!*" he shouted into the darkness of the doorway. "*In hep nehebka, neb mahotep mene ra!*" He waited, glancing into the darkness anxiously.

But still nothing happened.

After the last fireball fizzled out, the Watcher lunged again, and again the Master was forced to retreat. "So what is it?" he roared, angry but still haughty. "I know there's got to be an incantation that will release them, and if this house really is a kind of sword in the stone, that means the spell is probably right in front of us somewhere, doesn't it?" He scanned the walls of the corridor as he continued to creep backward.

The Watcher charged forward, cornering him. Screaming, the Master tried to get away, but this time it was too late, and to keep the sword from crashing down on top of him he was forced to grab the Watcher's wrist. As he did so, a hiss of lightning spread out from where their flesh made contact, and continued to flash and crackle as the two began to wrestle.

Lauren and Garrett watched breathlessly. Despite the Watcher's vaporous appearance, the Master was able to grip it as if it were solid. But every time their flesh made contact, the room lighted up from the pyrotechnic mixing of their energies. They fought viciously, savagely, the enormous strength of each at first appearing to be a perfect match for the other. But then finally the Watcher began to gain an edge.

Grabbing the Master firmly by the shoulders, it sent him

crashing into the wall, and then lunged at him again. But this time when the Master went to roll out of the way, it anticipated his move and met him with the sword, slicing his hand off neatly at the wrist.

The Master screamed with agony as a stream of greenish bilelike liquid began to spurt out of his severed wrist. "Damn you!" he cursed as he wrapped his other hand tightly around the stump to try to stanch the bleeding. Then, with eyes glowing volcanically, he opened his mouth and screamed again. But this time, in addition to a ghastly and earsplitting wail, out of his mouth issued a torrent of strange and disgusting substances: great volumes of something that looked like sheets of black spiderweb, rubbery clots of black congealed blood, small black feathery things, and gallons of sticky black liquid that solidified into a network of tendrils and fibers as soon as they hit the Watcher.

For several seconds the Watcher was immobilized as it cut through the sticky mess with the sword. And although it was obvious it would be free in moments, suddenly an excited gleam came into the Master's eyes.

"But of course! That's got to be it!" he said, turning toward the doorway. "It *has* been right under our noses all along!" Keeping one eye trained on the Watcher, he quickly began to recite the words: "*In girum imus nocte . . .*"

The Watcher cut through the last tendril of the discharge.

". . . *et consumimur igni.*"

The Watcher stepped out of the shroud and started for the Master.

But it was too late.

The house shuddered as a long and baleful howl came from the darkness.

And just as the Watcher was about to reach the Master, through the doorway burst such a gale of wind that even the Watcher was no match for its force. Struggling to keep its grip on the sword, it held its arms close to its body as the hurricane wind sent it crashing into the opposite side of the corridor.

Lauren screamed, bracing herself against one of the baulks lining the walls and clutching Garrett closer to her side. And even Fugate cowered in terror.

But the Master only laughed. "Yes! Yes!" he shrilled, somehow keeping his balance as he held his arms out welcomingly to the wind.

For several seconds it continued, keeping everyone but the Master pinned against the wall. Then, in one single, explosive flash, it started.

The first things to hit were the locustlike demons, their metallic armor still wet with condensation. They swarmed through the doorway in droves, diving and darting like angry bees. At first they appeared mindless in their frenzy. But then one stopped and hovered just inches from Lauren's face, and as she stared into its large and eerily sentient eyes, she realized it was not mindless, but dangerously intelligent. It hissed at her, baring its ferocious teeth, and she screamed and knocked it away with her fist.

It was just about to attack her again when the Master intervened. "Not her! The Watcher! Get the Watcher!"

Hissing at her one last time, the locust headed for the Watcher, and the other locusts in the room quickly did the same. They descended in a gnashing, glistening cloud, nipping and biting the Watcher viciously.

The locusts had not even finished raining down when still other creatures started to pour through the doorway —the insectlike demons that resembled houseflies and wasps, and the ghostly sylphlike beings with the dark, sunken eyes. They whirled around the room like an unearthly snowstorm, keening and shrilling, and flexing their long-frozen appendages. And then, as soon as they had assessed the situation, they descended on the Watcher in droves.

With the Watcher preoccupied, the Master was free to

continue his own attack, and he opened his mouth and vomited up another wave of the black, weblike substance. It wrapped around the Watcher like a sticky shroud, encumbering it further, as the sylphs and the demons continued their attack.

At first the Watcher fought heroically, killing vast numbers of the creatures with each swing of its sword. But finally the onslaught became too much and the Watcher fell to its knees, and dropped the sword of light on the floor.

Shrieking with glee, the Master rushed forward and reached for the sword, intending to finish the Watcher off. But it was a fatal error, for as soon as he touched the magical weapon, it exploded, and blew off his remaining hand.

However, instead of dispersing, the fragments of the sword swirled through the room like a glittering maelstrom, and then quickly reconstituted themselves in the Watcher's hand.

With the balance of power thus offset, the Watcher struggled back to its feet, and once again started hacking away at the swarm. As it did so, it also began to speak:

"*Trinitas, Sother, Adonay, Eloim.*"

"No!" the Master screamed.

"*Sabahot, Messias, Jehovam, Infinitas.*"

Abruptly, the wind that was surging through the doorway faltered and shifted direction as the keening of the swarm became tinged with fear.

"No!" the Master repeated, as he swelled his chest and readied himself to launch another attack. But this time Watcher was ready. "*Zazay!*" it roared, sending a crackling ball of blue lightning hurtling from its outstretched fingers and into the Master's chest. "*Salmay, Angerecton!*" it shouted, unleashing another barrage, and causing the Master to fall and start sliding toward the doorway.

"*No!*" the Master repeated, the stumps of his arms scraping uselessly on the floor.

But like a tide being pulled back by the moon, the wind just continued its reversal, roaring and sucking the swarm back into the darkness.

Finally, only the Master and Fugate remained—the Master clinging piteously with his stumps to the side of the door, and Fugate still cowering against the wall.

The Watcher prodded Fugate in the back with the sword and sent him scurrying to the Master's side.

Fugate started to cry. "You're not going to send *me* in there, are you?" he blubbered, looking down into the darkness.

The Master was infinitely less contrite. "Goddam you, you son of a bitch! You may have won this time, but I'll be back! I'll—"

But the Watcher just ignored him and swiftly kicked him down the stairs.

Seeing the Master vanish into the darkness, Fugate's eyes widened even further, and his crying became convulsive. "No, please, I'll be good! I'll do whatever you say! I'll—"

But the Watcher just pushed him into the darkness and calmly shut and bolted the door.

It wearily turned around and leveled its gaze at Lauren and Garrett. With the door already shut, Lauren thought it unlikely that it was reserving the same fate for them, but after everything she had just witnessed, she still had no idea what it was going to do next. She waited breathlessly, terrified, as it stared at them for a moment longer.

Finally it spoke. "You must leave now," it murmured simply. Then it turned and once again started down the corridor.

"Wait!" Garrett called. But even as he shouted the word he knew it would not stop. That was not its purpose. It had fulfilled its purpose, and now its only job was to continue its wanderings, its penance.

It quickly vanished back into the cavernous house, and after it did, they gathered themselves together and started their own trek back through the maze of halls. As they did, they remained silent, each beginning to piece together at least part of the answers to all of the questions that had plagued them.

From the way the Watcher behaved, Garrett now knew it was the forces of light that had inspired Sarah Balfram to build the house. He knew that the same power of good was also responsible for setting the Watcher up as the guardian of the doorway.

For her part, Lauren now understood why so many of the murderers who had committed crimes in the house had subsequently vanished without a trace, and why the threshold of the great doorway was so scuffed and bore the traces of so many fruitless struggles. She was also beginning to realize that the purpose of the house had never been to unleash evil, but to trap it: to draw it in, and entice and beguile it. The house was indeed a store-place, but not one that was merely holding its inhabitants for some future and apocalyptic offensive. It was a store-place that kept its quarry forever.

Most important of all, Garrett realized that it was wise that he had not stopped trusting everything. Had he stopped, their doom would have been sealed. However, he also realized that in this situation at least, it had been mere serendipity, the luck of the draw, that had allowed him to make the right choice.

There were things that were evil in the universe, unfathomably evil.

And there were things that were good.

And there were things like the Watcher that were of such complexity, and possessed such subtlety of shading, that they were not really categorizable as either. Things that transcended such simplistic moral pigeonholes.

But for Garrett, all that mattered as they descended the main staircase was that the nightmare was over. Both he and his mother had survived.

When they reached the front entrance hall, Lauren packed them each a small bag, and then with flashlights in hand they left the house and started toward Clearwater Lodge. Although the prospect of making such a trek at night still filled her with trepidation, somehow the cosmic implications of the house—the notion that there were forces at work on the earth whose only purpose was to combat evil—gave her courage to brave the journey.

And she did not want to spend the rest of the night in the house.

Halfway to the lodge, a car passed them. But they hid in the bushes as it approached, and seeing only one person in the car, a man, they decided not to reveal themselves or try to wave it down. They did not know who the man was, and Lauren simply did not want to risk it.

However, several hours later, as dawn was beginning to tinge the sky, they saw a camper driven by an elderly couple. They waved it down, and the couple gave them a ride the rest of the way to the lodge.

EPILOGUE

The motorcade cut through the darkness like the cars of a Ferris wheel at night—three black limousines, all with headlights gleaming. They stopped beneath the colonnade of majestic black spruce, and the doors of the first limo opened. The first man out, a short stocky man in a Bermuda shirt and wearing a gold Rolex on his darkly tanned arm, ran up toward the house.

"Holy shit, Stephen, so this is it? You weren't kidding when you said this place was huge!"

Stephen slid out of the back door of the limo like a sulky child, his hands buried in the pockets of his black leather pants. "What did you think, I was lying?"

A tall, beautiful Asian woman in a black Ungaro suit stepped out behind him and ran one of her bright-red fingernails across his shoulder. "Stephen's just upset because he still can't believe his wife really doesn't want him back."

"Fuck off, Miko!" Stephen snapped. "I've been over that bitch for a month now."

Miko placed her hands on her hips and pretended to look offended. "Touchy, touchy."

"No, that's not it," said a heavyset, tuxedoed young man with curly, extremely long hair. In one hand he carried a champagne bottle and in the other a glass with most of its contents emptied. "Stephen's upset because Chris stopped and picked up that couple whose car broke down, and now we're stuck with them for the night."

"Oh, Pig, you don't know anything," Miko argued.

"Don't call me Pig," the heavyset man shot back.

"Will you all just shut up!" Stephen said as the other two limos began to empty their passengers. "They're going to hear you."

As the doors of the two limos opened, out piled a crowd of people, most of them fashionably dressed and carrying bottles of champagne. Among them were a frumpy couple who seemed conspicuously ill at ease among this entourage—a short, nervous little man with a Don Ameche mustache, and a petite blond woman with large, almost frighteningly alert-looking eyes.

"Were you able to follow us all right, Chris?" asked the man with the gold Rolex.

"No problem at all, Georgie," returned the muscular driver of the last limo. "How about you folks?" he asked, turning toward the frumpy couple. "You fare all right back there with the rest of these rowdies?"

Several of the people in the crowd jeered the driver playfully.

"Oh, we were fine," the petite blond woman gushed. "We're just very grateful you happened along when you did, aren't we, Arnie?" She looked at her companion, and seeing that he seemed too tongue-tied to respond, elbowed him in the ribs.

"Y-yes. Very grateful," Arnie stammered.

Georgie smiled. "What did you two say your names were?"

"I'm June and this is Arnie," the blond woman bubbled. Her eyes zeroed in on Stephen. "I just wanted to thank you again for giving us a lift. I don't know what we would have done sitting out there on the highway all alone—"

"It's nothing," Stephen said curtly. "Let's get up to the house. I'm thirsty."

"So you *are* pissed about Chris picking those two up, aren't you?" Miko whispered as she walked along beside him.

"It's just that he works for me."

"Well, what did you want him to do, just leave 'em sitting on the side of the road?" asked Pig.

"No, I didn't want him to just leave them. But I would have appreciated it if he had asked me first instead of just stopping and inviting them to come along with us. I mean, I was looking forward to a real blowout of a party tonight. But with these two along . . ."

"Oh, I don't know," Miko said. "Arnie seems a bit out of his element, but June certainly seems to be adapting very well. Who knows, she may turn out to be a real party girl."

"That's what he's afraid of!" Pig chuckled, gulping down some more champagne. They all laughed and ran the rest of the way to the house.

When they reached the front door, Stephen opened the door and they went inside.

Several people in the crowd whistled. "Whoa, man, this place is great!"

"Isn't it," Stephen agreed.

"Why did you say Lauren left?" Georgie asked.

"The old guy I hired to run the generators wandered off and fell down a ravine. He must have been senile or something, because he broke his neck. But you don't have to worry. I've got a young guy running the generators now."

"But didn't you say this place has a history of that kind of stuff?" Georgie asked with a lurid and hopeful grin.

"Yeah, a real dark past!" Stephen said, smiling ghoulishly. He spun around and wriggled his fingers in the air. "So everyone be careful!" he shouted.

A chorus of delighted giggles and ahs rose from the crowd, as they broke like billiard balls and started to run through the house. For the first half hour they did nothing but explore, and each time Stephen showed them one of the house's architectural oddities, their partying only became more abandoned. Georgie, Chris, and the third limo driver—a tall Swedish kid named Ben—kept the champagne flowing, and Pig saw to it that the stereo in the drawing room was cranked into high gear.

But as the party started to gravitate toward the front porch, Stephen's attention was once again drawn to June and Arnie. June, although still playing the roll of wide-eyed and overly smilish spectator, had at least begun to drink champagne. But Arnie was still stiff and uncomfortable.

"So what do you think their story is?" he asked, turning toward Miko.

Miko, who had been talking to a handsome young Italian, turned and sidled up beside Stephen like a cat. "Whose story? Oh, are they still bothering you?"

Stephen just folded his arms. He did not know why the presence of the frumpy couple annoyed him so much. Perhaps he really was still brooding over Lauren.

He looked in Miko's dark and penetrating eyes and decided to open up. "Yeah, they're bothering me a lot, but I don't know why. Something about them just rubs me the wrong way."

Sensing a new level of seriousness in his voice, Miko appraised the couple again. "Well, let's see what we can figure out about them just by looking at them." She laughed and gave Stephen a sip from her champagne glass, and he loosened up a little.

"Okay," he said, delighted by the idea.

She perched one of her venomously red fingernails against her lip. "First, I don't think they're married."

"Come on! You think they're just screwing? I don't believe it."

Miko held her ground. "No, look, neither of them is wearing a wedding ring."

"But Miko, that guy doesn't look like he has the balls—"

"I didn't say they were fucking each other. I just said I didn't think they were married."

Stephen's doubt increased. "So what are they doing together? What's their relationship?"

"Well, I don't think they're related. They don't look anything like each other. I don't even think they're friends. They don't behave like friends together. They stay close to each other, but neither of them ever smiles at the other, or gives any of the other cues that friends give to each other." Miko ran her finger around the rim of her glass. "No, if you ask me, I'd say they just met."

Stephen glanced skeptically in June and Arnie's direction. "Okay, now that you mention it, they do seem a bit stiff with each other. Kind of like two frightened children."

"No, he's frightened. He's not happy at all about being here. But she's having a ball. Yeah—she's a little nerdy, but look at the way her eyes keep lighting up. She's never been at a party like this and she's loving every minute of it."

Stephen sighed. "But you still haven't explained what they're doing together. I mean, if they just met, why were they traveling together?"

Miko shook her head. "I don't know. Maybe they're on

some kind of business trip together." She grinned. "Or maybe she's a damsel in distress. Maybe they met at a coffee shop or something and she asked him if he would give her a ride. That would explain why they don't seem to know each other. It would also explain Arnie's unease. Maybe it's been a long time since he's been with a woman. Maybe this is all really new to him."

Stephen began to buy it. "Okay, I think you may be right, but still none of what you're saying explains why they give me the creeps."

Miko looked at him with astonishment. "The creeps?"

Even Stephen was a bit surprised by his admission. "You know, *that's* it. I didn't realize it at first, but the reason I've been so teed off about Chris's stopping and picking them up is there's something about June that I just don't like."

"Oh, well, that's easy. I can tell you what that is."

He looked at the Asian woman quizzically. "What?"

Miko took another sip of her champagne. "Everything!"

Stephen laughed.

"No, look, I'm serious. First, if you look at her really close, she's really quite homely. Oh, on the surface she presents a neat little package, but look at each of her features by themselves. For example, her hair's pretty, all right, but you can see her scalp through it. There's nothing more unattractive than a blonde whose hair is so thin you can see pink scalp through it everywhere."

Stephen's laughing became more uncontrolled, but at the same time he was becoming increasingly mesmerized by what Miko was saying.

"Go on. Go on."

"And her teeth. I mean, they're straight and they're white, but there are spaces between each of them. They're like little snaky pegs. That's icky." Amused at her own wickedness, Miko also started to laugh.

"Finally, there are those eyes. I mean, it looks like she's got her finger in an electric socket they're so wide and perky."

They had once again started to convulse with laughter when suddenly June looked right in their direction and smiled. She was too far away to have heard them, but something about the knowing, even delighted way her eyes gleamed made them go silent.

"You don't think she could have heard us?" Miko asked under her breath.

"No," Stephen snorted, but suddenly he wasn't so sure. Angered that he could be made to feel so self-conscious by someone as insignificant as June, he started down the porch steps. "Come on, we're going to wipe that shit-eating grin off her face," he whispered.

"How?"

He raised his hands into the air. "Hey, everybody down to the lake! We're all going to go skinny-dipping." Then he turned to Miko and said quietly: "That ought to embarrass the middle-class hell out of her."

Miko clapped her hands together mischievously. "Perfect, darling," she said, nipping him in the ear as she ran toward the lake.

The crowd whooped and followed.

When they reached the lake, Stephen looked back and was pleased to see that June and Arnie were tagging along. However, to his surprise, Arnie was the only who seemed discomforted by the events enveloping them. Far from being unsettled at the idea of skinny-dipping with a group of strangers, June appeared to be delighted. She strode down the lawn with her arms swinging wildly, and when she reached the edge of the lake, she quickly slipped out of her clothes, her sagging, middle-aged body gleaming in the moonlight, and plodded down into the water.

Nettled, Stephen decided that he could at least put Arnie on the hot seat.

EPILOGUE 269

"Hey, Arnie, come on in. The water's fine!" he goaded
as he took off his clothes and marched down into the lake.
He looked back and saw that on hearing the words, Arnie's
agitation only increased. It was the response Stephen had
desired, but seeing how mortified, and even frightened,
Arnie looked, Stephen suddenly felt contrite.

He was just about to call Arnie and tell him that he did
not have to join them if he did not want to when June
abruptly intervened.

"It's all right, Arnie. Come on in!" she called.

"No, thank you. I'd rather not."

"But I want you to, Arnie," June returned sweetly, but
with an undertone so insistent it was obvious she was not
going to take no for an answer.

Arnie looked first at Stephen and then at the growing
crowd of rowdy, naked people splashing in the water.
Then he looked back imploringly at June.

"*Arnieee,*" she pressed, and falteringly Arnie began to
take off his clothes.

Even Miko was a bit put off. "Well, I guess my theory
about their having just met is wrong if she's already got
him that pussy-whipped," she sniffed.

Stephen agreed and was just about to say something else
when suddenly Georgie came charging down into the water
and threw a volley ball out over everyone's head. "Water
hockey, anyone?" he shouted.

The crowd roared and dove for the ball.

For the first twenty minutes everyone played, laughing
and fighting over the ball with equal gusto. But finally,
people began to tire and leave the lake, and the only players
remaining were Stephen, a few of the other men, and June.

It annoyed him that his ploy to embarrass her had failed
so miserably, but what unnerved him all the more was
how boisterously she was playing. Despite her size and
age, she fought for the ball with a vigor that put even
Chris, the muscle-bound chauffeur, to shame. She was also

aggressive to the point of rudeness and displayed no qualm about knocking men twice her size out of the way and occasionally even hitting them, just to keep control of the ball. And always, after she indulged in one of these graceless tactics, she would give a raucous and throaty laugh, her head thrown back and her strangely peglike teeth flashing faintly in the moonlight.

"What *is* her story?" Miko asked as she swam over to Stephen from the lake's edge.

A thwacking sound rang out, followed by a howl of pain, as June slapped Ben in the back and stole the ball from him. She guffawed coarsely.

"I don't know," Stephen complained, "but I'm going to find out."

He swam over to where Arnie was wading timidly in the shallows.

"Hey, Arnie, what the hell is wrong with your wife?"

"She's not my wife," Arnie returned quickly.

"Well, what is she? Is she your girlfriend?"

Arnie began to fidget as if he did not know how to answer the question. But before he could say anything, June quickly swam over to where they were standing.

"We're just friends. Aren't we, Arnie?" she said, hugging him tightly against her naked and doughy body.

"R-right. Friends," Arnie agreed.

"Well, I don't know how you define friendship, lady, but it seems to me that you play a little rough," Stephen shot back.

A glimmer of delight rippled through June's unnaturally wide and luminous eyes. "You're right. I do like to play rough." She gave another of her unctuously artless smiles.

Her frankness startled Stephen. "Well, if it's rough you want, maybe we should raise the stakes a little?"

"What did you have in mind?"

"How good a swimmer are you?"

"I'm an excellent swimmer."

Stephen glanced over to a large log floating several hundred feet away in the middle of the lake. "Do you think you're a good enough swimmer to make it to that log and back?"

Miko became frightened. "Stephen, please."

"That would be child's play," June returned.

By this time both Chris and Ben had swum over to see what the excitement was about.

"What about you two?" Stephen asked. "Do you think you could make it over to that log and back?"

"I don't know. It's pretty far," Chris hesitated.

"Ah, it's not that far. I could do it," Ben countered.

Stephen looked back at June. "What do you think, June? Do you think you could beat us if we did a little race?"

"Easily," June murmured. "But only under one condition." She gave Arnie another hug. "Arnie here has to do it with us. I never do anything without Arnie."

Arnie went white. "Oh, no, June. I don't think I could begin to swim that far."

"Sure you could, Arnie."

"No, June, I . . ."

June gave him another steely glance. "*Arnie.*"

All the life seemed to drain out of Arnie, and he gave in. "Okay, June. Okay."

June looked back at Stephen. "Then you're on!"

"Great!"

Miko looked at Stephen worriedly. "Stephen, are you sure?"

But before she could say anything else, June pushed Arnie roughly in the direction of the log and they were off.

They swam madly through the moonlit waters, June, Arnie, Stephen, Ben, and Chris, and several times as they advanced Stephen thought Arnie was not going to make it. The sound of the little man's breathing was so strained and raspy that it could even be heard above their splashing, and once he stopped and looked as if he was going to go under.

But when he did, June just urged him on, callously and insistently, and he somehow marshaled his strength and continued.

Halfway there, Ben and Chris turned back, and Stephen's lungs began to ache so much he almost did the same. But when he looked and saw how effortlessly June seemed to be keeping ahead of him, his pride reasserted itself and he pushed on.

Finally, they reached the log, and Stephen grasped hold of it desperately, gasping for breath. Arnie also clung to the log for dear life, his face so blood-gorged and his breathing so strained he looked as if he was about to have a heart attack. Only June seemed unscathed by the race, and she smiled triumphantly as she treaded water a few feet away.

Seeing the agony Arnie was in, Stephen could no longer contain his anger. "Arnie, why in the fuck do you let her do this to you?"

For several seconds Arnie's gasping remained too convulsive for him to answer, but then finally he summoned the strength to speak. "Why do you let her do it to *you*?" he croaked.

"Do what?" Stephen asked, not understanding.

For the first time a flash of life surfaced in Arnie's eyes, accompanied by a glint of something that seemed almost like pity. "Let her manipulate you into challenging her just so she could get you out here alone?"

Stephen was still confused. "June manipulate me?" He looked at the little blond woman bobbling in the water, and she leered back at him with strange amusement.

"Don't you see?" Arnie entreated.

"*Arnie*," June cautioned.

But despite his exhaustion, the mote of fire that had

kindled in Arnie only increased. "No!" he exclaimed. "I'm not going to take it anymore. Your threats just aren't going to work anymore."

"What do you mean, threats? What kind of threats?" Stephen asked, his perplexity growing.

At this Arnie lost all patience. "Don't you see, yet? Don't you understand?" He lowered his head frustratedly toward the floating log and then lifted it up again. "I don't know who she is. I don't even know *what* she is—"

But as soon as the words left his lips, June slithered beneath the water.

Arnie panicked. "Oh, God, no!" he cried as he tried vainly to clamber up onto the log. But it just slipped and spun away.

Stephen had no idea why June's momentary submersion should cause Arnie so much alarm, but Arnie's terror seemed so real Stephen also began to panic.

"What is it?" he shouted, looking around desperately and trying to make some sense out of what was happening. "What do you mean, you don't know *what* she is?"

"Oh, God!" Arnie screamed and started to jerk around as if something was grabbing at his legs. He looked at Stephen one last time before he went under. "I didn't know what she was! She was just walking along the side of the road—!"

Then he vanished beneath the water.

Paralyzed with disbelief, Stephen continued to just look around, half expecting to see June and Arnie come laughing to the surface at any moment.

But when they didn't, he finally grasped the danger he was in and started thrashing violently toward the shore.

He had only swum a few feet when he felt something brush against his leg. He kicked at it, and for a moment he thought he might have pushed it away. But then he felt it bump against him again, this time holding tight.

And he too vanished beneath the water.

★ ★ ★

Lauren read about Stephen's death in the papers a few days later. When she had learned he was returning to the house for the summer, she had tried to warn him, but he would not listen. Nonetheless, her failure to convince him of the danger he was in still left her so racked with guilt that it was several days before she realized his death meant she was now a very wealthy woman.

For the next several weeks she continued to deliberate, trying to decide whether she should tell anyone else about the house or not. But finally she resolved to keep silent. She knew no one would believe her.

In time, as the weeks turned into months, she and Garrett even stopped talking about the house between themselves.

But Garrett did not stop thinking about the house. Not a day passed that he did not try to figure out which had played a greater role in saving their lives—chance or his willingness to trust in the unknown. But try as he might he could not decide, and the best he could come up with was that there were no easy answers.

More and more he realized that every situation had to be decided on its own. And that one had to go into each situation with equal amounts of optimism, willingness to believe, and suspicion. It was a twisting path that one had to follow to learn what exists in the innermost heart of another, a road without short cuts, and one that required great care in the walking. It was sometimes a road that brought one to one's destination quickly. And sometimes it was fraught with setbacks and wrong turns. But always it was a road that could not easily be anticipated. It was, in a word, a labyrinth.